continued . . .

"Another smokin'-hot Wild Riders story you will love reading."

—*Fresh Fiction*

"Jaci Burton's *Riding on Instinct* took me on the ride of my life."

—*Wild on Books*

"Thank you for giving us a love story where there is room for compromise and the good guys not only win, they take down the bad guys with a minimum of bloodshed and loss of innocent life." —*Night Owl Romance*

RIDING TEMPTATION

"Full of intrigue, sexual tension, and exhilarating release. Definitely a must-read."

—*Fresh Fiction*

"*Riding Temptation* has it all—action, suspense, romance, and sensuality all wrapped up in a story that will keep you on the edge of your seat and have you clamoring for the next story in the Wild Riders series!"

—*Wild On Books*

"Kudos to Ms. Burton for creating this exciting new series!"

—*Romance Junkies*

RIDING WILD

"A wild ride is exactly what you will get with this steamy romantic caper. This sexy and sizzling-hot story will leave you breathless and wanting more."

—*Fresh Fiction*

"A nonstop thrill ride from the first page to the last! Grab a copy of *Riding Wild* and take your own ride on the wild side of life!"

—*Romance Junkies*

"What an exciting and wonderful book!"

—*The Romance Studio*

"*Riding Wild* is a must-read for anyone who loves sexy romances filled with plenty of action and suspense."

—*Kwips and Kritiques*

WILD, WICKED, & WANTON

"*Wild, Wicked, & Wanton* starts off with a bang and never lets up!"

—*Just Erotic Reviews*

"This is the best erotic novel I have ever read! I absolutely loved it!"

—*Fresh Fiction*

"Jaci Burton's *Wild, Wicked, & Wanton* is an invitation to every woman's wildest fantasies. And it's an invitation that can't be ignored."

—*Romance Junkies*

FURTHER PRAISE FOR THE WORK OF
JACI BURTON

"Burton delivers it all—strong characters, an exhilarating plot, and scorching sex—and it all moves at a breakneck pace. Forget about a cool glass of water; break out the ice! You'll be drawn so fully into her characters' world that you won't want to return to your own."

—*Romantic Times*

"Realistic dialogue, spicy bedroom scenes, and a spitfire heroine make this one to pick up and savor." —*Publishers Weekly*

"Jaci Burton delivers."

—Cherry Adair, *New York Times* bestselling author

"Lively and funny . . . The sex is both intense and loving; you can feel the connection that both the hero and heroine want to deny in every word and touch between them. I cannot say enough good things about this book." —*The Road to Romance*

CHANGING
the
GAME

JACI BURTON

HEAT | NEW YORK

THE BERKLEY PUBLISHING GROUP
Published by the Penguin Group
Penguin Group (USA) Inc.
375 Hudson Street, New York, New York 10014, USA
Penguin Group (Canada), 90 Eglinton Avenue East, Suite 700, Toronto, Ontario M4P 2Y3, Canada
(a division of Pearson Penguin Canada Inc.)
Penguin Books Ltd., 80 Strand, London WC2R 0RL, England
Penguin Group Ireland, 25 St. Stephen's Green, Dublin 2, Ireland (a division of Penguin Books Ltd.)
Penguin Group (Australia), 250 Camberwell Road, Camberwell, Victoria 3124, Australia
(a division of Pearson Australia Group Pty. Ltd.)
Penguin Books India Pvt. Ltd., 11 Community Centre, Panchsheel Park, New Delhi—110 017, India
Penguin Group (NZ), 67 Apollo Drive, Rosedale, Auckland 0632, New Zealand
(a division of Pearson New Zealand Ltd.)
Penguin Books (South Africa) (Pty.) Ltd., 24 Sturdee Avenue, Rosebank, Johannesburg 2196,
South Africa

Penguin Books Ltd., Registered Offices: 80 Strand, London WC2R 0RL, England

ISBN-13: 978-1-61129-829-1

PRINTED IN THE UNITED STATES OF AMERICA

For all the women who love sports

ONE

GAVIN RILEY KNEW ELIZABETH DARNELL HAD BEEN avoiding him for the past several months. And he knew why.

She was afraid he was going to fire her just like his brother, Mick, had.

Oh, sure, Mick played in the NFL and Gavin played Major League Baseball, so in a lot of ways they were similar. And since Mick was Gavin's big brother, many people thought Gavin followed Mick's lead, especially in business matters. After all, Mick had hired Elizabeth first, and Gavin had followed suit.

But people assumed wrong. Gavin made his own decisions about business and didn't do everything his brother did. Even if Liz had messed with Mick's personal life, had hurt Mick's girlfriend and her son, and had done just about everything humanly possible to piss his brother off. She might have apologized and set things right with Mick, Tara, and Tara's son, Nathan, but it had been a case of too little, too late.

There were things a sports agent did that were valuable to an athlete's career. But screwing with an athlete's love life could be the kiss of death for an agent.

Liz had never once touched Gavin's love life. In fact, Liz threw women at him like a pimp. Beautiful women. Actresses, models, the kind of women that made Gavin look good. Gavin had no complaints. In fact, Liz had done the same thing for Mick until Mick had fallen in love with Tara Lincoln and put an end to Liz coupling Mick with the latest and greatest starlet on the cover of whatever magazine would get him the most exposure. But Liz had tried to get Tara and her son out of Mick's life, which had resulted in Liz getting fired.

And that's why she'd been avoiding Gavin, no doubt afraid Gavin had sided with Mick and was ready to do the same, which Gavin found pretty damned amusing. Elizabeth watched over her clients like a hawk, and for her to go to complete radio silence was like giving up and letting the vultures swoop in and take over her prime real estate.

Not that Gavin was the best player around, but she'd sat on him since she signed him, not letting any other agents get within talking—or signing—distance.

Maybe it had something to do with that night Mick had fired her.

Mick had walked out of the locker room, leaving Elizabeth alone with Gavin.

Liz had come up to him looking all teary-eyed and vulnerable, two things that were totally uncharacteristic of her.

Then she'd kissed him. And walked away.

Not that he'd thought about that kiss over the past months.

Much.

Except after that she'd disappeared, hadn't called him, e-mailed him, seen him, or stalked him in any way—also uncharacteristic of her. So had it been the kiss that had sent her into hiding or the fear if he saw her he'd fire her?

Did she really think he couldn't hunt her down if he wanted to cut ties with her?

It was time for her to come out and face the music.

She couldn't avoid him forever, especially not at this sports banquet where she had several clients—him included, though she'd been doing her best to steer clear of him.

He'd lain low most of the night, letting her flit around and focus on a few of his baseball peers. He always enjoyed watching her work a room full of hotshot jocks. Elizabeth commanded attention. It didn't matter whether a room was filled with the hottest females around—a guy would have to be either limp-dicked or dead not to notice her. Hair the color of his favorite red sports car, incredible blue eyes, creamy soft skin, and legs a man could only hope to have wrapped around him someday. And she showed it all off with practiced precision. She was a walking sex bomb with a wicked brain. A lethal combination.

Gavin would be lying if he didn't admit to being tempted by Liz. But he never mixed business with pleasure, and he took his opportunities elsewhere. Liz had been a great agent, had locked him up tight with the Saint Louis Rivers Major League Baseball team right out of college, and she'd worked her ass off to make him rich, get him product endorsements, and keep him in his position at first base. He never wanted to do anything to change that.

Besides, he doubted Elizabeth was his type.

Gavin was pretty damned particular about the women he chose. And ballbusting women like Elizabeth? Definitely not his type.

But they needed to get a few things straight, and she could only avoid him for so long.

The banquet was winding down, and most everyone was leaving. Liz was with Radell James and his wife, walking toward the main ballroom doors. Gavin shot out a side door and hung back, unobserved, while she said her good-byes.

She looked good tonight in one of her usual business suits. Black, which seemed to be one of her favorite colors, and tailored to within an inch of its life. The skirt hung just above her knee, and those shoes she wore played up her toned calves, too. She walked through the front doors of the hotel and outside with Radell and his wife.

Gavin stepped outside unnoticed while Liz talked with Radell. Gavin stood in the background and watched until Radell and Teesha's taxi arrived.

After they left, Liz leaned against the brick wall and closed her eyes. She looked tired. Or defeated. Her guard was down.

Time for Gavin to make his move. He stepped in front of her.

"You've been avoiding me, Elizabeth."

Her eyelids shot open, and her eyes widened with shock. She started to push off the wall, but he pinned her there by placing his hand on the wall by her shoulder. There was a planter on the other side, so she had nowhere to go.

"Gavin. What are you doing here?"

"It's the sports banquet. You knew I was here. In fact, I'd say you danced around tables doing your best to not run into me tonight."

She blinked. Her sweetly painted mouth worked, but nothing came out for a few seconds. He didn't think he'd ever seen her at a loss for words before. Her gaze darted from side to side like a cornered animal looking for escape.

Finally she relaxed and the old Elizabeth was back, her game face on. She tipped her finger down the lapel of his jacket.

"I wasn't avoiding you, sugar. I picked up a new client, so I had to babysit him a bit and introduce him to all the right media people. Then there was Radell, and we had a few things to discuss that were important. I'm so sorry we haven't had a chance to catch up. Did you need me for something?"

"Yeah. We need to talk."

In an instant, the warmth fled. Her expression narrowed. "About what?"

"You and me."

Something flashed in her eyes, something hot he'd never seen before.

Or maybe never noticed before. As soon as it was there, it was gone.

Maybe he'd just imagined it. But Gavin didn't imagine things, and what he'd seen caused a tightening in his balls. It was like the kiss that night, throwing him for a loop and making him second guess everything he thought about her. He'd always maintained his distance from Liz because they had a professional relationship. Besides, she didn't pay much attention to him other than in a professional capacity. She never fawned over him in the same way she did with a lot of her other clients. He figured she didn't have a personal interest in him, which suited him just fine since he had no problem finding women, and women had no problem finding him.

But what he'd just seen in her eyes had been . . . interesting.

"You and me? What about you and me?" she asked.

"You finished with all your client stuff?"

She nodded.

"Let's go somewhere and . . ." He skimmed his gaze down her body, lingering where her silk blouse lay against her breasts. He dragged his gaze back to her face, searching for a reaction.

She swallowed, and the muscles of her throat moved with the effort.

Elizabeth was nervous. Gavin didn't think he'd ever seen her nervous before.

This was perfect.

"Talk."

"Talk?"

"Yeah." He pushed off the wall and signaled for the valet, gave him his ticket, and grabbed Elizabeth's hand, bringing her with him to the curb while he waited for the valet to bring his car.

Fortunately, the sports banquet was in the city where the Saint Louis Rivers spent spring training. Damned convenient and no travel biting into his schedule. He traveled enough during the season, and having to add one more event where he had to hop on a plane would have been a drag.

He tipped the valet when he brought the car. He and Elizabeth got in, and he zipped onto the highway.

"Where are we going?"

"My house."

She arched a brow. "You have a house? Why not one of the hotels?"

"I stay in enough hotels during the season. I want a place to myself during spring training."

They drove in silence. Gavin made the turn north toward the beach.

"A house on the beach?"

"Yeah. It's remote and I can run in the mornings."

She half turned in her seat. "Dammit, Gavin. Are you going to fire me? Because if you are, I'd rather you just do it right away. Don't drag me out here to your house, then expect me to take a cab back to the hotel."

Gavin fought back a laugh. "We'll talk when we get inside."

"Shit," she whispered, then folded her arms in front of her and propped her head against the window for the remainder of the drive.

He turned off the highway and took the beachfront road, pulling into the garage. Elizabeth let herself out of the car and followed him inside, looking like a prisoner on her way to an execution.

He flipped the lights on and opened the sliding door leading out to the back porch.

"Nice place."

He shrugged. "It'll do for now. Want a beer or some wine?"

"Why? Trying to soften the blow?"

He slipped his hands into the pockets of his slacks. Ignoring her question, he asked again, "Wine, beer, something else?"

She inhaled and let out an audible sigh. "Glass of wine would be nice, I guess."

He opened a bottle of wine, poured a glass for her, then grabbed a beer from the fridge.

"Let's go outside."

The house had a great back porch, though he supposed out here it was called a veranda or balcony or something. Hell, he didn't know what it was called, only that it overlooked the ocean and he liked sitting out here at night to listen to the waves crash against the beach.

There was a long cushioned swing for two and a couple of chairs. Liz sat in a chair, and Gavin took the other one.

She took the glass he offered and tipped it to her lips, taking several deep swallows of wine. "Is there a particular reason you dragged me out here to your beach haven instead of telling me what you needed to at the hotel?"

Yeah. He wanted to set her off balance. Liz was always in control. Besides, he didn't want her to stalk off or find an excuse to leave.

And . . . hell, he really didn't know why he'd brought her here, other than he wanted to know why he hadn't seen her in months. She was on his tail constantly, until the thing happened with his brother. Since then she'd all but fallen off the face of the earth.

"You usually call me twice a week, and I see you at least once a month."

She shrugged. "You were busy with the end of your season. I was busy, too. Then there were the holidays."

"You always make it a point to be wherever I am so we can have dinner. And when was the last time you missed the holidays with my family?"

She snorted. "Your brother fired me. His fiancée hates me. I hardly think it would have been appropriate to spend the holidays with your family."

"It wouldn't have mattered to my mother. She loves you and thinks of you as family. Personal is different from business."

"Not to me it isn't. And I'm sure it isn't to Mick and Tara, either. I wouldn't have wanted to interfere in your family celebrations. I know I'm not welcome there anymore."

She looked away, but not before he saw the hurt in her eyes.

This was a new side to her. Gavin looked closer, suspected she was full of shit since he knew she had no feelings. She was just bitter about losing Mick as a client.

"You could have arranged to see me outside of family gatherings."

She studied her nails. "My schedule has been kind of full."

"Bullshit. You went into hiding after Mick fired you."

Her head shot up. "I don't hide. Losing Mick was a giant financial hit. I had to scramble to sign clients to lessen the burden."

Gavin laughed. "You've made a ton of money off Mick, me, and the other guys. I don't think you're hurting."

"Fine." She set her wineglass down and stood, moving toward the railing to stare out over the ocean. "You can believe whatever you want to since you've already made up your mind. And if you're going to fire me, then get it over with so I can get out of here."

Gavin stood and came over to her. "You think I brought you here to fire you?"

She faced him. "Didn't you?"

He was struck by the vulnerability on her face. He'd never seen it before. Elizabeth always had a hard edge to her, a confidence she wore that made her stand out like a star. Right now it wasn't there. She was vulnerable, hurt, and afraid.

Maybe it wasn't an act after all. He'd been convinced she wasn't capable of actual emotions.

It would appear she was capable of hurting, and he didn't know what the hell to do about that.

Moonlight danced across her hair, making her look like a goddess lit by silver fire. For the second time that night Gavin realized that Elizabeth was a beautiful, desirable woman. He'd always thought of her as a vicious shark, which was a great place to file her in his head because she was the business side of his life. Oh, sure, she was always great to look at, and he had to admit he'd admired her body more than a few times, but he'd never thought of her as someone who had . . . feelings or emotions.

But as the light played with her eyes, he thought he saw tears welling up in them. And something else lit up her eyes when she looked at him, something he'd seen in many women's eyes before.

Desire. Need. Hunger.

Couldn't be. Liz was cold. He'd seen her drive a three-hundred-pound lineman into the ground with her sharp tongue, take a cold-hearted team owner by the tie and squeeze millions from him without so much as blinking. Liz was ruthless and had no soul. She would cut your heart out before she ever showed you she was vulnerable.

He'd seen what she had done to Tara and her son, Nathan, and hadn't once thought about how it would affect them. She'd wanted to cut them out of Mick's life. Emotion and how they felt hadn't entered the picture. They were an inconvenience and needed to be removed.

Whatever act she was putting on for him now was just that—an act, a way to gain his sympathy or distract him so he wouldn't toss her out on her ass. Losing clients was bad for business. And Liz was all about business, all the time. As far as he knew, she didn't have a personal life. She ate, breathed, and slept business twenty-four hours a day, seven days a week.

So yeah. Elizabeth, vulnerable? That was a freakin' laugh. Those tears were manufactured, and he wasn't buying it. And the idea of her wanting him? No way. She'd usually been straightforward with him, so he didn't understand what game she was trying to play.

"Liz, what are you doing?"

She frowned. "Excuse me?"

"What are you trying to do here?"

She rolled her eyes. "I have no idea what you're talking about, Gavin. You brought *me* here, remember?"

She drained her glass of wine and held it out to him. "Either get on with the reason why you brought me here or refill my glass. You're making me crazy."

Ditto. He grabbed her glass and took it into the kitchen, finishing his beer along the way.

When he came back outside, he found she'd kicked off her shoes and taken off her jacket. Wind whipped strands of her perfect hair loose. They flew in the breeze, wild and untamed.

He'd like to see Liz wild and untamed, but he'd bet she gave orders in bed, too.

He never thought about Elizabeth and sex in the same sentence, preferred to keep the two topics separate.

So why now? Was it the look she'd given him earlier?

Dammit. He didn't want to think of her that way.

She shivered and rubbed her arms.

"Want your jacket?

"No. I'm just cold by nature."

He could make a remark about that but decided to let it slide, handed her the wine, and poured himself a whiskey from the bottle he'd brought outside with him. Beer just wasn't cutting it.

It was time to get down to business and tell her why he'd brought her out here tonight.

"I screwed up with Mick," she said, staring at the water, not looking at him. "I thought I could control him, that I knew what was best for him. Turns out I had no idea. I wasn't listening to him when he told me he wanted Tara. I thought it was a fling. But he was in love with her, and I didn't want him to be in love with her."

This was new. Liz opening up to him? They talked business, and sometimes had a few drinks and laughs when they were together, but they mostly talked sports. Nothing personal. Ever.

"Why didn't you want him to be in love with her?"

"Because if he was, things would change."

"What things?"

"Mick was so easygoing. I could fix him up with an actress or model for promo, and he'd go along with whatever I suggested. His face was on the cover of so many magazines, and his name was everywhere. I made him famous."

He moved up next to her. "His arm made him famous, Liz."

Her lips curled in a wistful smile. "That was part of it. You guys don't understand PR at all. You think all you have to do is what you do out on the field, when it's so much more than that." She emptied her glass again, then set it on the table. "Being good at your sport is only a small part of making you into an icon. The gossip magazines, the media, your pictures, and your endorsement deals . . . everything else is what makes you."

She turned to face him. "You could be the best goddamn first baseman in all of baseball, but if I don't get you the deals to hawk deodorant or razors or underwear, if the public doesn't find out who you are, doesn't see your face eight times a day on commercials and in print media and online during your season? No one's going to care, Gavin. No one's going to care that you had a .338 batting average with forty-one home runs, that you won your sixth consecutive Golden Glove, and that you were the National League's MVP. No one's going to care. They care because the media tells them to care. And the media cares because I tell the media to care.

"All you guys want to do is play your sports, have your parties with your women, buy your expensive cars, and make sure you look good. You want those endorsement deals so you're financially secure, but you don't realize how cutthroat it is out there, how hard it is to get those deals. Because for every one of you, there are forty other guys clamoring for the same spot. That's what you pay me for. Not just to negotiate your contract, but to get all those deals for you and to put your face on the cover of *Sports Illustrated* and to make sure you end up in *People* magazine. That's what you pay me for. That's why you need me."

She pushed off the railing and stumbled into the kitchen.

Hell. He had no idea what *that* was all about. He knew damn well what she did for him. She was on a roll, wasn't she?

But he liked the feisty Elizabeth much more than vulnerable, sad Elizabeth. He was just going to let this play out and see where she went with it.

SHIT. LIZ LEANED AGAINST THE COUNTER AND TOOK A long swallow of wine, wishing she'd never agreed to come here with Gavin.

Spilling her guts like that had been stupid. She never talked to Gavin like that. Everything with him was always superficial. She told him how great he was, or she set him up for a photo shoot. And she renegotiated his contract and got him the best deal. That was it. That was all they ever discussed.

She always kept her distance from him, usually met him in crowds and at public events where she'd be safe.

And she had a damn good reason for it.

One, she was four years older than him. She didn't date younger guys. Ever.

Two, she was in love with him and had been for years.

Three, he was totally, utterly, and completely oblivious to it, and she intended to keep it that way.

Oh, sure, she flirted with him, just like she did with all her clients. Surface stuff, nothing but fluff. She never wanted Gavin to think she treated him any differently than she did her other clients. And he was mostly clueless, because he paid very little attention to her except when it came to business, thankfully.

But she did treat him differently, because she felt differently about him. She kept her distance because of how he made her feel.

When it had happened, she couldn't say. God knows she'd tried to keep it from happening. But there was just something about him. Maybe it was his dark good looks, his mesmerizing green eyes, the way his dark brown hair fell over his brow, or the sexiness of his goatee. Maybe it was his lean body that he honed into shape with daily workouts at the gym and playing noncompetitive sports outside his own sport of baseball. Maybe it was the way he catered to kids on the ball field, always taking the time to sign autographs or stop and talk to them. He was a big jock and worth millions, but he'd never developed a giant ego about it like many of her clients did. He was a genuinely nice guy.

But what she really loved about him was his smile. There was something wickedly devilish about Gavin's smile. It was a secret, mature kind of smile, the kind of smile that made a woman want to know what he was thinking about.

She'd been curious about his smile when she'd first met him and he'd looked her over in the way a man looks at a woman. But as soon as she'd signed him, that had been the end of it. He'd never looked at her that way again. Oh, she'd seen him cast that smile at other women, and in many ways she'd regretted signing him on as a client, even though she'd given him 100 percent of herself as an agent.

But she'd woefully, wistfully regretted not having him direct that wicked smile at her.

Until tonight. Tonight, outside the hotel, he'd looked at her that way for the first time since he became her client. He'd looked at her like a man looks at a woman he's interested in having sex with. Her breath caught and for one brief moment she'd wondered . . .

"You hiding in here?"

She jerked around to face Gavin, her fingers clutched tight to the empty glass of wine.

"Refilling my wineglass."

His gaze shifted. "Glass is empty."

"So it is." She lifted the wine bottle. "And so is the bottle."

Gavin went to the wine cooler and pulled out another bottle, grabbed the opener and yanked the cork out. His warm fingers slid over her chilled ones as he held the glass steady as he refilled it, his gaze never leaving hers.

"Your fingers are still cold."

There was that look again, that smile he'd given her outside the hotel earlier tonight, the one he'd never let her see before. Her belly tumbled, and oh, God, her nipples hardened. She wondered if Gavin could tell through her flimsy bra and silk blouse.

"I'm fine."

"Okay." He held on to her hand, and she tucked her bottom lip between her teeth.

"You'll have to spend the night."

She swallowed. "What?"

"I've had too much alcohol to get back in the car tonight. I'm not driving. You'll have to stay here."

"Oh. Uh . . . I could call a cab."

He smirked. "You could. But you don't want to, do you?"

What? What the hell was he talking about? Was he hitting on her? Oh, no. Oh, hell no.

She went for her bag and dragged out her cell phone. "I'm calling a cab."

He grasped her wrist and leaned into her. "We're not done talking, Liz."

He wasn't referring to having a conversation. She knew it, and so did he.

"Why now, Gavin? Why, after all these years, are you doing this now?"

"Why do we have to dissect it?"

Her heart pounded so loud she wondered if Gavin could hear it.

He laid her phone on the counter, pulled her fingers away from it.

Call a cab. Go home. Get out of here now before you do something incredibly stupid, Elizabeth.

"I don't have sex with my clients, Gavin."

His lips quirked. "You want me to fire you so I can fuck you?"

Her body was going up in flames. Why was he doing this to her?

"Not particularly."

"Do you want me to fuck you?"

She couldn't breathe. How was she supposed to answer that?

Lie, you idiot, just like you've been lying for the past five years.

He moved to the center island like a predator, caging her between it and him by placing his hands on either side of her hips.

"You're panting, Liz. Do I scare you?"

"No."

He leaned in closer, his hips brushing hers. And then she felt the hard ridge of his cock, and every ounce of common sense fled.

He bent and pressed his lips to her neck, his hair brushing her cheek. She inhaled, breathing him in, realizing this was the closest she'd ever been to him. He smelled like fresh soap and everything she'd ever dreamed of. She gripped the granite counter so tight her fingers hurt.

She tried swallowing again, but she'd gone dry. At least her throat had gone dry. Below her waist she was wet, primed and ready for him to slide inside her and give her what she'd fantasized about for the past five years. Her pussy throbbed with anticipation; her breasts hot and swollen. Her clit tingled, and if he rubbed against her just the smallest bit, she could come just thinking about how good it could be between them.

"Gavin," she squeaked.

"Touch me, Elizabeth," he murmured, sliding his tongue across her neck. "Put your hands on me, and tell me this is what you want."

Damn him. Damn, damn, damn. How could she not give him what he asked for? How could she not take what *she* wanted?

But this would change everything between them. And would undoubtedly cost her Gavin as a client.

Gavin pushed his hips against her, and she melted. She slid her arms up and tangled her fingers into his hair. She pulled on his hair to bring his face up, and the wild need she saw in his eyes matched her own.

His mouth was on hers in seconds, lighting the fire she'd banked for all these years. It exploded when his tongue slid between her teeth.

She'd dreamed of his lips, the taste of him. He tasted like whiskey and the promise of hot sex. He licked her bottom lip, nibbled at it. Her fingers were lost in the soft thickness of his hair, the only thing soft about him as his mouth ravaged hers. She knew there'd be nothing easy about Gavin. He was hardness and pain, and she reveled in it as he drove his tongue inside her mouth and tangled it with hers, sucking her tongue hard until tears sprang into her eyes.

She let out a ragged moan. Gavin grabbed her hips and lifted her onto the counter, settling between her legs, grabbing her butt to draw her heated center against him. He pulled her blouse out of the waistband of her skirt, lifting it over her head in one jerky motion.

He skimmed his hand along her throat and between her breasts. Elizabeth leaned back and watched as he laid his tanned, dark hand across the cup of her bra.

"Sexy, Elizabeth." He lifted his gaze to hers, then looked back to her bra as he pulled the cup aside, revealing her nipple, which was hard and puckered. "Such a pretty nipple, too."

She held her breath when he bent and put his lips over her nipple. The second she felt the hot suction, she gasped, her fingers moving into his hair again. She couldn't believe this was happening. All the hot fantasies she'd stored up of her and Gavin together were coming to life.

She'd never believed her dreams could become reality. She might be a little drunk tonight, and she knew he was, too, and this would probably never happen again, so she was committing every moment of it to memory so she'd never forget it. The pull of his lips on the tight bud of her nipple, the sight of his dark head against her pale breast, the scent of him as she inhaled a deep breath, and simply the way she felt—totally consumed by him.

It was her every fantasy to be taken by him. She'd known it was going to be like this.

And she'd never, ever tell him how much it meant to her. She had to keep herself under control, didn't want him to know how much power he held over her.

Never give a man power over you, or he'll destroy you.

She lived by those words, and yet right now she was in languorous splendor.

She'd take back control later. Now she gave it up willingly as Gavin dragged the other bra cup aside and lavished attention on her other nipple, using his fingers on the nipple he'd made wet with his mouth. And when he looked up at her, his eyes now filled with a darkness that melted her to the countertop, she waved the white flag in surrender.

He pushed her skirt up over her hips and laid the palm of his hand over her sex, smiling up at her in the way she'd always wanted him to—that secret smile he'd always reserved for other women, never her.

"You've got some very sexy underwear, Elizabeth. Do you always dress this way, or did you wear these tonight with the intent to seduce someone?"

She fought to find her voice. "I always dress this way."

"When was the last time you fucked someone?"

Her eyes narrowed. "None of your business."

He swept his hand up across her sex, and she gasped. "Answer me."

"No."

Pleasure shot through her as his fingers teased her, then stopped. "When was the last time you fucked a man, Elizabeth?"

She knew better than to give him that kind of control. She'd already given up too much. "When was the last time you fucked a woman, Gavin?"

He swept his fingers along the side of her panties, and she swore if he got anywhere near her clit she'd come. "You want me to lick your pussy, don't you? You want me to make you come, don't you?"

Her sex throbbed; her mind awash with the visuals of his head buried between her legs, his soft tongue lashing her pussy until she screamed in orgasm. "Yes. Make me come, Gavin."

"Then answer me. "

"Why do you need to know?"

He shrugged, his fingers lightly teasing the satin material of her panties. It was a breath, a whisper of touch across her sex. Enough for her to feel it, yet . . . not enough. "I want to know. Tell me. How long has it been?"

"Two years."

He frowned. "Is that the truth?"

"Yes."

"Damn, Liz. Look at me."

She dragged her gaze to his. He grabbed the tiny wisps of material at her hips and ripped. She gasped; he smiled, then dragged the remnants of her very expensive panties away. Her naked butt hit the granite counter, and she shivered.

"Cold?"

"A little."

He swept his hand under her butt and lifted her, then planted his mouth on her sex.

Oh, God. Oh, God. Oh, God. It was so good. She lifted, watching him as he slid his tongue in a wide arc across her clit, then dragged his tongue down her pussy lips, shoving it inside her.

"Gavin," she whispered, trembling at the sensations of his tongue rolling along her flesh.

It had been so long since a man had touched her. She didn't allow it for so many reasons. Sex was so complicated, and often she got so little out of it.

Thoughts fled as she gave up and allowed herself to feel, to experience the magic as he sucked her clit, ran his tongue up and down her pussy, licked her until she fought for every ragged breath.

He grasped her wrists and held her, his fingers digging into her skin, the pain only intensifying the sensations as he took her to the edge of control.

And embarrassingly, she wasn't going to last. She wanted to because this was the sweetest pleasure she'd ever felt. It was magic, and she was only going to have it once. But the rushing tide of orgasm wouldn't hold, and she lifted, cried out, and came, her climax a shock wave of sensation that zapped her nerve endings with unbearable pleasure. Gavin tightened his hold on her while he lapped up everything she had to give.

Her muscles quivered, and he helped her sit up, his face wet from her. Her hand shaking, she used her thumb to swipe across his chin. He grabbed her thumb and sucked it, his gaze still dark with unquenched desire. He handed her wineglass to her, and she took a couple long swallows to quench the raw thirst in her throat, but it didn't quench her thirst for him.

She was afraid it would take a long time for that thirst to be slaked.

He lifted her into his arms and placed her on her feet. All she wore was her skirt and bra, which was off-kilter. He was still completely dressed, his hard cock visible against his dark slacks.

He grabbed her hand. "Come on."

He led her down the hall, her bare feet padding along the wood floor toward the master bedroom that was all burgundy and cream and wide windows overlooking the ocean. She wished it was daylight so she could see outside, but there were open French doors leading to the terrace, a soft breeze blowing inside, and a lazy fan circling over the . . .

Oh, my God.

A bed that could sleep at least six people.

Now she understood the appeal of this house for Gavin.

It was the bed. Had to be the bed.

She wondered how many people he'd had in that bed at one time.

"You rent this house before?"

"I own this house, Elizabeth."

Yes, it definitely made sense.

"Plan many orgies?" she asked as she wandered into the room and stopped at the foot of the massive four-poster.

He frowned. "Huh?"

"That bed is not made for one, or two, people to sleep in."

He continued to give her a confused look, then glanced at the bed and back at her. "Oh. I sprawl. I like a big bed."

"Gavin, that goes beyond big bed. That's the kind of bed a polygamist would covet."

"I don't have orgies, Elizabeth." He grabbed a remote off one of the nightstands, pushed a button and the drapes started to close.

"Oh, please, don't shut all the night out. I like it open and breezy. It's not like you have peeping neighbors or anything."

He clicked the button and reopened them.

"Thank you."

He tossed the remote to the table. "Undress."

She put her hands on her hips. "You like giving orders."

He moved in front of the bed and casually leaned against the footboard. "Don't make me tell you again."

She tilted her head back and laughed. "Or, what? You'll spank me? You want my clothes off, Gavin, get your ass over here and undress me."

His eyes went dark, and oh, God. There it was. That not-quite-there smile, the one that screamed secrets.

Except his smile fled, and he stared her down, the heat swirling in his eyes. And then he advanced on her.

For a second, she trembled.

And she never trembled.

Whether it was excitement or raw desire she didn't know, but he was on her in seconds, her bra ripped and tossed to the ground. He grabbed her skirt, and she felt the strength of his hands at her zipper.

"Wait. Fine, I'll do it."

He stopped and stepped back, a smirk on his face as she drew the zipper down and let the skirt fall to the floor.

"Asshole," she said as she stepped out of it. "That underwear cost a fortune."

He didn't apologize, instead raked his gaze over her naked body, and any anger she felt fled in the face of the heated, hungry look on his face.

He unbuttoned his shirt, pulled it off, and tossed it on top of her skirt, then undid the button on his pants and jerked the zipper down. He kicked off his shoes and dropped his pants then his boxer briefs. His erection bobbed up, making her lick her lips and crave the feel of his cock in her hands and mouth.

He was magnificent and everything she could have imagined. Lean, with muscled abs and thick biceps, tan and sexy, and as he jerked her into his arms, she couldn't think of any place she'd rather be, even though she knew there were a thousand reasons they shouldn't be doing this.

And a million reasons why she wanted to.

TWO

ELIZABETH'S BREATH CAUGHT AS GAVIN JERKED HER against him, turned her around so her back pressed against his chest.

Her heart pounded, her body on fire, the need and desire so fierce it nearly drove her to her knees.

"You sure about this? I won't ask again."

She was shaking, the tension in the room so thick she felt she could reach out and touch it.

"I'm sure."

In actuality, she was sure of nothing. *Never give up control, Elizabeth.*

She blinked several times, blocking out the warning.

His warm breath billowed against her neck, making her shiver. He reached for her hair, pulled out the barrette and the carefully crafted pins holding it in place, then tangled his fingers in it, smoothing it out over her shoulders.

"Your hair is beautiful." He pressed his nose against the strands.

"Smells so good. You always wear it up. You should wear it down more often."

He smoothed his hands over her shoulders, down her arms, and back up again. Goose bumps pricked her skin, but she wasn't cold. She was so heated internally now she was on fire.

"Turn around, Elizabeth."

She pivoted, and the heat in his eyes was a blast furnace of need. She'd never been looked at the way Gavin looked at her now, as if he were so hungry for her he couldn't wait to have her.

It was raw, primal, and made her shiver with anticipation.

He grazed his knuckles across her cheek, the action so tender it made her knees weak. He laid his palm on her neck, then let his hand slide down her collarbone and over her breasts, cupping one in his hand.

"Your body is perfect. Soft." He swept his thumb over her nipple, and she gasped. "Made to be touched. Why haven't you let anyone touch you in so long?"

He rolled her nipple between his thumb and forefinger, the sensations shooting to her pussy, making her come alive with need and desire. She reached out and grasped his arms. Her legs shook, and she was afraid she was going to drop. But Gavin reached around her back to hold her and bent his lips to her breast, taking a nipple between his lips to suck.

"Oh, God, yes," she cried, needing that pain to satisfy her pleasure. She tangled her fingers in his hair, the desire to touch him only amplified by the sensation of his lips and teeth on her. He grazed her breast, sucking the skin.

When he let go of her, she was panting and dizzy with need.

He lifted her and carried her to that gigantic bed and laid her on the edge, her legs dangling over. He reached into the drawer and pulled out a condom, put it on and leaned over her.

"Look at me, Elizabeth."

She did, and he was everything she could imagine: his body tan and all lean muscle, his biceps bulging as he held her lower body suspended in his arms.

"I'm going to fuck you, hard. I'm going to use your body until I come inside you. And then we're going to play. All night long."

She waited, her pussy wet with need.

He positioned his cock at the entrance to her pussy and eased inside her.

She'd expected him to use her, to shove inside her. She hadn't expected this tenderness from him, and it was almost more than she could bear.

He laid his palms on either side of her and took it slow until he was fully seated inside her and then he held, waiting for her body to accommodate him. It had been so long since she'd had a man inside her, since she'd felt this kind of heat and thickness swelling in her.

His eyes briefly closed, and she saw the tension in the furrowing of his brow as her pussy quivered and tightened around his cock. She slid her hands along his muscled forearms, felt the sheen of sweat gathering there.

Then he began moving slow and easy, withdrawing partway out, and sliding in again. She raised her legs and planted her feet flat on the bed, lifting to pull him deeper inside her.

He lifted, watching her pussy as he fucked her. "You have a nice, tight, hot pussy, Elizabeth," he said. "I like fucking you. I've thought a lot about fucking you over the years. I didn't want to, but I did."

The way he looked at her tore away the veil of secrets she tried so hard to hide from him.

"Did you ever think about fucking me?"

"Yes. A lot."

He smiled, watching where their bodies were connected.

"I never knew it would be this good." He lifted his gaze to hers.

"And now you're mine. Do you understand that? You don't give this pussy to anyone else while we're playing. You're mine."

Oh, God. He was driving inside her, telling her she belonged to him, that she couldn't fuck anyone else. If any other man said that to her, she'd tell him to go fuck himself.

But she wanted Gavin. She'd always wanted Gavin. She'd never wanted anyone but him. His dark and delicious words thrilled her.

And she was so close to coming she had to grit her teeth and pull back to keep it from happening. Watching the way he fucked her was like a slice of magic, a fantasy come true. And to know he'd taken possession of her like this was something she could have never imagined.

He dropped her legs and bent down over her.

"You want to come, don't you?"

"Yes."

He ground against her and tears sprang to her eyes. She was so close. So damn close she wanted to let go, but she waited.

"It would feel so good for you and I to come together, wouldn't it?"

"Yes. Dammit, Gavin, yes."

"You want to come with me, Elizabeth?"

"Yes. God, Gavin, yes. Please let me come."

He dug his fingers into her hips and pumped hard, rolling his hips over hers as he ground against her.

Her climax shattered her, releasing the tension that had built up until she burst. She cried out as she came. Gavin pushed through the tightening of her pussy with fierce strokes, then glued himself to her and groaned with his own orgasm while she spiraled out of control. He laid over her and kissed her while her orgasm seemed to go on endlessly. He continued to move within her until the earth-shaking climax reduced to sweet pulses.

He withdrew, left her for a moment, then came back and turned her over onto her stomach, smoothing his hands over her buttocks. He laid a kiss on each cheek before sliding his hands down her legs.

"You have a fine ass, Elizabeth. And these legs of yours are amazing. I've always loved looking at your legs."

He climbed onto the bed and kneeled in front of her. "Get up onto your hands and knees."

She loved his power and his commanding presence in the bedroom.

She took control in every other aspect of her life. It was fun to give control up to him here; it excited her and made her tingle with anticipation.

"Suck my cock and get it hard again."

She licked her lips and opened her mouth, grasped his cock in her hand and took it between her lips. Her pussy was still throbbing from having him inside her, still quaking from the aftereffects of her orgasm. She slid her tongue around the crest of his shaft, then brought him inside with the suction of her mouth.

Gavin held on to the back of her head and slid his cock deep into her mouth.

"That's good. Christ, your mouth is hot. Take it deep, Elizabeth. Suck it hard."

She rolled her tongue over his shaft, then moved her head up and down over him. Gavin moved to the side to hold on to her wrists.

"Yeah, like that. Fuck, that's good. Suck me, Elizabeth. Get me good and hard and wet. Then I'll fuck you and make you come again. You want that, don't you?"

He was stretching her arms, holding them above her back, making her work on his cock with only her mouth. And all she could think of was his glorious shaft in her pussy, fucking her until she came again. She craved the orgasm, could think of nothing else but him pounding away inside her. He reached for her breasts, rolling the nipples tight between his fingers. The slight pain made her suck him harder.

"Yeah. Suck it hard like that. Now swallow it." He pushed into her throat, and she took everything he gave her. He seemed to know exactly how much she could take, because he'd pull back, then slide his shaft along her tongue, only to push deep inside her mouth again.

"Lick my balls," he commanded, and he pulled his cock from her mouth, lifted it out of her way so she could have access to his ball sack. She slid her tongue underneath to lick his balls, wished she was free so she could pull them into her mouth, but she was limited by the position he held her in. And through it all, he continued to tweak and roll her nipples, and the pain was delicious.

She'd missed having a man touch her, lick her, and fuck her. She'd missed so much about sex.

Gavin was a goddamn master at it.

She swept her tongue under his balls, flicking, teasing, licking him.

"Yeah, oh, yeah, I like your tongue."

He dropped her arms and dragged her up onto her knees, pulling her against him. His mouth met hers in a searing kiss that made her nipples tingle, his tongue diving inside to take possession.

"Now lay on your belly."

He threw a pillow in the center of the bed, and she lay across it.

"Spread your legs."

She widened her legs, and he put on a condom, then kneeled between her thighs. She felt his body brush against hers, and then he was inside her, and just like before, her pussy quivered. She grabbed hold of the sheets as he began to move slowly within her, easing out and then sliding inside her again.

He brushed her hair aside to kiss and nip at the nape of her neck. "Don't come yet, Elizabeth. You know it'll be good if you wait."

She fisted the sheets and held on, knowing she could come right now. Sucking his cock had built the anticipation, and she was primed and hot. The sheets rubbed her clit, increasing the friction, making her ready.

He rose up and grabbed her hips, thrusting harder, faster. "You make my dick hard. Your pussy is so tight. Lift your ass higher."

She lifted, and he powered inside her with a fierce thrust that drove her into the mattress. Her clit rubbed the pillow, and she was so close to climax she had to fight not to come. She wanted Gavin coming with her.

He dug his fingers into her hips as his strokes became relentless. "Are you ready, Elizabeth?"

Sensation pummeled her. She was ready to tear the sheets apart if she didn't get to come soon. "Yes, Gavin. Yes."

He reached underneath her and found her clit, rubbed the knot that burst with pleasure. "Let go. Come with me."

With his next thrust she splintered, burying her face against the comforter as she screamed with the intensity of her climax. Gavin glued his body to her ass and rocked against her, shuddering as he came.

When she finally fell, he was there to sweep her hair away from her face. He rolled her onto her side and pulled the pillow away. He left only long enough to bring them both something to drink, then gathered her into his arms and pulled her against his chest, rubbing her back and shoulders.

It was quiet. Neither of them said anything. Gavin turned off the lights and pulled the covers over them.

Elizabeth stared out the windows at the moonlight streaming in and listened to the lulling, peaceful sound of the waves.

This entire evening had been a revelation. She was still a little shaky about it all. She thought he'd brought her here to fire her. Instead, he'd fucked her, and it had been magical, more than she could have ever asked for.

The question was . . . now what?

THREE

NOW WHAT?

Gavin sat outside and watched the seagulls swooping down at the water's edge searching for breakfast while he nursed a cup of coffee and pondered the naked redhead asleep in his bed.

Not just any naked redhead, either, but his agent, Elizabeth.

What a surprise she'd been last night. In more ways than one.

He would have never expected Elizabeth to be his match in the bedroom. She'd turned him on in ways he'd never imagined.

Sure, he'd had a bit to drink last night, and fucking her hadn't been on his mind. It had just happened. But whoa, it had been good.

And he wanted more.

But it was an all-around bad idea. First, because she was his agent, and they needed to keep their relationship strictly business.

Second, she had screwed over his brother, and that still didn't sit right with him.

Third, she wasn't his type at all. He liked his women soft and easygoing. And easygoing and Elizabeth didn't belong in the same sentence.

He still wanted more of her.

He could have some fun with her. Okay, a lot of fun with her. It wasn't like they were going to be dating. He didn't date women. He fucked them. They partied, had fun together, and that was it. He had a career in baseball, a high-profile lifestyle, and women got into that. They wanted to be seen with him, and they understood how it was. Though there were always those who thought they could be the next Mrs. Gavin Riley.

He wasn't looking for a Mrs; not right now. He was too busy having fun.

"Morning."

He turned to see Elizabeth leaning against the doorway. She'd helped herself to one of his T-shirts, and God help him, she looked so damn different. She was usually dressed to perfection in designer clothes and high heels, and wore her hair up. This . . . this was spectacular. The T-shirt was long on her, hit above her knees. It was gray and worn, and hugged her curves. Her hair spilled down around her shoulders, was all messed up and stuck up in places, and she had a sleepy look on her face, pillow marks on her left cheek, and her lips were swollen.

Goddamn, she made his dick hard.

"Morning."

"I grabbed one of your shirts. And helped myself to a cup of coffee. I hope you don't mind," she said, lifting the cup to show him.

"I don't mind. Come on out here and sit down."

She sat in the swing this time and sipped her coffee, pulling her legs up on the seat. She inhaled and closed her eyes. "I can see why you like it here at the beach, Gavin. What a beautiful way to wake up in the morning. So relaxing to just sit and watch the ocean waves and the birds. You don't get this kind of view in Saint

Louis. Not that I'm at the office or at my condo all that often anyway."

Who was this person? He'd found out more about Elizabeth in the last twelve hours than in the seven years he'd known her. "You travel a lot. Me, too. It sucks. I come down here during the off-season a lot to go fishing and just to get away from the winter."

She brushed her hair away from her face. "Understandable. It's nice to have a place like this."

"I'm sure you could buy a place down here. You can afford it."

"Mmm," was all she said, then put the cup to her lips. "I should get dressed and head out. Mind if I use your shower first?"

"You have somewhere you need to be?"

She shifted her gaze to his. "Not really."

"Then why the hurry?"

"My stuff is at the hotel. I need to check out today."

"Where are you going?"

"Back home."

His lips lifted. "It's February. Cold in Saint Louis."

"Yes, it is."

"You could hang out here for a while, soak up some sun."

She rested the cup in her lap. "Are you inviting me to stay?"

Was he? He had no idea what the hell he was doing. All he knew was that he had fun with Elizabeth last night, and his dick wanted more of her. That was all he wanted.

"You're not gonna deny we had great sex last night."

She stared at him. "It was really great sex, Gavin."

"Then hang out with me down here. We'll have more of it."

"So you're not firing me."

His lips curled. "Not yet."

"Asshole." She pushed off the swing and sauntered into the house. He went inside to refill his coffee. Elizabeth was in the kitchen refilling hers.

"So are you staying?"

"Right now I'm going to take a shower. I need to go get my bags and check out."

"I'll call the hotel. They can check you out, and I'll have your things delivered here."

She leaned against the counter, cup in hand. "Thinking of holding me prisoner here for the next month?"

He leaned his hip against the counter. "I don't know. Think you've got what it takes to keep me interested that long?"

Her eyes sparkled. "That sounds like a challenge, Gavin."

He sipped his coffee. "Can you cook?"

"Not at all. Can you?"

"You don't grow up in my house without learning to fend for yourself. My mother didn't want her children to be tossed out into the world as useless human beings."

"So now you're calling me useless?"

"You're what, Elizabeth—thirty-four or something? One would think you would have learned to cook by now."

"I'm thirty-two, and you're a prick."

He laughed. "Not the first time I've been called that."

"I'm not home enough to cook, and who am I going to cook for? Myself?"

"Aww, poor Elizabeth. Single and alone. Am I supposed to feel sorry for you now?"

"You're baiting me, trying to get a rise out of me."

"Shouldn't you be trying to get a rise out of me?"

She let her gaze drift down his body and linger at his crotch, then looked back up to his face. "Why? What's in it for me?"

"Get my dick hard, and you get an orgasm out of it. After a two-year drought I figure you're gonna wanna come as much as you can while you're here."

She snorted. "You think you're that good, huh?"

He laid his coffee cup down and stalked over to her, pulled the cup from her hand and put it on the counter. He wrapped one arm around her waist, lifted her T-shirt, and laid his palm over her naked sex.

She was already wet, her eyes wide pools of green as he slid his finger inside her and rocked his hand against her, then took her mouth in a hard kiss.

She melted against him, her tongue sliding against his, her pussy coating his fingers with her sweet cream. He spread her juices over her clit and massaged the nub.

She whimpered against him, and he was relentless, driving his palm against her sex, dipping his fingers inside her to fuck her pussy. She lifted onto her toes and sought release.

And he gave it to her, keeping his mouth on hers, his arm wrapped around her to hold her steady while she cried out and clung to his shirt.

Her body quivered against his, and he let her down slow and easy, withdrew his fingers, liking the way she stared up at him with a little bit of shock and disbelief.

He flipped her around and bent her over the kitchen counter, flipping the T-shirt over her back, unable to resist roaming over the bare skin of her back and ass. Her skin was the softest silk, and in between her legs was sweet honey. He swept his hand between her legs again, and she lifted, spreading her legs, palming the counter, and letting out a gentle moan.

She was wet from her orgasm, and his cock throbbed with the need to be inside her. He put on the condom he'd had in his pocket, dropped his shorts and kicked them away, nestled between her legs and shoved up inside her, wrapping his arm around her as a barrier to keep her belly from hitting the granite counter, because he needed to pound hard inside her. His balls tightened as her sweet pussy gripped him in a tight vise of unbearable pleasure, and he knew he wouldn't be able to hold on for long. Nothing this good could last. She was tight and hot, and he was going to come.

He slid his hands under the shirt and grasped her breasts, filling his palms with her nipples and squeezing her flesh.

"Gavin," she cried, lifting off the counter, her hair spilling over his arms.

"Come on my cock, Elizabeth. Make yourself come."

Her hand slid between her legs, and she rubbed her pussy, her fingers brushing against his balls, teasing him as she teased herself.

He rolled her nipples between his fingers, plucking them into tight points. She whimpered.

"I'm coming, Gavin. I'm coming."

He held tight to her and pushed deep into her as he came, jettisoning deep bursts of come as his orgasm shot through him, leaving him panting and drawing in deep breaths.

When he withdrew, he turned her around and kissed her, making sure she understood without a doubt what he was capable of. He left her mouth wet, licking her lips and a look of uncertainty in her eyes as he swept his thumb over her bottom lip.

"Honey, I *am* that good. I know what you want, and I can give it to you. Anytime you want it. Anytime I want it. That's why you want to be here with me."

He picked up his cup, refilled his coffee.

"Shower's all yours. I'll go call the hotel and have your things brought over."

He walked away feeling pretty damn good about how things were going between them.

ELIZABETH WASN'T SURE SHE'D MADE THE RIGHT choice at all.

She swept away the fog in the bathroom mirror and stared at a woman she didn't know.

What the hell had possessed her last night? And this morning.

She'd had sex with Gavin Riley. She'd broken every damn one of her carefully constructed rules about not getting personally involved with one of her clients. And especially not Gavin.

And now her clothes and laptop were being brought here, and she was going to stay with him?

Good God. This whole nightmare had epic clusterfuck written all over it, and the thirty minutes she'd spent in Gavin's opulent shower had provided no clarity.

The woman with the wet hair staring back at her in the mirror was a grade-A idiot. She should grab her luggage and run like hell. This was going to end in disaster.

"Elizabeth?" Gavin knocked twice.

"Yes?"

"Your things are here, but I figured you probably hadn't intended to stay more than last night, right?"

"True."

"You don't have anything to wear, do you?"

"Not really."

"Okay. Get dressed, and I'll take you shopping so you can get some clothes."

She stared at the door. Shopping? He was going to take her shopping?

What. The. Fuck.

She felt like Alice in Wonderland, and she'd definitely just fallen down the rabbit hole.

Curiouser and curiouser, for damn certain.

She came out of the bathroom with a towel wrapped around her.

"I put your suitcase in my room."

She arched a brow. So did Gavin.

"You didn't think I invited you here to stay in one of the guest rooms, did you?"

"No, I suppose not." She padded into Gavin's bedroom, where he'd laid her luggage on the bed. She popped it open and grabbed her makeup bag and some clothes.

After she dried her hair and put it up in a twist, she applied makeup and put on a pair of jeans and a T-shirt, thankful she always packed at least one casual outfit just in case she got stranded somewhere. She slipped on her heels and went in search of Gavin, who was outside on the terrace. His beautiful shoulders and arms were showcased by the sleeveless cotton shirt he wore. He had on shorts and tennis shoes and a Saint Louis Rivers baseball cap.

Very casual.

"I'm ready."

He turned and looked down at her feet, then frowned. "Heels? We're in Florida. You need sandals."

She gave him a disdainful *pfft*. "Honey, I live in heels."

"Not on the beach, you don't."

"Try me."

He shrugged. "Whatever you want."

He drove her to one of the nice Palm Beach malls. Everything was outside, the sun was shining, and tall palm trees lined the walkway.

Now they were in her element—shopping. She breezed in and out of a few stores, picking up a few pairs of Capri pants and some shoes, underwear and sundresses.

Gavin laid back and held bags for her while she went on a tear. She knew herself, knew what she liked and what looked good on her. She didn't really own that much resort wear since she never took much downtime. These would all be new things for her.

He paid particular attention in the upscale lingerie shop, of course, his eyes gleaming when she fingered the sexy and sinful bras and panties. Armed with several items, she stood in front of him at the counter.

"I'm not paying a fortune for new lingerie if you're just going to ruin it by ripping it off me."

The saleswoman behind the cash register gaped at them. Elizabeth didn't care.

Gavin took the bundle from her hand, laid them on the counter, and whipped out his credit card. "No guarantees of that. You look smokin' hot in this stuff. If we ruin them all, we'll just come back for more."

She shrugged. "It's your dime."

That saleswoman would have plenty to gossip about after they left.

The temperature in the store rose a few degrees, and Elizabeth took a step back, irritated by the hardening of her traitorous nipples. The young saleswoman shot Gavin a look of pure lust, but he kept his gaze on Elizabeth.

Fine. Score a point for Gavin.

"You need something sexy to wear when we go out at night."

"We're going out at night? Where to?"

He shrugged. "Don't know yet. Maybe I'll take you dancing."

She ignored the tiny little thrill at the thought of being in Gavin's arms while he toured her around a dance floor. "I thought you just wanted to fuck me."

He stopped and slid his finger across her cheek. "I do. I will. But we have to come up for air and leave the beach house. You want to have some fun outside the bedroom, don't you?"

Something fluttered in her belly, something that felt an awful lot like stirrings of emotion. "Gavin, why are you doing this?"

"Doing what?"

"This. Keeping me here with you. Shopping with me. Talking of going out places. I don't get it."

He directed her into a store. "Quit asking questions."

He motioned to one of the saleswomen. "She likes black. So anything *but* black."

Elizabeth rolled her eyes. "Definitely lots of things in black for me."

She selected several black cocktail dresses, but by the time she went into the dressing room, they were gone, replaced instead by a red dress, a champagne-colored dress, and another in a soft burgundy.

"These are the wrong dresses," she said to the saleswoman.

"Your gentleman selected these. Said for you to give in and try them on."

She rolled her eyes, but the dresses were pretty, so she put one on. The red one first, which she paraded for him. He shook his head so she tried the burgundy one next.

"Nice, but not good enough."

She put her hands on her hips. "This is why I go for the black dresses. They always work."

He smiled at her. "Go put the last one on."

She flounced off to the dressing room, determined to prove him wrong. The champagne dress was fitted, had thin straps, and hugged every single one of her curves. She looked at herself in the mirror and was stunned at how the color accentuated her hair and her skin tone. She would have never thought to go with a color like this.

She came out of the dressing room, and Gavin's eyes rocketed to her.

He stood, came over to her, and turned her to face the mirror. His fingers grazed her shoulders.

"You're beautiful, Elizabeth. The dress makes your hair look like fire."

She'd been told she was beautiful before, but they had been surface compliments. Gavin spoke with his eyes, the way they raked
over not only her body, but her hair, her face. His eyes meet hers.
The warmth she saw there . . .

Was entirely her imagination.

"Thanks. I guess it's okay."

"It's more than okay. It gives you a sweet innocence instead of
the hard edge you always go for when you wear black. I'm getting
this dress for you." He signaled to the saleswoman. "This one."

"Yes, sir."

Men didn't buy her clothes. She was independent, had more than
enough money to buy her own things. Anything she wanted. That's
why she'd worked so damn hard the past ten years, so she could be
independent.

Never dependent again.

She sidled up to Gavin at the counter. "I can buy this dress for
myself."

He turned to her. "Yes, you can. But I chose it because I want to
see you in it, so I'm buying it for you. Is that okay?"

"Yes, I suppose."

"And while I'm buying this, why don't you change into that yellow flowery sundress you bought? It's hot outside, and you must be
dying in those jeans."

"Good idea."

She changed clothes, shaking her head while she did.

THEY FINISHED THEIR SHOPPING AND LEFT THE MALL.
Gavin took them to a seaside grill, where they had fantastic cock-
tails along with amazing seafood.

"So, are you a good seafood cook?" she asked, spearing her last
mouthwatering bite of lobster salad.

"I'm an excellent seafood cook. What would you like me to fix for you?"

"I love seafood. Anything you cook, I'll eat."

"I'll have to take you fishing, see what we catch."

She studied him over her pomegranate martini. "I don't fish."

He stared right back at her over his glass of whiskey. "You've tried it before and hated it."

"Not exactly."

"You've never fished."

"I've never fished."

"So I'll teach you. You'll love it."

Challenge. Again. "If you want me to go out on a boat with you, great. I'll sunbathe. You fish. And don't you have to play baseball or something?"

He smirked. "I still get free time and use every minute of it."

"Once spring training starts, you'll have games almost every day."

"Not every day. And games don't take up the entire day. Why, are you trying to get out of our agreement?"

"I said I'd stay, didn't I?"

"Good. You can come to my games. Or do whatever work you have to do. Schmooze some clients. Pick up new ones. Plenty of teams play around here. Do what you do best, as long as you're in my bed every night."

Her body zinged with awareness. She'd wanted to be with Gavin since the first moment she'd laid eyes on him, when he was twenty-two and she was almost twenty-six. She had felt like a dirty old woman back then.

Now he was twenty-nine and she was almost thirty-three.

"I'm older than you are, you know."

He laughed. "Where did that come from?"

"I just don't get the sudden attraction. You've never paid any attention to me before."

"Oh, I noticed you before."

"Still, we don't have anything in common. The fishing thing, for instance. Plus the age difference."

"I know how old you are, Elizabeth, which isn't even a factor. You think I can't handle you? Want me to show you again?"

She laughed and took a sip of her drink. "No, thank you."

He leaned back in his chair. "Bored with me already?"

She inhaled a shaky breath. "Not quite. You still have a little tread on your tires."

His gaze went dark. "Yeah, I'll show you a little tread on my tires. Go in the bathroom and take off your panties."

"Excuse me?"

"You heard me."

"No."

"You want me to take them off of you out here?"

"You wouldn't."

"Wouldn't I?" He finished his whiskey and slid his hand under the table, lifting her sundress.

She slapped his hand away, then the realization hit.

He'd asked her to change clothes.

"You planned this."

His lips curled. "Maybe."

She looked around the fairly crowded restaurant. Granted, no one was looking at them. They had a semicircular booth, which meant they could scoot together and . . .

No. She wouldn't dare.

"Do it, Elizabeth. You're already wet thinking about it, aren't you?"

Her gaze shifted to Gavin, her thoughts gravitating to how he would do it. What if they got caught? How could she stay quiet?

The danger aspect of it thrilled her. She wanted it, wanted him to shove his fingers inside her and make her come. Now. "Yes."

"Go take your panties off and let me make you come."

She grabbed her purse and hurried to the ladies room, dashed into a stall and slipped off her panties, tucking them into her purse. She stopped at the mirror on her way out. Her face was flushed, her pupils dilated with arousal. She was back at the table in no time, her pussy throbbing, her nipples beading against the soft fabric of her dress.

She scooted next to him and reached for her drink, taking a long swallow to quench her thirst.

Gavin leaned over and whispered in her ear while he lifted her dress to her thighs. "The tablecloth is long and will cover anything I'm doing. Put the napkin over your lap, and put some of those shopping bags against your other side."

She pulled the bags against her, effectively blocking anyone's view.

"Now spread your legs for me, babe, and let me touch your pussy."

She widened her legs, and his fingers danced along her inner thigh, sliding down over her sex. She leaned back, needing him to rub her clit, fuck her pussy, take her over the edge, and give her the climax she could already feel building inside.

"Make yourself comfortable. That's it. Put your elbow against the back of the booth. Turn and look at me like you're listening to me in conversation. Look at me the whole time, Elizabeth, because I want to see your eyes when you come."

His fingers slid between the hardened bud and down along her pussy lips, circling over and back up. He was toying with her. She laid her head in her hand, looking like she was relaxed and enjoying conversation with Gavin, but she was primed and tense.

"Gavin, please."

"Yeah, baby? Tell me what you want."

"Care for another drink?"

She jerked in surprise, but Gavin seemed cool and relaxed as he turned his head to smile at their waitress.

"I think we're fine here, Amanda."

Elizabeth shuddered out a sigh.

"Look at me, Liz."

She did, and he used his fingers, gliding them over her pussy. She was damp, needy, and she wanted to take his hand and shove his fingers inside her.

"Tell me what you want."

"I want your fingers inside me, fucking me."

He dipped the tip of one finger along the surface of her pussy, coating it with her moisture, then moved it back up to sweep across the bud of her clit.

"Stop teasing me. Fuck me. Make me come."

"The tease is the best part, Elizabeth. Do you know how hard my dick is right now? Do you know how much I want to be inside you or have your mouth wrapped around me? My balls ache. And when we leave here, you'll make me come. But right now, it's all about you and your pretty pussy, and getting you off."

She licked her lips, imagining putting her mouth on him and feeling him shoot down her throat, or him pushing his cock into her until she screamed in orgasm. But right now he dipped two fingers inside her, and she lifted her butt off the seat and pushed against his hand.

"Easy, baby. Take it easy." He swirled the pad of his thumb over her clit, keeping his fingers moving inside her.

Her mouth dropped open, and she inhaled, losing sight of where she was. She gripped his arm and dug her nails into it as he shoved his fingers inside her. His movements were maddeningly slow, taking her right to the brink, where she held, watching his face, realizing he knew where she was.

"I'm going to come, Gavin."

He stilled his movements. "Quiet, Elizabeth. Remember that no one can know. You control this."

She took a deep breath and nodded.

"Now come for me. Let me see it."

He swept his thumb across her clit with expert precision and shoved his fingers inside her.

Her eyes widened as she came with a rush of sensation. She wanted to buck against his hand, to let go with a loud cry. Instead, she dug her nails into his forearm and held them there while the tidal wave of pleasure took her to ecstasy.

Gavin smiled and held on to her while she rode that wave. He protected her the entire time by casting surreptitious glances around the restaurant until the wild crest of her climax settled. He withdrew his fingers and smoothed her dress back down over her legs. He leaned forward and brushed her lips with his. "Your face is flushed."

She smiled at him. "I can't breathe." She still felt her heart ramming against her ribs.

That was the most exhilarating experience she'd ever had.

"Will there be anything else?"

Their waitress smiled at Elizabeth.

"Oh, I think I'm done now," she said, and Amanda took her plate away.

It was only then that Elizabeth reoriented herself to time and place. She'd completely lost her sense of being, had forgotten there were other people in the restaurant who no doubt had been walking by. She'd been so tuned into Gavin and his touch, his focus, that she'd lost her senses.

Gavin was a very dangerous man.

"Ready to go?" he asked, handing the waitress his credit card.

Elizabeth was ready to go, all right.

Ready to go insane from playing this game with him.

FOUR

GAVIN STOOD IN THE BOX AND READIED FOR THE BALL, studying the pitcher's stance, trying to figure out what he was going to throw. The pitcher wound up, threw, and Gavin swung the bat. Wood connected and the ball soared into the outfield.

It felt good to swing the bat again, to feel the power. He liked seeing the baseball disappear deep into center field.

It was only practice, but as he took a few more swipes, his muscles loosening under the Florida heat and humidity, he felt the typical anticipation of the upcoming season.

By October he was dead tired, burned out, and desperate for a break. By February he was eager to get started again, ready to play the game. Every season it was like this.

He loved baseball. It had been in his blood since he was five years old and his father had stuck a bat in his hand and pitched him his first ball to hit. Something about seeing that ball skip across the dirt and through Mick's legs or over Jenna's head had made him feel a sense of accomplishment he couldn't get anywhere else. And all through T-ball and Little League, and in high school and college, he knew there was only thing he wanted to do with his life.

Play baseball. Because he was damn good at it.

After his turn at the plate, he grabbed his glove and went to his position at first base to shag grounders and work on his fielding.

They were having a scrimmage with Tampa Bay today. Warm-ups were finished and Tampa Bay's batters were up first, so Gavin stayed at first base. Wasn't even an official preseason game, but it was a game, and damn he was ready.

While the pitcher warmed up, he glanced into the stands and saw Elizabeth sitting in the second row on the first baseline. Sunglasses shielded her eyes. She wore her hair up, as usual, but she at least wore a sleeveless blouse and those pant things that came up to her calves. Capri pants. That's what she'd called them when she got dressed this morning.

And high heels. He shook his head.

She was on the phone talking to someone, and her face was buried in her laptop, typing away at something.

In other words, she wasn't paying attention. Not even when the announcer called batter up and the crowds applauded loudly.

She might as well have stayed at the house for all the attention she paid to the game.

Gavin focused his attention on the batter, who struck out. Gavin rolled his shoulders and got into position, bending over and readying for whatever might happen. Batter two hit a grounder toward first base. Gavin scooped it up and touched the base before the runner was halfway down the line.

Two outs.

Third batter popped up in right field.

It was time for Gavin's team to bat. Gavin waited in the dugout, since he was third in the lineup. Jose batted first since he had a good average, was fast, and could steal bases. He hit a grounder just past the shortstop and got on base. Dave popped up so Jose had to hold at first base, which brought Gavin up to bat. He stood at the plate and held at the first pitch, too high. Second pitch looked low and inside, but the umpire called it a strike. Third pitch was right down the middle and Gavin swung. It dropped in front of the left fielder, and Gavin ran for first. Jose, one fast motherfucker, ended up at third.

Gavin took a quick glance at the seats. Elizabeth still had her head buried in her laptop, not paying attention to the game.

He was irritated by how much it irritated him. So she wasn't watching. What difference did it make? She was his agent and they were fucking. It wasn't like she mattered to him or anything.

Focus back on the game, he got into running position and stepped off the base when Dedrick came up to bat. As their cleanup hitter, Dedrick was a powerhouse with a bat and held the team home-run record. Gavin leaned right.

First pitch was a strike. Second was in the dirt, but the catcher smothered it, saving a run. Dedrick got a piece of the third pitch but sent it behind him into the stands, foul. He connected on the fourth pitch and let it sail over the left field wall for a home run. Hell yeah. All Gavin had to do was make a slow trek around the bases.

As Gavin made his way to homeplate, despite the fans wild cheering, Elizabeth didn't once look up.

Dammit.

They ended up winning the practice game seven to two. Gavin showered, talked to the press, and signed a few autographs. Elizabeth met him at the dugout when he was finished.

"Next time I need to bring a hat. The sun is hot," she said as they walked to his car.

"Did you enjoy the game?"

"Yeah. It was great."

As if she had any idea. "What was the final score?"

She tilted her sunglasses down her nose. "Seven to two. You won and you scored twice. You're crowding the plate a little, though. You need to step back, or someone's going to bean you in the head."

Huh. So maybe she was paying attention.

He opened her door for her and she slid in. He tossed his gear in the trunk, feeling stupid for being mad. He slammed the trunk door and got in the car, started it up and headed back to the house.

When they got inside, Elizabeth went into the kitchen. "You want something to drink?"

"A beer would be good."

He went outside and sat on the porch. She brought out two bottles of beer. He twisted the top off both, handed one back to her.

"Don't really see you as a beer drinker," he said as she took a seat on the swing.

She took a long swig. "You don't know all that much about me, Gavin."

"True enough. Why don't you tell me?"

"I'm not really here for you to delve into my background, am I? I'm here because you want to fuck me. So let's just leave it at that."

He'd hit a nerve. Something she didn't want him to know about. But she was right. He didn't know much about her other than she'd started working for one of the top sports agencies right out of college, apprenticed with one of the best agents, and pushed her way into getting her own clients by the time she was twenty-three. Right off the bat she'd signed some pretty impressive figures. Since then she'd picked up a portfolio of some of the best the sports world had to offer in a wide variety of sports—athletes from football, baseball, hockey, basketball, tennis, and NASCAR. She was known as an agent and public relations magician, and she was highly sought after. Athletes came to her, not the other way around.

But losing someone as high profile as Mick had hurt her, put a dent in her credibility. He wondered how much.

Actually, he wondered a lot about her, realized he knew nothing about her personal life at all. He'd never bothered to ask.

"Where did you grow up, Elizabeth?"

She didn't answer right away, instead took a long swallow of beer. "Arkansas."

His brows rose. "Really? For some reason I thought you grew up in the East."

"You thought wrong."

He sat on the chair across from the swing and tipped his beer to his lips. "Where in Arkansas?"

"A small town. You wouldn't even recognize the name if I told you."

"You're a small-town girl? I never would have believed it. You have big city written all over you."

"People can change who they are, reinvent themselves."

"Is that what you did?"

She lifted her gaze to his. "Yes."

"Why?"

"Because I wanted to get away from the girl who grew up in Arkansas and become someone else."

"Who were you back then that was so bad?"

"I don't want to talk about this, Gavin."

She swirled her thumb over the top of the bottle. It was obvious she was uncomfortable talking about her past. But something made him push.

"Why not? Everything we are today is partly due to who we were back then. I want to know about you."

"Why? Why does it matter? We're just fucking. You don't need to know me."

"We're not just fucking. We're talking. We're spending time together."

She laid the bottle down and came over to him, leaned against him and smoothed her hand down his arm. "I'd rather just fuck."

He could push her to answer his questions. She'd cave eventually. But her scent was hot and sexy, and her breasts were pressed against his chest, and okay, they were just fucking. He didn't know why he was curious about her past.

Right now he was curious how far she was willing to go to make him forget the questions he wanted to ask about her.

She smoothed her hands down his arms and over his chest. "I love the way you feel, Gavin, the way you smell." She raised up and pressed her lips to his neck, so she could stroke her tongue across his throat. His pulse kicked up a fast beat. He liked her mouth and he wasn't a passive kind of guy, so he swept his hand behind her head and kissed her, tasting beer and mint.

The late afternoon sun beat down on his back. Sweat gathered and slid down his spine, but he wasn't about to move, not when he had a beautiful, sexy woman sliding her hand into his shorts and winding her fingers around his hard cock.

It was still daylight, but there was plenty of privacy on the deck, especially since he'd pulled the shades down on the sides, leaving only the front visible. And with him shielding Elizabeth and the beach a hundred yards away, someone would have to come up to the porch to see what was going on.

Not that he much cared since she had a stranglehold on his cock and was stroking him with deliberate intent.

"You trying to kill me?" he asked, his gaze riveted to the motions of her hand.

"No, not kill you." She stroked and squeezed, and it took every ounce of strength he had to stay upright. "Make you my slave, maybe."

It was working. He'd do anything for her right now. Time to even the odds.

He unbuttoned her blouse and pulled it aside, revealing a light pink bra with lace across the top. He traced the lace with the tip of his finger, slowly, watching her breasts rise as her breath caught and held.

"Now who's trying to kill who here?" she asked.

He swept his thumbs over her nipples, the silk material unable to hide the hard bud from his questing fingers. But what he really wanted was to feel the softness of her flesh under his hands. He flicked the clasp of her bra, and the cups sprang free so he could fill his hands with her breasts. She pushed her breasts against him, her nipples hard as she rubbed them across his palms. He slid his thumbs over the nipples, and she backed away, out of breath, then dipped her hands under his shirt, snaking her fingers over his belly and chest.

He held on to the railing of the deck and watched her, her shirt blowing in the wind. She seemed not to care that her breasts were exposed. And he sure as hell didn't care; in fact, he loved the view of her hard pink nipples and her perky round breasts.

She lifted his shirt off and threw it on the chair, leaned in and licked around one of his nipples. He sucked in a breath because it made his dick twitch, so she slid her tongue over the other and flicked her tongue over his nipple until it was hard and he was try-ing damn hard not to squirm. She seemed to know exactly how that got to him. Not that he was complaining, because he liked her mouth on him.

And when she dipped down to a crouched position, taking his shorts with her as she bent, he drew in a deep breath. He took a quick glance behind him. He could see people playing in the water in the distance, but no one seemed to be paying attention to what was happening on his deck.

Good, because Elizabeth dropped to her knees, grabbed his cock, and flicked her tongue over the swollen head.

He ached for her mouth, anticipated when she'd put her lips

around him, but he liked seeing her pretty pink tongue lick around his cock head. She dragged her tongue along the underside of his shaft, then wrapped her hand around him and stroked, lifting his cock to lick his balls.

God, he liked watching her play with him, especially when she licked his shaft from stem to stern and put her lips around the head of his cock, lifted up, and took him inside.

The heat of her mouth was intense, and when she pressed down, squeezing his cock head between her tongue and the roof of her mouth, he thought he was going to explode right then. She flicked her tongue over the crest, then dragged her tongue along the underside of his shaft, letting him feel every slow inch being pulled deeper into her mouth.

This slow play made sweat drip down his back. He wished he had a camera so he could take a movie of her mouth on his dick, her tongue darting out to circle his cock head before she swallowed him whole again.

Gavin gripped the deck rail, pushing his hips forward to shove more of his cock between her lips. She reached out and grasped the base of his shaft and held him, squeezed him, pumping his cock between her lips and sucking him hard until he felt the stirrings of orgasm. He held back, beads of sweat dripping down his brow. He wanted to prolong the sensation. But when she swirled her hands over his cock, then pumped him within her tight fist and shoved his cock deep into her mouth and took him all the way to the back of her throat, he couldn't hold back.

He reached down and held her hair in his hand, tilting her head back.

"I'm going to come in your mouth, Elizabeth."

She let his cock pop from between her lips and smiled up at him, licked the wide crest of his cock head, then slid his shaft into her mouth again.

Christ, she was beautiful, her lips swollen from sucking him, her eyes glazed over with passion. He grasped the back of her head and shoved inside her mouth, making her take all of him as his orgasm tunneled through him in a rush. She shifted and met his gaze and pressed her lips around him, swallowing as he let out a groan and erupted. He tightened his hold on her hair and held her there as he emptied everything he had, his legs shaking the entire time.

Elizabeth licked the head of his cock and released him. He tugged up his shorts, drew her to a standing position, and pulled her against him, her bare breasts sticking to his sweaty chest. He held her, kissed her, tasting himself on her lips and tongue.

He turned her around, placed her against the railing, and snaked his fingers between her breasts, watching her nipples pucker. Her breathing picked up as he bent and captured one bud between his lips, sucking it between his teeth to nibble.

She tangled her fingers in his hair, her soft moans driving him to suck harder, to tease one nipple between his fingers while he licked the other.

She held on to the railing while he dropped down onto his knees on the deck, unbuttoning her pants and sliding them down to her ankles, revealing a wisp of pink silk that matched her bra. He took his time gazing up at her, loving the half-dressed look and the breeze whipping strands of her hair across her cheeks.

He ran his fingers up her legs, slipping his fingers across the dampened silk of her panties. He swept his thumb over the hard bud of her clit, felt her legs shake as she thrust her pussy at him.

"You're hot here. Wet."

She stared down at him. "You made me that way. Sucking you turns me on."

His cock thrust against his shorts, already hard again, eager to slide between her legs and fuck her until they both came. But he restrained himself because what he really wanted was to taste her, to slide his tongue between the soft folds of her sex and feel her body come apart.

He raised up, pulled her panties aside, and pressed his mouth to her pussy.

"Ohhh."

Elizabeth lifted against him, pressing her sex against his mouth, feeding him the softness of her. She tasted like tart honey, hot and sweet. The sounds coming from her as he made a slow glide with his tongue only ratcheted up his need to make this good for her—as good as she'd made it for him.

He tucked his tongue inside her pussy, fucked her with it and felt her legs quiver.

Oh, yeah.

"Gavin," she cried out, and he tilted his head back, watching his redheaded goddess with her hair wild from the wind, her shirt flying out, and her breasts exposed to his view. Her legs were parted, and her pussy glistened from his mouth and her own desire.

She was beautiful when open to him this way, giving him everything, unrestrained.

He slipped a finger inside her pussy and swiped his tongue over her sex, lingering at her clit.

"Oh," she said, tilting her head down to watch him. "Yes. Fuck me with your fingers, Gavin. Make me come."

He loved watching her let go, loved seeing her so turned on and near the edge that she told him exactly what she needed. Her eyes were glazed over, deep in passion, and he knew all she was thinking about was climaxing. That's exactly where he wanted her—poised on the edge and ready to fly.

He circled the bud with his tongue, then put his lips over her clit, put two fingers inside her pussy, and started to pump fast, watching her face as she came.

She was beautiful when she was in orgasm, an almost-pained

expression on her face as she rocked her pussy against him and shuddered all over, her breasts rising and falling as she panted and reached down, grabbing his hair and holding him in place as the waves rolled over her.

When she finally settled, he rose and took her mouth, reaching into his pocket for a condom and sheathing himself, then entering her. She cried out as he drove inside her, felt her tighten around him as she wrapped her arms around him and kissed him deeply.

He grabbed her hair and held her while he pumped hard and fast. She was still spasming from her orgasm, the convulsions squeezing his cock in a stranglehold of sensation. Her tongue wrapped around his, and he sucked on it, needing to come inside her, wanting her to go off again. When he heard her whimper, he knew she was ready again, and he powered up inside her and held, then rocked against her until she splintered.

He went with her this time, losing himself inside her heat, kissing her as he came until they were both shaking, breathless and wet with sweat from their efforts.

"It's hot out here," he said when he pulled away. "How about a swim?"

She laughed, pulling her pants up. "Sounds good to me."

They threw on their swimsuits and ran into the ocean, which felt damn good after the heated fires they'd just been through. And even more, she surprised him. She didn't mind getting her hair wet, couldn't care less that her makeup ran in rivers down her face. In fact when he mentioned it, she didn't turn around to swipe at the mess under her eyes. Instead, she laughed it off and splashed water at him.

He hadn't expected that of her. She was always well dressed, her hair flawless—everything about her perfect. In the ocean her hair fell over her eyes, and she kind of resembled a drowned rat.

And she didn't seem to care at all.

There was a lot about Elizabeth that was totally unpredictable.

And she'd given him one hell of a blow job to keep him from finding out more about her.

He wondered what she was hiding.

Time to up the stakes in this game he was playing and see if he could get a little truth from her.

FIVE

THEY WERE GOING DANCING TONIGHT. GAVIN HADN'T been joking when he'd told her he wanted her to have dresses so he could take her dancing.

How utterly bizarre. She knew his mother had been a dance teacher at one time, but she just didn't see Gavin as a dancer. He was rough around the edges, a shot of whiskey and hang out at the bar kind of man. A man's man. Not a woman's kind of man.

But hey, if he wanted to get dressed up and go to a club, who was she to say no? She had plenty of guy friends she went clubbing with, though they were all gay and she usually went with the guys and their boyfriends. And had a wonderful time doing it. Nothing romantic about it, of course, at least not for her, but she had a blast clubbing with her friends.

Guy friends. She had a lot of guy friends. Girlfriends? No, not too many of those. Okay, none of those. She wasn't the type of woman who made female friends. She wasn't sure why. Maybe it was because she was in a man's business. All her clients were men. She didn't get friendly with their wives and girlfriends, at least not on a social level. Friendly enough that the women knew she wasn't after their men—just their men's careers. But friend friendly? No. Never.

She knew her way around men, was comfortable around them. Women were strange and bitchy, and she didn't know how to relate to them at all. Even in college she'd gravitated toward the guys, had always had more male friends than women friends.

What did that say about her? She had no idea. Maybe she was missing something by not having girlfriends to confide in all these years.

Then again, she didn't reveal her secrets anyway, so she wasn't missing a damn thing other than all-night chat sessions that were boring and tedious, and lots of drama she didn't want or have time for. Men didn't do drama, which was probably why she'd always liked them better.

She'd spent the day catching up on work since Gavin had a game and after-game interviews. They were going out late tonight.

She finished dressing and came out of the bedroom. Gavin wore black slacks, a white shirt, jacket, and tie.

"You clean up nice," she said.

He turned, scanned her from head to toe appreciatively, and smiled. "The dress looks incredible on you."

She lifted her head a little higher and turned around for his inspection. She had to admit he had a decent eye for clothes, which surprised the hell out of her. She'd never have chosen this dress for herself. Then again, she mostly wore black. This champagne-colored dress did bring out the color of her skin and made the red in her hair stand out.

She hated when someone else was right.

They drove to an incredibly ritzy restaurant in Palm Beach,

where Elizabeth was surprised to see they were meeting two other couples, guys that Gavin played with on the Rivers and their wives.

"Figured you wouldn't mind if we met up with a couple of my friends and their wives, and shared dinner with them."

She managed a tight smile. "Not at all."

She did mind, mainly that he hadn't told her. And okay, she'd thought they were having a night alone.

She shook hands with Dedrick Coleman and his wife, Shawnelle, and Tommy Maloney and his wife, Haley.

Shawnelle was gorgeous, just like her husband. She had beautiful dark skin, the most unusual whiskey-colored eyes Elizabeth had ever seen, a sexy modern Afro, and a curvy body with breasts that would no doubt make Gavin's eyes bug out of his head all night long. Then again, Dedrick was six foot three of delicious eye candy himself. So maybe if Gavin was going to ogle, Liz would, too.

Haley was a petite little blue-eyed blonde who looked about sixteen. Elizabeth could only hope she was of legal age. Tommy was one of the Rivers youngest players, so that explained why Haley looked like jailbait. She probably *was* that young.

Delightful.

This meant the guys would talk baseball all night, and she'd be expected to make—ugh—girl talk with the women.

They got their table and ordered drinks, and just as she suspected, the men put their heads together and launched into a discussion about today's game and the upcoming season. Elizabeth waited to be engaged by the ladies. It didn't take long.

"Elizabeth, how long have you and Gavin been dating?" Shawnelle asked.

Oh, we're not dating. We're just fucking each other brainless until one of us gets tired of the other.

Probably not a good icebreaker.

She forced her sweetest smile. "Oh, we're not dating. I'm Gavin's agent and happen to be in town for some business, so he invited me along to dinner."

Gavin pulled himself out of his guy conversation. "She lies. She's hanging out with me at my place during the preseason."

"Interesting," Shawnelle said, her amber eyes studying the two of them.

If looks could kill, the one Elizabeth shot at Gavin would have left him instantly dead where he sat.

Gavin lifted her hand and pressed a kiss to her knuckles.

"Okay, I'm confused. So are you two dating or aren't you?" Haley asked.

"Dating? Oh, hell no. We're just having sex, honey," Elizabeth said, profoundly grateful when her martini arrived.

"Oh," Haley said in a tiny little voice.

Shawnelle just laughed, took a long swallow of her cocktail, and said, "Get it while it's good, girl."

Elizabeth leaned back in her chair, deciding to tune out Gavin and have some fun. "It's definitely good."

Shawnelle's gaze raked over Gavin as she stirred her drink. "Mmmmhmmmm, I imagine it is with him." She turned her gaze back to Elizabeth. "What is it with these guys and their sex drive. I swear to God Dedrick damn near wears me out every night."

Haley looked dumbfounded, like she couldn't believe they were talking sex in the middle of a restaurant.

The girl needed some educating. Much too naïve. This could be entertaining.

"No idea. One would think they'd be worn out after all the work-outs and the games. But no. They could go all night long. All after-noon long."

"And the mornings, too," Shawnelle added.

"Yes. They wake up hard and they stay that way."

Shawnelle laughed and patted Elizabeth's hand. "And we like them that way."

Elizabeth chanced a glance at Haley.

Yup. Deer in the headlights look. Probably appalled. The poor kid.

Gavin leaned over and brushed his shoulder against hers. "What are you three talking about?"

"Sex. We're horrifying Haley."

Gavin shook his head. "Tommy, you'd better rescue your bride. I think Elizabeth and Shawnelle are corrupting her."

Tommy laughed and rubbed Haley's shoulders. "They corruptin' you, darlin'?"

She shook her head. "No. I'm learnin' a few things though." She waved her hand at Tommy. "Y'all go back to talking to each other and leave us ladies alone. There are some things I need to learn."

Elizabeth sipped her martini. So, maybe Haley wasn't as revolted as she thought. Or as naïve.

It turned out that talking with women wasn't as bad as Elizabeth thought it would be. Throughout dinner Elizabeth learned that Shawnelle was an absolute riot with a bawdy sense of humor. She and Dedrick had been married seven years. Shawnelle was a lawyer, worked for the district attorney in Saint Louis. And Haley, though barely twenty-one, wasn't naïve at all. She had a natural curiosity, was open and honest, and wanted to learn . . . everything. Including everything about sex. She and Tommy had only been married six months, but young Miss Haley loved sex. She'd lived a sheltered life in Mississippi, and she loved Tommy with every breath she took. Marrying Tommy had been her ticket out of her repressive small town, and she never wanted to go back there.

But Tommy, Elizabeth found out, was a little unpracticed in the sex department, so Haley wanted to soak up some knowledge about the art of seduction and getting her man to open up a little bit.

Shawnelle and Elizabeth looked at each other, nodded, and decided they could definitely help Haley out.

The dance club was away from the beach and private. Gavin had snagged them an invitation since the owner was a fan of the Rivers. The ambiance was dark, moody, and low-key, unlike the loud beach-type laser bars that blasted your ear drums out. Elizabeth was profoundly grateful.

She loved dancing and hot, up-tempo music, but she also wanted to be able to have a conversation without screaming herself hoarse. She was way too old for that nonsense.

They were shown to a VIP table against the wall. Private, with an attentive waitress. Just the way Elizabeth liked it. They ordered drinks and settled in against the cushioned booth.

"You enjoy dinner?" Gavin asked.

"I did."

"Sorry I was occupied with Dedrick and Tommy. I really didn't bring you out to dump you on Shawnelle and Haley."

"I'm a big girl, Gavin. This may come as a shock to you, but I can take care of myself."

"I'm sure you can. You were probably born not needing anyone."

Their drinks arrived before she could shoot a retort to his smart-ass comment. As soon as the music started, Shawnelle was ready to dance. Dedrick wasn't, so Shawnelle stood, smoothed down her dress, and looked at Elizabeth and Haley.

"Come on, girls. Let's go rock the dance floor."

"Oh, I don't think so." Elizabeth shook her head.

Haley grinned. "Sure. I'm game."

Shawnelle put her hands on her hips and stared down at Elizabeth. "You. Up. Dance floor. Now. No excuses."

Elizabeth was about to object, but the steely look in Shawnelle's eyes and the fact that the music was pretty damn good made her shrug. "Okay, fine. We'll dance."

"Yay!" Shawnelle took her hand and dragged Elizabeth out of the chair and toward the dance floor.

It didn't take long for the music to get her moving. Plus, Shawnelle and Haley were—she had to admit—a whole lot of infectious fun. It was obvious Shawnelle was comfortable with her body and didn't mind shaking it. Haley was simply in love with her life and enjoyed the freedom she had now, so the two of them danced around Elizabeth while she moved her hips from side to side.

When she twirled around, she found three sets of male eyes staring at them with rapt interest.

Which gave her an idea.

She flipped around and moved toward Shawnelle. "I think we can help Haley with her sex life while we're out here on the dance floor."

"Oh, yeah? How's that?"

Elizabeth motioned toward the VIP table, and it didn't take but a few seconds for Shawnelle to make the connection.

"I see your point. Haley, honey, sandwich yourself in between Elizabeth and me, and let's do a little dirty dancing."

Haley's eyes went wide. "Huh?"

Elizabeth moved in closer to Haley. "You want your man to want you, right?"

"Yes."

"Then you gotta turn him on," Shawnelle said.

"Men love to see women together," Elizabeth explained.

Haley looked up at her. "They do? Why?"

Elizabeth shrugged and bumped her hip against Haley's. "No clue. Something about the fantasy of girl-on-girl action gets their motors running."

"Which means that you and me and Elizabeth are going to give your husband something to fantasize about. And when you get him in bed with you tonight, you're going to ask him just how hot he thought it was."

Shawnelle slipped her arm around Haley's waist, and Elizabeth did the same.

"What do I do?" Haley asked.

"Look at us like you want to eat us for breakfast," Elizabeth said.

"And move your body like you do when you're in bed," Shawnelle added. "Tommy's imagination will do the rest."

"Oh, okay. I can do that."

Haley was a quick study. Though petite, she could move her hips. She tilted her head back, turned on her charm, and gazed at Elizabeth and Shawnelle like they were goddesses and she wanted whatever they were offering.

The three of them undulated against each other to the slow, sexy beat of the song; snaked their hands up and down rib cages, waists, and hips; rocked crotches against asses; and put on quite a show for the guys. By the time the song finished and Elizabeth headed back to the table, it was patently obvious that Tommy wasn't the only man at the VIP table turned on. Gavin's dark gaze latched on to hers. He stood and held out his hand for her. She caught the telltale ridge of his erection. She took a couple sips of her drink and started to sit.

"Not yet. Let's dance."

"Okay."

He led her out onto the dance floor and pulled her into his arms. As she suspected, he was a very capable dancer.

"We've never danced together before," she said as he moved her into the center of the floor.

"We haven't?"

"No." She'd been to parties with him before, events where there had been dancing. He'd either had a companion already, or she avoided getting that close to him.

"I guess I just never noticed that before."

She shrugged. "No reason for you and I to dance together, was there?"

He scrutinized her with a look. "Guess not."

Shawnelle and Haley were both dancing with their husbands. It gave Elizabeth a great deal of pride to see Tommy's hands on Haley's ass. Haley looked like she'd just reached nirvana. Her eyes were closed, and she laid her head against Tommy's chest. Elizabeth wouldn't be at all surprised if Haley ended up having dynamite sex tonight.

"Enjoy that show you put on?" Gavin asked.

She turned her attention back to Gavin. "Immensely. Did you?"

He snaked his hand down her lower back to the top of her butt and pressed in, making sure she could feel his erection. "A lot. I take it you've bonded with Shawnelle and Haley."

She grinned. "You could say that."

"I had no idea you were into women."

She tilted her head back and laughed. "I'm not. That was for Haley."

He frowned. "I don't get it."

She pressed against him to whisper in his ear. "She's trying to sex up her husband a little more. Things in the bedroom haven't been exactly great for the two of them. We were helping out."

Gavin leaned back. "Oh. Well, after your performance on the dance floor, that should do it."

She slid her fingers over his goatee. "Worked for you, didn't it?"

"You saying I need sexing up?"

She pressed her thigh between his legs, rubbed against his erection. "Honey, any more sexing up and you'll kill me."

He brushed his lips against hers. "Glad I'm able to satisfy you."

Butterflies danced in her belly. Gavin was dangerous to her in so many ways. She should have turned around and run like hell back to Saint Louis when he asked her to stay with him.

But it was just sex. At least to him. He had no idea how she felt about him. As long as she remembered that, she could survive this.

SIX

GAVIN DRANK A WHISKEY OUT ON THE DECK, LISTENING to the sound of the waves. This was always his favorite part of the night. Sometimes he'd sit here for hours, just listening to the sound of the ocean.

But tonight he was plotting. Elizabeth might have distracted him earlier with amazing sex, but he still wanted answers from her.

Why he cared about who she was before, he had no idea. It really didn't play into what they had right now, but for some reason he wanted to know. And for some reason she didn't want him to know. And he thrived on competition, on winning.

She was in the bathroom changing, washing her makeup off, taking her hair down.

Time to make his move.

He laid the glass down on the kitchen counter and headed into the bedroom.

She stood in the bathroom brushing her hair, wearing only a

cream strapless bra and matching panties. He went into his drawer and pulled out four neckties, grateful for the occasional media interviews he had to give that required him to dress up. He threw the ties on the seat at the foot of the bed, then went into the bathroom to press a kiss on the soft skin between her neck and shoulder. She smiled at him in the mirror, the softness of her green eyes mesmerizing him. He saw something in them. A vulnerability or something else he couldn't figure out, and he was struck by a punch to the gut so strong it almost knocked him to his knees.

What would it be like to see a woman like Elizabeth in his bathroom every night, to have someone to come home to instead of an empty house?

He'd never wanted a woman in his life before, never craved companionship. He liked his life just the way it was, liked being able to travel, to come and go as he pleased without having to answer to anyone. He had no ties and no obligations.

His life was perfect and he had no plans to change it.

But he liked having Elizabeth here, liked seeing her female doodads on his bathroom counter, loved seeing her dressed only in her bra and panties, loved ogling her creamy skin, loved feeling her next to him in bed at night.

Hell, he liked waking up next to her.

Whoa. Gavin wasn't the domestic type. And Elizabeth sure as hell wasn't, either. And if he was looking to settle down, get married, and start having some kids, she was the last woman on earth he'd choose to do it with.

Not the soulless cold shark.

But was she soulless and cold? Or was that just a part she played in business?

What did he really know about Elizabeth Darnell?

Time to find out.

She turned to him, wrapping her hand around the back of his neck. "Ready for bed?"

"You could say that." He took her hands and led her to the side of the bed, reached around and unhooked her bra, then bent and pulled her panties down.

He undressed, glad to be rid of his clothes so they were both naked.

Elizabeth reached out and fanned her fingers over his chest. "Mmmm, I like where this is going."

"Do you? We'll see. How about you lay in the middle of the bed. I'm going to tie you up and have my way with you like you did with me this afternoon."

Her eyes flashed with desire. "You weren't tied up this afternoon."

"Do you trust me, Elizabeth?"

She arched a brow. "That's a loaded question, Gavin."

"Then trust me enough to know I won't hurt you. Because I won't. I never will."

She sucked in a breath. "All right. But you know I can't spread my limbs as wide as your giant orgy bed."

He laughed. "I know. I'll take care of it. Go spread out in the middle of the bed."

She crawled onto the bed, her sweet ass and pussy on display for him as she did. His cock tightened and hardened as she rolled over onto her back, then lifted her arms up over her head and widened her legs. He couldn't resist palming his shaft and balls, and giving them a squeeze. Just looking at her spread out on his bed like that gave him a lot of ideas.

First he had to secure her. He grabbed the twine he'd pulled from the garage, measured the length he'd need from the posts at each end to her legs and ankles, allowing for the length of the neckties, then cut four strips. He tied the ends of the twine to the end of each necktie, then secured her ankles and wrists, giving her enough room to move comfortably but not enough to roll and get away.

She watched him the entire time without saying a word, her nipples beading hard, moisture gathering at the entrance to her pussy. He swept his finger along the seam of her sex and brought his finger to his mouth and sucked.

"This get you wet?" he asked, positioning himself on his knees between her spread legs.

"Yes."

"Why?"

"Because I wonder what you're going to do to me."

He cupped her ankles above the restraints and smoothed his hands up her legs. Her skin was smooth silk, buttery soft. Having her under his control like this was tempting, made his cock so hard it was painful. He wanted to slide inside her right now and fuck her until he came. But that would ruin the fun and anticipation for both of them.

"The answer is easy. I'm going to give you pleasure. I'm going to make you come. You're going to make me come."

Her breasts rose as she inhaled a deep breath.

He laid his hands on her hips and swept his fingers over her belly. She flinched, sucking her stomach in. He bent down and pressed a kiss to her navel, then dragged his tongue south. He heard her breath catch and smiled.

She didn't think he'd go right for the holy grail, did she?

He stopped at her pubic mound, pulling his tongue up to her belly button again, dipping the tip into her navel.

"Dammit, Gavin."

Oh, he was just getting started. If she thought he was torturing her now . . .

He swept his hands over her rib cage, rose up, and straddled her, letting his dick rest against her pussy as he took her breasts in his hands, filling his palms with the globes as he rubbed his cock against the softness of her sex.

She lifted her butt, sliding against his cock. He smiled down at her but didn't let her have it.

"We're not nearly ready to fuck yet, Elizabeth."

"Bastard," she said, her eyes green slits of frustration and desire.

He rolled his thumbs over her nipples, then bent down and took one in his mouth, keeping the other entertained by squeezing it between his fingers. Her cries of delight made his balls quiver. He cupped her breasts in his hands and rolled his tongue over both, sucking and licking them until Elizabeth started to pull against the ties at her wrists.

"Fuck me, Gavin. Lick my pussy. Do something to make me come."

Now he had her. He leaned over her and brushed his lips against hers. She lifted her head, her tongue meeting his in a hungry kiss. He tangled his fingers in her loose hair, loving the soft wildness of it. He spread it over the pillow under her head, then kissed her jaw and her neck. He ran his tongue across the side of her neck, her shoulder, her collarbone, before taking a lazy trail over her breasts and belly again.

"You're making me crazy."

She was losing patience. Good. He wanted her willing to do anything.

He licked his way to the top of her sex, his tongue hovering near her clit. He inhaled the sweet scent of her sex, the tangy aroma of her arousal, then lifted his head to see her looking down at him with hunger and demand.

Oh, yeah. His gaze still focused on her, he dragged his tongue along the crease of her inner thigh, across her wet pussy lips, avoiding her clit, licking all around her, taking her so close he saw the muscles of her biceps bulge as she pulled at the restraints.

"Gavin!"

And yet he wouldn't lick her there just yet. He circled the bud with his tongue, flattened his tongue across her pussy lips, dipped inside to lap at her juices, held on to her hips and legs when she started to buck against him.

"Goddamn it, Gavin, this isn't fun."

Oh, yes, it was.

Because when he dragged his tongue up her pussy and laid it right on her clit, she moaned a long, low sound that made his cock swell, made him grind his pelvis against the mattress, made him want to come inside her.

And then he stopped, rose up on his knees.

She jerked her head up.

"You have got to be kidding me. You are not stopping."

"Tell me about Arkansas, Elizabeth."

Her eyes widened. "Are you out of your fucking mind? Get your head back down there between my legs and lick my pussy. I'm not talking about Arkansas. Not now, not ever."

He laid his hand on her sex, dipped his fingers inside her, and pumped once, twice, felt her shudder, felt her pussy tighten around his fingers.

"Fuck you, Gavin. Untie me."

He withdrew his fingers and took all that wet cream and painted her clit with it, teased the nub until it hardened and bloomed under his finger.

She dropped her head and moaned, her hips rocking under his hand.

And then he stopped. "Tell me about Arkansas, Elizabeth."

"Screw you. This is supposed to be fun between us."

"I'm having fun."

She stared up at the ceiling. "I'm not."

"Aren't you?" He swept his fingers along the seam of her pussy again, circling her clit until her lips clamped tightly closed and her jaw tightened. "You want to come, Elizabeth. I know how good this feels." He slid two fingers inside her and began to move. "You want me to fuck you, to make you come. I want to come in you, to feel your pussy squeeze me until I shoot off inside you."

She refused to look at him. "Then shove your cock in me and fuck me."

"I want to know you, to know all about you. I want to know where you came from, who you were before."

She lifted her head and tears filled her eyes. "No, you don't. You don't want to know that, Gavin. Please."

He pulled his fingers out of her, laid down on top of her. "What hurts you about that? Tell me."

"Damn you. I can't. Don't make me talk about it. This isn't a game to me."

Was she manipulating him, or was that the truth? With Elizabeth, he was never sure.

And what did she mean by it not being a game? Being tied up, talking about Arkansas, or something else?

He swept his hand over her hair, turned her to face him. "Talk to me."

"Let me go, Gavin. Just let me go."

He kissed her. She whimpered against his lips, fighting him at first, but then she gave in. Gavin untied the restraints at her wrists, and she wrapped her arms around him, tight. He swept his arm around her back, and something elemental passed between them, something fierce and primal as he fit his cock at the entrance to her pussy and slid inside her.

Elizabeth lifted, and Gavin reached underneath to hold on to her ass, pulling her closer to him as he ground against her, still kissing her, his tongue licking against hers as they met each other in a hot melding of passion that caught him by surprise. Maybe he felt bad for asking more than she was willing to give, but his guilt was torn away as desire took over and he fucked her with deep strokes.

Elizabeth raked her nails across his shoulders and moaned against his lips. It was as if neither of them wanted to break the contact. He wanted to untie her legs but didn't want to break his hold on her as he rolled his hips against her, giving her the contact she needed against her clit. She bit his lip, and he dug his fingers into the globes of her ass, dipping her pelvis up to drive harder inside her.

Her pussy gripped him as he felt the first waves of her orgasm clench around his cock. She cried out, and he swallowed her cries with his own loud groans as his orgasm crashed into him and left him holding tight to Elizabeth.

It wasn't until he pulled out and went to untie her that he realized he'd fucked her without a condom.

His hands were shaking as he released the restraints and rubbed her legs, wondering how the hell he'd lost control like that. He never, ever lost control.

He crawled up onto the bed and pulled her into his arms. "God, Elizabeth, I'm sorry."

"It's okay."

"No, I mean I didn't use a condom. That has never happened before. I am always protected."

She lifted up and looked at him. "Gavin, I'm on birth control. And I haven't had sex in two years. I told you that. You don't have to worry about me. I'm safe."

Jesus. She thought . . . Jesus.

He dragged his fingers through his hair. "Honey, I'm worried about hurting you, not the other way around. But I'm tested regularly. Clean bill of health. And I've never, ever had sex without a condom. Until tonight. I don't know what happened."

She laid her head back down. "Don't worry about it. It's not like I'm going to pop up pregnant or try to trap you."

That wasn't at all what he was worried about.

"And about me asking you questions."

She stilled. "Forget it, okay?"

"Okay."

But he wasn't going to forget it.

SEVEN

ELIZABETH WAS WAITING FOR HIM OUTSIDE HIS LOCKER after the game the next day.

"I thought we'd go have dinner at this new Italian restaurant in West Palm Beach."

She'd brushed aside the night before, hadn't said anything further about it. Gavin wanted to talk about it, but every time he'd try to bring it up she changed the subject. He wasn't the sharpest tool in the shed, but he could grab a clue.

"Italian it is." He grabbed his bag, put his arm around her, and they pushed through the doors to the parking lot.

He stopped dead in his tracks when he saw his brother leaning against a car.

Mick's smile died instantly when he spotted Gavin with his arm around Elizabeth. Mick pushed off the car and came toward them.

"Oh, shit," Elizabeth whispered, stepping away from him.

"Hey," Gavin said as Mick approached. "I didn't know you were in town."

Mick hugged him, but he wasn't smiling. "Yeah. I had a meeting in New York, so I thought I'd take a quick flight down here and catch one of your games."

He nodded at Elizabeth. "Liz."

"Hi, Mick."

"So, what's going on?"

Gavin shrugged. "Preseason stuff. You know the drill."

"That's not what I meant and you know it. What's going on with you and Elizabeth?"

Elizabeth turned to Gavin. "I'm going back to the house. I'll let you catch up with your brother, okay?"

Gavin nodded. "Sure."

He watched her walk away. She looked miserable. "Give me a second, Mick."

He caught up with Elizabeth. "Hey. I'm sorry. I didn't know he was in town."

She lifted her head. There were unshed tears in her eyes, but she masked her unhappiness with a wide smile. "It's no big deal. You catch up with your brother. I'll see you later."

Uncaring whether his brother saw or not, Gavin cupped her cheeks and pressed a soft kiss to her lips. "I won't be long."

Elizabeth grasped his arms. "You take your time and enjoy catching up with Mick. I have some contract stuff to work on anyway."

He waited while she got into her car and drove off. When he turned around and walked back, Mick had a furious look on his face.

"Want to go get something to eat?" Gavin asked.

"What the fuck is going on?"

"Look. I'm hungry. Let's eat and then we'll talk. Follow me."

It was a chickenshit excuse, but Gavin needed a few minutes alone in his car to get his bearings before facing his big brother. He drove them to a restaurant several miles away from the ballpark where they could grab some burgers and where Gavin could get a beer. Since Mick was an alcoholic, he ordered a soft drink.

Once the waitress took their food orders and brought their drinks, Mick leaned forward.

"What the fuck, Gavin? Elizabeth? Are you out of your mind?"

Gavin's chin lifted, irritation making him grip the glass tightly in his hand. "What about Elizabeth?"

"You know what she did to Tara and Nathan. Her betrayal of them hurt them. It hurt me."

"And she knows it. She apologized and she fixed it. And you fired her. What the hell do you want from her, man? Blood? A limb, maybe?"

"I can't believe you're seeing her. How long has this been going on?"

Gavin's lips lifted. "Now you sound like Mom."

"Not funny. I'm serious here. Or maybe I should ask if you're serious. Are you just fucking her? Or maybe you're just fucking *with* her. Surely you don't care about her. Do you have any idea how screwed up this is?"

Once again it was all about Mick. How many times in Gavin's life had the world revolved around his brother? First it was football, then his alcoholism. The family had always rallied around Mick. Gavin supposed being the oldest had its advantages. You got to do everything first. Mick had always been the shining example that Gavin had to follow. And then when Mick had fallen from grace with his battle with alcohol, he'd dragged himself up by his bootstraps and shown everyone what a hero he was and become an NFL star.

Oh, sure, Gavin had his own successes in baseball, but really, after everything Mick had been through, Gavin's success in the major leagues was pretty much an afterthought.

And now with Elizabeth, she was the agent Mick had fired. So Gavin wasn't supposed to date Elizabeth because she had screwed over Mick's fiancée? Even Gavin's girl wasn't good enough for Mick?

Fuck that.

The waitress brought their burgers, and the conversation was put on hold temporarily while they dove into their food. Unfortunately, Gavin's voracious appetite waned as he thought about Mick's attitude toward Elizabeth and Elizabeth's reaction to seeing Mick there.

"So, are you going to tell me what's going on?" Mick asked, pouncing as soon as Gavin pushed his plate aside.

"I don't know what you're fishing for, Mick."

"You and Liz. What's the deal?"

"Stay out of my personal life, Mick. Shouldn't you be concentrating on your own?"

Mick's gaze narrowed. "Don't bring her around the family."

"Mom loves Elizabeth."

"Not right now, she doesn't."

"Has she told you that?"

"She doesn't have to. She knows everything that went down with Tara and Nathan."

"And she said . . . what, exactly?"

Mick tossed his napkin on the table. "You know she doesn't like people who interfere in other people's lives. And she doesn't like people who hurt kids."

Which meant Mom hadn't directly said anything negative about Elizabeth. "You're just making this all up as you go along. Look, Mick, I get that you're defending Tara. If she were my woman, I'd do the same. And I understand you're still pissed at Liz for the way she manipulated all of you. But my relationship with her isn't the same, and you can't judge me . . . or her . . . for it. You need to stay out of it."

Mick shook his head. "Sorry, but you're my brother, and you haven't always made smart decisions where women are concerned."

"Oh, so now you're saying I'm stupid."

"I didn't say that. But you know Liz. Or at least I thought you did. Can't you see what she's doing?"

"She isn't *doing* anything. We're having some fun together and that's all. It doesn't have anything to do with you. Leave it alone."

Mick stared long and hard at him. It reminded Gavin of when they were kids fighting over a toy. But Elizabeth wasn't a toy. And this time Mick wanted Gavin to throw her away.

"I think you're making a mistake. She's only with you because she's trying to keep you as a client."

"I'm not that stupid, Mick."

Mick leaned back and grabbed his glass of soda, finished it and took the bill the waitress presented. He took out cash and handed it to her with a smile. After the waitress left, Mick's smile died as he turned his attention back to Gavin. "Just clear your head and try not to think with your dick. She's playing you."

"Thanks for thinking so highly of me."

"I care about you, Gavin. I don't want to see her hurt you the way she hurt me and Tara."

"I think you need to get over your grudge against her and move on with your life. Plan your wedding to Tara. Forget about what Elizabeth did."

They walked outside to their cars.

"Thanks for coming down here to see my game."

Mick finally smiled for the first time. "You're looking good."

"Thanks."

They hugged. "At least think about what I said."

"Give Tara my love. And Mom and Dad, too. I'll be back home soon."

Mick inhaled and let it out. "This isn't a game, Gavin."

Gavin hadn't felt that way before.

So why did he suddenly feel like it was? A game between Gavin and his brother, and Elizabeth was right in the middle of it.

EIGHT

"YOU'RE OUTTA THERE!"

Gavin tossed the bat in the dirt and headed for the dugout, mentally cussing out the umpire who'd called him out on strikes.

That last ball was low and inside and out of the strike zone.

"That last ball was right in your hitting zone, Riley."

Gavin lifted his gaze to the Rivers coach, white-haired, heavyset Manny Magee.

"Yeah, yeah. I'll get 'em next time, Manny." Gavin flopped onto the bench.

"Your first game you were hitting them like there was an eight-year-old pitching tennis balls to ya. The past five games you haven't hit shit. What the hell, Riley?"

Elizabeth had been gone for five days. The last five games he'd totally sucked.

Not that the two were related. At all. Gavin didn't believe in women and their mojo on players, good or bad.

"I'll work on my hitting, Manny."

"You're damn straight you're going to work on your hitting. I need to see some lightning out of you, Riley, and soon. Because you suck."

Great. He needed a hitting nosedive while in the preseason. Not.

"Where's your good-luck charm?"

"Huh?" Gavin turned to Dedrick. "What good-luck charm?"

"Elizabeth. When she was here, you played good. Shawnelle said she hasn't been to the past few games, and you've sucked. Which makes her your good-luck charm."

"Oh. She had to head out of town for a few days on business. And she's not my good-luck charm. I've been playing baseball for five years without her help, Deed."

Dedrick spit sunflower-seed shells onto the ground. "Yuh-huh. That was before you started sleepin' with her. Now she's your good-luck charm."

Gavin rolled his eyes, glad the game was in the ninth inning so he could get away from Dedrick's knowing looks. He showered, did his media bit, and got the hell out of there, craving the quiet of his house.

There was no correlation between Elizabeth being gone and his shitty hitting streak. He'd just been a little preoccupied since she'd left the other morning, because he figured it was his fault she was gone. And she wasn't coming back. He knew he shouldn't have pushed her about Arkansas. The very next morning she'd packed up her things and said she had a client who was going to be drafted into the NFL next month and there was a snag she had to deal with. She said she'd be back as soon as she took care of it.

He knew it was more than that.

Even worse, he missed her, which made him feel all kinds of stupid, because he wasn't supposed to miss her. They'd only been together a few days. No big deal, right?

So why did he miss her? He had games almost every day, followed by meetings and practice and media bullshit to keep him busy.

But the nights he spent on the deck looking out over the ocean were lonely. Like tonight. He leaned against the railing and listened to the give and take of the sea in the darkness. It used to fill him with peace.

Now it was a lonely sound.

And goddamn it, it had never been lonely before. In a couple days he'd gotten used to having Elizabeth around.

Time to get over that. What he needed to do was find a woman, go have a few drinks and some fun. He'd forget about her as soon as he slid his dick into some willing female. And his batting would likely improve, too.

He went inside, laid his drink on the counter and picked up his phone, stared at it for a few minutes, then put it back on the counter.

Shit. He didn't want to go out with some boring chick who didn't challenge him.

Elizabeth was a pain in the ass. Mouthy. Opinionated. Obstinate.

But she challenged him.

His phone rang and he swept it up off the counter.

Elizabeth.

"Hey," he said as soon as he pressed the button.

"Hey, yourself. You home?"

"Yeah."

"Good. I'll be pulling into your driveway in about ten minutes."

He hung up and ignored the rush. So, she was back. She was coming back to him, to his house, just like she said she would.

Dude, you gotta be careful. Wasn't this his game to play? Because it sure seemed as if she'd played him. Had she run off because he'd gotten too close, because he wanted too much information?

He fixed himself another drink and picked up the place since he'd been mainly tossing clothes all over for the past five days. By the time Elizabeth came to the door, the house looked sort of presentable again. He went out and grabbed her suitcase from the trunk of her car. She smiled at him.

"I could have dragged that in."

He rolled it and talked to her as they walked to the front door. "Then what good would I be?"

She grinned at him. "I can think of ways you can be useful."

He grinned back at her. "How was the trip?"

She shrugged out of her suit jacket and folded it over the back of the sofa. "Exhausting. Exhilarating. Negotiations are fun but nerve-racking, especially since it's the draft. You don't really know if a team is going to commit to a player or not, so everything you're talking about has to be couched very carefully so you don't blow it."

He handed her a glass of wine and sat next to her on the sofa. "Who was the client?"

She arched a brow. "Blane McReynolds. Offensive lineman out of Indiana. Promising future and great talent. We're pretty certain Tampa Bay is going to draft him. Why?"

"Just curious about which young hotshot you signed."

She kicked her high heels off and propped her feet on the table in front of the sofa. "Honey, I'm always signing a hotshot or two. Have to keep the young blood rolling in for when the old timers aren't any good to me anymore."

"You're so devoted to your clients."

She batted her lashes. "Always. Anyway, we're pretty secure about Tampa Bay, and they have the second pick in the draft. Their offensive line is shit, and they need to build with strong talent, especially at offensive tackle, which means they're looking hard at Blane. He's pretty thrilled about that, but you never know. Teams change their minds. Nothing's for certain. The poor kid is a basket case.

He's worked his whole life for this." She turned to him. "You remember what it's like."

"Yeah, I do. And you did a great job for me."

Her lips lifted. "Thanks. I was practically a rookie myself back then."

"Didn't seem that way to me. You went in there balls to the wall and didn't take no for an answer."

She laughed. "I didn't even know what I didn't know back then. With you or with Mick. God, I was fearless."

"You still are."

She kept her gaze on his. "Thank you, Gavin. A little shot of confidence is welcome. I needed that."

So maybe she had been gone for a reason. And maybe she wasn't playing games with him. "You got a backup team for this kid?"

She grinned, and he could hear the excitement in her voice. "Yes. Two, in fact, are interested in Blane. Both with first-round picks, but they could go another direction, too." She scrunched her shoulders, then took a long swallow of wine. "This stuff makes my head hurt."

"Turn around."

"Why?"

"I'll rub some of the tension away."

She gave him a wicked smile. "Now that sounds good."

She turned and presented her back to him. He started off light, using his thumbs on the muscles, which were definitely hard as rock. His fingers kept slipping on her silk blouse.

"Take your blouse off so I can get to your skin."

She pulled the blouse out of the waistband of her suit, then drew it over her head. Gavin sat back and admired the muscles of her back as she moved, the way the hairs on the back of her neck curled. He bent and pressed a kiss there.

"Mmmm, that might be more relaxing than the shoulder rub."

"You say that now because I haven't really started rubbing your shoulders yet. I'm a master at it."

She gave him a look over her shoulder. "That experienced at it, are you?"

He brushed his lips across hers, then turned her head to face forward. "That good at it. Just relax and drop your head forward and let me perform my magic."

She giggled but dipped her head toward her chest, and Gavin went to work, starting easy at first, then when her body became more pliant, he began to dig into the muscles. Elizabeth moaned, and he felt the muscles melt under his fingers.

"Oh, God, you are good at that. You must have women melting at your feet."

He laughed. "I don't think I've ever massaged a woman before."

She lifted her head and half turned. "Really? You're lying."

"No. I just pay attention to the trainers and what they do to me when my muscles tighten up. Figured it would work the same for you."

"Huh. You surprise me, Gavin."

"Yeah? In what way?"

She turned her back to him again and shrugged. "In a lot of ways."

"Wanna give me a list?"

"No. Your ego is inflated enough."

He pressed in on her muscles again, sliding his thumbs into the nape of her neck. "Now that hurts my feelings."

"No, it doesn't."

"You're right. It doesn't."

She laughed, then went quiet as he slid his fingers up into her hair, pulling the barrette and pins out and shaking it loose.

"Why don't you wear your hair down?"

"It gets in my way. Up is more professional."

He sifted his fingers through the softness of her hair, lifted the strands to his nose. She smelled like flowers. "Down is sexy."

"I don't need to be sexy to negotiate a contract."

"Couldn't hurt."

She laughed. "I need to be taken seriously, Gavin."

"Oh, come on, Elizabeth. You use your sexuality like a negotiating point."

She flipped around to face him. "Are you kidding me? That's what you think?"

"Yeah."

She narrowed her gaze and backed away. He grabbed her arm and pulled her toward him.

"Don't be offended. I don't mean that you're, like, trading sexual favors or anything. I mean, you're a beautiful woman. You dress professionally, but you can't hide your sexuality. It's just . . . there. But no, you don't show off like a sex bomb or anything."

"I have no idea what you mean, then. I don't offer sexual favors to gain a client or to get a client a good offer."

"I didn't say that. But you give off sexual vibes. It's a natural thing for you to flirt. And you can't deny that you're one of only a few women in your field. You use being a beautiful woman to your advantage. You capture men's attention because of your beauty and your presence. There's nothing wrong with that. I never meant that you used sex."

"Oh. I see what you mean. Well, of course I use it to my advantage. It's a marketing tool, and especially in the beginning I needed every advantage I could to get me in the door. Now my reputation gets me there because I'm damn good at what I do. And if your brother didn't realize that, then it's his loss."

Gavin raised his hands. "Whoa. How did the topic get turned to Mick?"

She stood, grabbed her blouse. "I don't know. I'm tired. It's been a rough few days. I'm going to take a shower."

She headed off toward the bedroom. Gavin grabbed his drink and took a long swallow.

Okay, his back rub obviously hadn't worked on her. He wondered what the hell had gone wrong the past five days to make her so upset?

ELIZABETH LET THE HOT WATER RAIN DOWN OVER HER head, hoping it would erase the past five days from her memory.

The Blane contract was going well, but that was the only positive to the trip. Steve Lincoln was dropping her. A Pro Bowl–caliber player and a free agent, he'd just signed with the Davis Agency, one of her top competitors.

Steve Lincoln was also a very good friend of Mick's, and it was a known fact Mick wanted Lincoln—a stellar fullback—to play for San Francisco, Mick's team.

And it was also becoming well known that Mick had fired Elizabeth.

And suddenly Steve fired Elizabeth.

Pretty easy to put two and two together and figure out who was behind Steve's sudden change in agents. Mick was out to ruin her.

She wasn't going to let it happen. And she wasn't going to let Gavin know about it.

Unless Gavin already knew.

Was that why he'd invited her to stay with him, so he could keep an eye on her while Mick did his behind-the-scenes damage? Maybe Gavin was talking to her baseball clients, too. He knew who all her clients were. Maybe it was a team effort between the two of them, and Gavin was fucking her senseless to keep her off balance.

Paranoid much, Liz?

It was a ridiculous idea.

Then again, she refused to discount anything. This was her livelihood, and she'd do whatever it took to save it. She'd worked too damn hard to build her business—her very name. Her personal feelings for Gavin aside, she wouldn't let anyone ruin her. She might have invested her heart in Gavin, but she'd stomp all over her own heart in order to save her business.

She grabbed the body wash and scrubbed until she was pink, then rinsed her hair and got out of the shower, dried off and tossed on a cotton sundress, combed her hair out and decided not to bother with drying it. She was exhausted.

She slipped on a pair of flip-flops and went in search of Gavin. He was out on the deck. The cool breeze coming off the water coupled with her wet hair made her skin break out in chills.

"Hey." Gavin rose from the chair when she came outside. "Your hair's wet."

"I'm too tired to dry it."

"I'll be right back."

He went inside. She shrugged and slunk into the swing, pulled her feet up and stared out into the darkness.

Gavin came back a minute later with a blanket. He'd turned the lights out inside, making it even darker outside. There wasn't a moon tonight, so there was no light casting over the water. Just the sound of the ocean and her own black thoughts.

Gavin put the soft blanket over her and sat in the swing with her.

"Thanks."

"It's cold out here and your hair's wet. Wanna go inside?"

"No. I like it out here."

"Me, too." He put his arm around her, and they sat there swinging and listening to the ocean, both of them quiet.

"Something bothering you?" He pulled her closer.

She didn't want to be close to him. She should have gone back to Saint Louis, but something brought her back here. She had no idea what it was.

You know exactly what brought you back here, idiot. You're in love with him, and he's probably using you. No, he's definitely using you. And he's probably setting you up, too.

She sighed, feeling stupid. She hadn't felt stupid in a long time. She'd vowed no man would ever make her feel like this. So why was she letting Gavin?

"It's just been a long few days."

"Want to talk about it?"

"Not really."

He played with the ends of her hair. "Elizabeth, if we're going to have any kind of relationship, you're going to have to start opening up to me."

She stilled, held her breath, afraid to move.

He's playing you. Don't trust him.

"Is that what we're doing, Gavin? Having a relationship?"

"I don't know. I missed you while you were gone. So maybe we are. Maybe I want to."

He'd missed her? The giant hole in her heart filled up with longing and need. Part of her wanted to crawl up next to him, throw her arms around him, and tell him she loved him, that she'd been in love with him for years. The other part of her wanted to close off her heart and run like hell. "Don't say things you don't mean. This is just sex."

He caressed her arm, letting his fingers trail up her neck. "I don't say things I don't mean. Not about this, anyway. I don't really know what this is between us. I don't have relationships with women, but I did miss you, so I'm pretty sure whatever it is that's between us has become more than just sex. I kind of thought you had left for good."

He sounded so sincere. She leaned back and studied his face, wished they weren't shrouded in total darkness so she could read him better. "You did?"

"Yeah. I figured I pissed you off tying you up and asking you to talk about your past."

"Oh. That. No. The sex was really good."

He laughed. "Yeah, the sex between us is really good. But there has to be more."

She looked out over the water, barely making out the white-capped tips rushing toward the shore. "More sex?"

He made a low growl in his throat. "You're trying to kill me. No, not more sex. If we're going to take this any further, then there has to be more than sex."

She wrinkled her nose. "More talking."

"Yeah."

"Talking's overrated."

"Now you sound like a guy."

"That's why you like me."

"Because you're a guy?"

She laughed. "No, because I'm not like your average woman."

"You're not at all like an average woman, Elizabeth. You're not like any other woman I've ever known. That's why I like you. You're complicated. A giant pain in my ass most of the time. You frustrate the hell out of me. And I like that about you. But I don't know anything about you, and that just doesn't work for me."

She swept her fingers across his goatee. "Mysterious is sexy, you know."

He cupped her chin between his fingers and brushed his lips across hers. Everything inside her tightened as he took her mouth in a deeper kiss that lasted long enough that she thought he might forget about the talking part. She leaned into him, rested her palm on his chest, felt his heart rate quicken. But then he pulled back.

"Yeah, mysterious is sexy if it's a one night stand. You're not a one-night stand. You're someone I want to get to know. Which means you're going to have to open up and start talking to me."

Once again he was heading down a track she didn't want to follow.

"You already know me, Gavin. It's not like we're strangers. You got a whole packet of information about me when you signed with me."

He looked at her as if she'd just fed him bullshit. Which she had.

"Are you fucking serious? How dumb do I look?"

"What?"

"Your business portfolio is supposed to pass as getting to know you? I'm not talking about your bio, Elizabeth. I know where you graduated college and did your marketing internship. I know which sports agency gave you your start. But you didn't start to exist in college. I want to know who you were before then. And if you don't trust me enough to tell me—"

"Okay. Fine." She pulled the blanket over her shoulders, wrapped her hair around itself, and pulled it into a makeshift ponytail. The wind had picked up, but the moody atmosphere outside matched her own. "What do you want to know?"

He tugged her closer and pulled the blanket over her legs. "Might as well start at the beginning. I want to know everything about you. You know everything about me."

She did know everything about him. His family had become her family over the past five years because she had no family of her own.

"Well, let's see. I was born and raised in Harrison, Arkansas. No brothers or sisters. My dad worked as a laborer, so he was in and out of work. My mom was a secretary, so she held down the full-time job. She was always working. I went to school, got decent grades. I was very lucky to get the scholarship to Brown—"

"Wait. We're already on college? You skipped everything."

"My childhood's pretty boring, Gavin. I went to school. Not much to tell."

"Did you have friends?"

"Yes."

"Tell me about them."

"I had a couple of girlfriends. They lived on the same block as

me. I wasn't allowed to hang out with them until the weekends so I
didn't get to—"

"Why not?"

"What?"

"Why couldn't you see them until the weekends?"

"Oh. My father wouldn't allow it. I had chores to do after school
and dinner to put on the table. Then I had homework at night."

He frowned. "But in the summer . . ."

"In the summer there were chores during the day. And I got sent
to my grandparents' farm a lot, so my parents didn't have to wonder
what I was up to during the times my dad was working."

"The farm, huh?"

"Yeah."

"Bet that was fun."

Her lips curled up remembering times on the farm, some of the
best—only—good memories of her childhood. "It was, actually. My
grandpa taught me to ride a tractor, and they had horses. My
grandma taught me to bake pies from scratch—'"

He sat up straight and turned to face her. "Aha! You *can* cook."

She laughed. "That was a long time ago, Gavin. I don't remember."

"So you say. I'll bet you could remember. How many summers
did you spend at your grandparents' farm?"

She tilted her head back, trying to remember. "I first remember
going there when I was about five. Last time I went I was sixteen."

"So eleven years. That's a lot of pie making."

Her lips lifted. "Sixteen was a long time ago."

He leaned back again, drawing close to her so he could nuzzle
her neck. "Would you make me a pie, Elizabeth?"

She nudged her shoulder at him. "You're out of your mind. I
don't cook. You're supposed to cook for me, remember?"

"I'll make you dinner if you bake a pie."

"I don't cook for anyone."

"But you'll bake for me, right?"

Sometimes he was like a kid. Exasperating. But it was one of the things she loved most about him. "We'll talk about it."

"No, we'll settle it right now. You're the great negotiator. You taught me that one yourself. We settle the deal while it's on the table."

"Bastard. And here I thought you never paid attention. Fine. I'll make you a pie. Or I'll try to remember how to do it. No guarantees. I might end up poisoning you."

"I'll take my chances. So, back to you being a kid. You got to see your friends on the weekends, right?"

"Yeah. I had two best friends, Lindsey and Denise. I got to swim in Lindsey's pool in the summers."

"Nice."

"It was. We used to do everything together. Sometimes I'd get to sleep over at their houses but not very often."

"Why not?"

"My father wouldn't let me. Said my place was at home with my family."

"Your father was strict?"

She snorted. "That's an understatement. He ruled our home with an iron fist. My mother had to report in every second of her life. Where she was going, what she was doing, who she was seeing. God forbid she wasn't at her desk if he happened to call her office. He'd go off into a tirade about that."

"Why?"

"He had to be in control. His whole life was about controlling people. Controlling her, controlling me. The world would stop turning if he didn't know what we were doing every moment of the day. That's why he didn't work much. How could he work and manage us at the same time?"

Gavin didn't say anything. Dammit, why had she offered up so much information? She'd only meant to talk about Lindsey and Denise, and the fun they had. She'd meant to keep it light. But, oh, no, she'd just had to talk about her father.

"I'm sorry about your dad. That must have been hard on you."

"I avoided him, defied him when I could."

"And your mother?"

She pressed her lips together, determined not to talk about it.

"Elizabeth? What about your mom?"

"She did whatever he told her to do like the good robot she was. He told her to be home at a certain time, and she was. Canned goods had to be organized in a certain way in the cabinet, and they were. Towels had to be folded just right, or she had to do it over again until they were. She had no friends, because why did she need friends when she had him to take care of, and God knows he was a full-time job. She was supposed to spend all of her time with him."

He reached under the blanket and took her hand in his. "I'm sorry. That's no life for a kid. There must have been a lot of tension in the house."

She shrugged, tried to pull her hand away, but he didn't let go. "It wasn't that bad. I managed just fine."

"It sounds like it was a nightmare."

She didn't want to answer, but something compelled her. "It was hell."

"But you survived it. And knowing who you are now, I'd bet he couldn't control you."

She laughed. "No, he couldn't. I wouldn't let him. He tried, and he did when I was younger, but by the time I hit high school, he was too busy managing every second of my mother's life and had to choose between her or me."

"And he chose her."

"Yeah." She sighed. "Lucky her."

"Do you see them at all?"

"Oh, hell no. I'm not going back there. Once I left for college, that was it. I wasn't going back there ever again."

"Don't you at least wonder how your mother is?"

Her shoulders slumped.

"I tried, Gavin. I tried to get her away from him, tried to get her to come visit me, because I sure as hell wasn't going back there. She refused, said Daddy needed her and she couldn't come."

"So she chose him over you." He swept his hand over her hair. "I'm sorry, honey."

She batted back the tears that threatened. It had been too many years since she'd cried over what she couldn't change. Never again. "She made her choice to put up with him and his demands. She has to live with it now. That doesn't mean I have to."

"So you never went home after you left for college?"

"No. Never. I was free and I wasn't going back. I was on full scholarship, and I worked during school. I had no reason to go back."

"So they never once came out to see you?"

"No. I'm sure my father was afraid if my mother left the state, she'd somehow escape him and he'd lose her. He was happy keeping her in that little town, and obviously she'd do whatever she was told."

"She never called you or wrote?"

"Oh, sure. She'd call and ask me to come home at the holidays or during summer. Whatever Dad wanted her to say. After I said no enough times she stopped calling."

He didn't speak for a while. She knew what he was thinking. "You think I'm a cold-hearted bitch, that I abandoned my mother."

"That's not what I'm thinking at all, Elizabeth. You weren't supposed to be responsible for her. Your parents were supposed to be responsible for you."

"They were. They fed me and put a roof over my head. I got a decent education and I wasn't abused."

She heard his soft laugh and tilted her head to look at him. "What?"

"Come on. You're smart, surely you know."

"Know what?"

"Elizabeth, your father was an abuser."

She shook her head. "No, he was a prick and a controller. But he never hit my mother or me."

Gavin turned in the swing to face her. "Honey, an abuser doesn't always hit. Abuse is emotional, too. Don't you think that's what your father did by controlling your mother, by forcing her to live in what was essentially a prison?"

Talking about it made her relive it, and she didn't want to go back there ever again, had sworn she wouldn't, not even in her mind. And she'd already spent way more time there tonight than she'd ever wanted to. She shrugged off the blanket and hopped off the swing. "I'm tired, Gavin. I had a long day and a long flight, and I'd really just like to go to bed."

She walked away, didn't look back to see if he was following, just headed straight for the bedroom, stripped off her dress, and crawled into bed without turning on the light.

She had to shut it all out, to forget, to shove the past where it belonged so it couldn't come back and haunt her again.

Within a few minutes Gavin joined her, his body chilled from the cold air outside. He wrapped his arms around her and pulled her against him. She resisted at first, but he wouldn't let go of her until she relaxed her body against his.

He didn't ask for anything, didn't say anything, just stroked her hair. The silence and his breathing finally calmed her, and she was able to shut her eyes.

But she couldn't shut out the memories. She'd never be able to make them go away.

NINE

RAIN AND WIND BATTERED THE DECK AND WINDOWS, coming down so hard Gavin couldn't even see the chairs.

The rain kept them shut inside. That was bad. No game today.

No sunshine, nothing to do but stay inside.

That could be good.

While Elizabeth slept during the morning, Gavin went to the store and bought food. He intended to cook for her, felt bad about making her talk about a past that was obviously painful for her.

She'd had a rough childhood. A very rough childhood with a father who'd been abusive to both her and her mother. And yet she'd managed to escape and grow up to be a strong, independent woman, which said a lot about her strength and character. He wanted to talk more about it, but it was clear she wasn't ready yet. Maybe she never would be, and it was her right to decide that.

But he admired her more for what he knew now about her. There were facets to Elizabeth he'd never known about, things about her that made him appreciate the woman she'd become. She'd done it all on her own.

Despite the game being rained out, he still had work to do. Workouts with the trainer and indoor batting practice with the batting coach. He left a note for Elizabeth telling her where he'd be, hoping she'd still be there when he got back.

He was gone most of the day. He had spent several hours on physical training, then batting practice, trying to figure out what the hell was wrong with his swing. The verdict—nothing was wrong with his swing. As he figured, it was mental. The mechanics were all in place; he just had to connect bat to ball. And he would, as soon as the rain stopped and he got the chance to stand at the plate and swing the bat again.

He had to do a few media interviews late in the afternoon, then he was cut loose for the day and on his way back to the beach house. He wasn't sure why he was surprised to find Elizabeth's car in the driveway, but he was glad she was still there. When he went inside, she was curled up on the sofa, a steaming cup of something on the table in front of her, her legs crisscrossed over each other and her laptop sitting in her lap. She wore a sundress and a sweater, had her hair in a ponytail, and didn't have any makeup on. She looked so young, almost like a teenager, when she lifted her head and smiled at him.

God, she was beautiful.

"Hi, honey. How was your day?"

He grinned and flopped onto the sofa next to her. "Just great. How was yours?"

"Productive, actually. Nothing like a rainy day to help one catch up with paperwork and phone calls. I got a lot done. You?"

"Workouts and batting practice and a few interviews. Trying to figure out why I've been oh-for-everything the past few games."

She frowned. "You have? Why?"

He shrugged. "No clue. My swing is fine. Mental block I think."

She leaned forward and kissed him. "Too much sex weakens you."

"I haven't had any sex. You were gone. That's probably the problem."

She gaped at him. "Oh. I didn't know we were being exclusive."

"I believe I mentioned that the first night we had sex." He arched a brow. "Tell me you didn't go around screwing everything with a dick while you were out of town."

She laughed. "I'm the one with the two-year drought, remember." She laid her hand over her heart. "I've been totally faithful to you."

"Ditto." He swept his hand behind her neck and pulled her mouth to his for a searing kiss that made his dick hard in an instant. God, he'd missed her, had missed fucking her last night. But last night she'd needed to be held, not fucked.

Now, though, as she climbed onto his lap and her breasts pressed against his chest, Gavin felt the warmth of her and inhaled her scent, and he didn't want to wait. He needed her. She was a fire in his blood and constantly on his mind. She made his balls quiver, and all he could think about was sinking inside her.

He shifted her underneath him, spreading them both out on the sofa, positioning himself on top of her. He nudged her legs apart and positioned his cock against her sex, feeling the heat soak through her underwear and his jeans.

"Five whole days without sex, huh?" she asked, lifting against him with a wicked smile.

"Six now. It's killing me."

She swept her fingers across his goatee, then slid her hand down his chest and between them, cupping his hard cock. "Poor baby. How you must be suffering. We should take care of that right away."

"Yeah, we should. How about right here?"

She gave his cock a gentle squeeze. "I'm just lying here waiting for you to get this inside me. I'm ready, Gavin. I'm wet and my pussy's throbbing. Fuck me."

He sucked in a deep breath, raised off of her only long enough to lift her dress up and take her panties off and unzip and remove his jeans, and then he was between her legs again, falling into her welcoming arms.

His mouth met hers at the same time his cock slid inside her. Unsheathed, he felt her, hot and slick, tightening around him as he thrust inside her.

He swirled his tongue around hers, and she wrapped her hand around his neck, her fingers diving into his hair. She lifted her hips and tightened her legs around him. He'd never felt anything like the sensations bombarding him all at once. His mouth on hers, his cock inside her, and his whole body pressed against hers. He fisted her dress, pulling the strap down on one side to reveal her breast.

No bra. He liked that. He bent and took her nipple in his mouth, feeling it harden against his tongue as he sucked.

"Gavin," she whispered, arching her back and feeding her nipple to him, still holding on to the back of his head and keeping him there. Her body was fluid motion as she moved against him, and he was caught up in a tight ball of tension, ready to skyrocket into an orgasm that he'd held back for all these days.

All he'd done was think about her—how she looked, how she smelled, how soft her skin was. He popped her nipple out of his mouth and looked down on it, then dragged his tongue up to her neck and grazed her throat with his teeth, watching the goose bumps prickle her skin.

She smelled like vanilla, like sugar cookies, and he loved the taste of her. She was like his favorite candy—hard on the outside but a soft surprise on the inside.

She was his Elizabeth, and he didn't think anyone knew her like he did. He didn't think she'd ever let anyone know her like he knew her. And that made her a treasure. His treasure.

He lifted up on both arms and looked down at her. She was painfully beautiful without her makeup on, her hair pulled loose from her ponytail, all messy and perfect. He lifted and thrust into her, watching her eyes when he rolled his hips over her to grind against her clit.

She might keep secrets from him about painful parts of her life, but here, when they were connected, there were no secrets. She was fully open to him and she let him see her pleasure, how much she enjoyed sex, how much she enjoyed what he did to her.

She wound her arms around his neck. He pulled her up. Her legs were still wrapped around his hips as she slid right into rhythm with him, moving against him, riding his cock as she balanced her feet on the edge of the sofa, held on to him, and rocked against him, taking him right to the edge so fast he had to pull back to keep from climaxing.

But she wouldn't let go. She tightened her grip on his neck and rode his cock, rolling her pussy over him and dropping down onto him, rubbing her ass against his balls until sweat poured down his face. He grabbed her ass then, gripping her tight and lifting her on and off him.

"Yes, like that," she said, keeping her focus on his eyes as hers went dark green. "Make me come for you, Gavin."

He dug his fingers into her ass cheeks and lifted her faster and faster, up and down on his cock. "Yeah. Come on, baby, come on me."

When she tightened around him and he saw her jaw drop, he let go, shoving inside her with the force of his orgasm. She cried out and came, and the convulsions around his cock intensified, sending him spiraling out of control. He wrapped his arms around her and let his orgasm rip through him. Both of them shuddered against each other as he poured everything he had into her until all his limbs were shaking and he was breathless and spent.

He smoothed his arms down her back, kissed her neck, and held her, not wanting to let her go.

"I'm starving," she said against his chest.

He laughed. "Good thing I went to the grocery store this morning."

They disengaged, cleaned up, and dressed, and Elizabeth picked up her cup from the coffee table, grimacing.

"It's cold now. Guess I won't be drinking any more coffee. How about a cocktail? Or do you want to get dressed and go out to eat?"

"I'm making you dinner tonight. I bought white wine. It'll go with dinner."

She stopped on her way to the kitchen and pivoted, arching a brow. "You are? Does this mean I have to make a pie?"

"Nah. I was just teasing about that."

She gave him a dubious look. "Okay."

She looked like she didn't believe him, but he went into the kitchen to start dinner. Elizabeth fixed them glasses of wine and sat at the counter, watching him drag out pans and ingredients.

"What are you making?"

"Pan-seared salmon with pasta and spinach cream sauce."

She laughed. "No really. What are you making?"

He slanted her a look. "That's really what I'm making."

"I'm stunned. And will be highly impressed if you don't poison me."

He laughed. "I promise not to poison you."

He put water on to boil, then put butter in a pan and added a piece of salmon. While that was cooking, he got out the spinach, washed it, and zested a lemon.

"You look like you know what you're doing."

He smiled at her and took a sip of wine. "I told you I can cook."

"I guess you did, didn't you."

Once the salmon was done, he set it aside, threw more butter into the pan, and tossed the spinach in there. Once the spinach had wilted, he added the lemon zest and some cream, and stirred it with one hand while drinking his wine with the other.

Elizabeth inhaled. "Gavin, that smells so good. What can I do to help?"

"Are you sure you want to? I don't want to ruin your cooking embargo."

"Ha-ha. What do you need me to do?"

He gave her instructions for the garlic bread, so she busied herself with slicing the bread and preparing it. She set the table while he tossed the bread in the oven. By then it was time to flake the salmon and add it to the pan with the spinach and cream. He'd already added pasta to the boiling water.

Everything was moving along at a fast clip, just the way he liked it.

Elizabeth came up behind him and wrapped her arms around him. "A man that cooks. I might just never let you go. Do you hire out for parties?"

He laid the spoon on the stove, turned around, and kissed her thoroughly, making sure she understood just how much he still wanted her. "Depends on the payment plan."

Her cheeks were bright pink, and he didn't think it had anything to do with the stove being hot. "Oh, I think I could definitely meet your payment demands."

He patted her on the butt, and she moved out of his way while he drained the pasta and added parsley to the salmon and spinach in the pan.

While that heated up, he pulled the bread out of the oven, put some pasta on their plates, and scooped the cream, spinach, and salmon on top of the pasta, finishing it off with some fresh parsley. He brought the plates over to the table where Elizabeth had already poured fresh wine.

He waited while she took the first bite. Her closed eyes and murmured sounds of approval made him smile.

"Holy crap, Gavin. Are you sure you wouldn't rather be a chef? This is fantastic."

"Thanks. And I like to eat but don't always like to eat out. Told you my mom is a good cook and insisted we learned to fend for ourselves."

She scooped another forkful into her mouth. More yummy sounds. He liked that.

"Fending for yourself is tossing a steak or burgers on the grill. This is cuisine. Men just don't cook like this."

He took a bite, enjoying her delight in his cooking. "This man does."

She waved her fork at him. "You are a rare breed, Gavin Riley. Don't tell too many women your secrets, or they'll be lining up in droves to marry you."

"You think so?"

"Hell, yes. You're gorgeous; you play Major League Baseball, which means you're a jock; you're a millionaire; and you can cook, too? Women will swoon. I should get media to do a photo spread of you in the kitchen."

He ate, watching the wheels turn in her head. Her eyes widened, and he knew the gears had clicked into place.

Shit.

"Oh, my God, the exposure would be fantastic. We could do the cooking angle, maybe get you on some of the cooking network shows, some of the morning shows, because they eat that up. The jock who can cook." She grabbed a forkful of food and ate another bite.

"What else can you cook?"

He arched a brow. "Why?"

"Well, is it fancy stuff like this?"

"This isn't a fancy meal, Elizabeth. It didn't take long to make."

"It doesn't matter. It looks fancy and it tastes incredible. So tell me what else you can make."

He ignored her. He was hungry, so he finished his food, drank his wine, and ate garlic bread, then fixed a second helping. Meanwhile, Elizabeth grabbed her laptop and ate while simultaneously typing notes.

"What was the name of this dish again?"

"Pan-seared salmon with pasta and spinach cream sauce."

She typed, then looked over the top of her laptop at him. "Now tell me what else you can make."

He sighed, pushing his plate to the side. "Pasta carbonara. Lime chicken with mango salsa. Steak fajitas with Spanish rice. Chicken Parmesan. I make a lot of stuff, Elizabeth. I don't even remember half of it."

She was wide eyed. "Really? This is great. We could do a cookbook. Or even a cooking show."

"No."

"What? Yes."

"No. I don't cook for a living. I play baseball."

"You could do both. Are you kidding me? Women will go crazy over you. This will sell tickets like nobody's business. I'll make you famous."

"Me cooking will not sell baseball tickets. That makes no sense."

"Of course it will. See, this is why I'm in charge of your PR and you're not. You just don't get the connection."

"Because there is no connection. And no, I'm not going to be your cooking baseball guy."

"But—"

"No, Elizabeth."

"Gavin . . ."

"No."

She inhaled and let out a huge dramatic sigh. "Fine."

She closed the laptop and took her dishes to the sink. Gavin sat back and finished his glass of wine, watching her take her frustrations out on the pots and pans.

She was cute when she didn't get her own way. He let her storm about the kitchen for a while, then went in with his plate and helped her finish up the dishes. She didn't speak to him or look at him, which meant she was either pissed or gearing up for round two.

"What do you do during your off-season?"

Round two.

"I come down here to fish, hang out at home. See my parents. Go see some of Mick's games. Relax."

She grabbed the dish towel and dried her hands. "Cook?"

His lips lifted. "Yeah. I cook."

"Alone or with your mom?"

He snorted. "I don't need to cook with my mom anymore, Elizabeth. I'm a big boy now and can handle the stove all by myself."

"Not what I meant. Do you try out new recipes alongside your mother? Does she help you, or do you come up with dishes on your own?"

"I spend a lot of the off-season on my own, so yeah, I cook for myself. Why?"

She folded the towel and hung it on the rack. "No reason."

No reason his ass. But he wasn't going to question her further because he didn't want to encourage her stupid notion of him and cooking and making anything promotional out of it. Wasn't gonna happen.

"Lizzie?"

She turned to face him. "Yes?"

"Drop this idea. I mean it."

She lifted one shoulder. "Okay. Sure. If that's what you want."

"It's what I want. I cook because it's fun and relaxes me. I don't want you exploiting it."

She nodded. "Understood, Gavin."

Somehow he didn't think she really understood. Elizabeth with an idea was like a dog with a meaty bone. Once she got hold of it, nothing was going to make her let go.

And that worried him.

TEN

THE SUN CAME OUT AGAIN AND BASEBALL RESUMED. Elizabeth was glad to get out of the house. She'd always hated being cooped up. Even in Saint Louis, she'd go out in the rain or snow if she had to.

Now that the preseason was in full swing, she actually enjoyed the crowds and the atmosphere of the games. For the past few days the Rivers had played on the road, which meant Elizabeth had stayed at the beach house while Gavin traveled. It gave her time to catch her breath and do some work.

Today was the Rivers' first day back on their home field. Gavin had come home late last night. She'd been asleep. He'd woken her up by crawling into bed and making love to her. She hadn't minded that at all. In fact, waking up to his warm hands and mouth on her, bringing her to orgasm before she was fully awake, had been an amazing surprise. He'd slid inside her while she was still climaxing, and he'd fucked her with a slow and lazy rhythm, kissing her neck, whispering that he'd missed her, until they'd both come, then fell asleep wrapped around each other.

She could get used to having him around.

Dangerous thought.

She sat with Shawnelle and Haley, and watched the game. Well, she had her laptop on and her face buried in it. But she was really paying close attention to every aspect of the game. Gavin just didn't know that. No sense in giving his already healthy ego too much of a boost. He already had her heart. She didn't want to give up her soul to him.

"Nice to see you back here," Shawnelle said. "Gavin's playing much better now that his lucky charm is back where she belongs."

Elizabeth dragged her gaze away from profit-and-loss statements and Gavin's position at first base to frown at Shawnelle. "What are you talking about?"

"Oh, everyone knows you're Gavin's good-luck charm," Haley said, leaning forward from Shawnelle's left side. "He played like total shit while you were gone those few days last week. You come back and boom—suddenly his batting improves."

Elizabeth laughed. "I don't think my presence has much to do with his batting average."

"Uh-huh." Shawnelle dipped her sunglasses down to her nose and gave Elizabeth a look. "Honey, you have everything to do with how that boy plays ball. We're not blind. We see how he glances up here to see whether you're paying attention or not. So pull your head out of that laptop and look at him. Let him know you're rooting him on."

"Oh, I'm rooting him on. And I'm definitely paying attention. I just don't want him to know that."

"Huh?" Haley's confused expression told Elizabeth the girl knew nothing about power plays.

"If he sees me hanging on his every play, then he'll think he owns me. It's bad enough I agreed to stay down here during pre-season. I can't give him everything."

Shawnelle arched a brow. "Seems to me you already have, haven't you? You love him, don't you?"

Elizabeth looked around, glad no one else was sitting near them. "I do not."

"Liar. Even I can see it, and I'm not the sharpest tool in the shed," Haley said.

Elizabeth sighed. "You're not dumb at all, Haley. And, Shawnelle, you're a pain in the ass."

Shawnelle smirked. "Not the first time I've heard that. I'm right, aren't I?"

"Yes." She stared down at her laptop.

"How long?"

"Five years." She lifted her gaze to Shawnelle and Haley. "He doesn't know."

"Of course he doesn't. Men are obtuse. You have to beat them over the head with a frying pan to get them to notice things."

"I proposed to Tommy because he was too shy to ask me, even though I knew he loved me and wanted to marry me. He's dumb as a cow."

Elizabeth snorted out a laugh. "What did he say?"

"He said he was gettin' around to askin' me." Haley rolled her eyes. "I figured by the time he got around to proposin', I'd be too old to have sex. Good thing I took matters into my own hands."

"Good thing," Shawnelle said. "And speaking of, how are . . . things between you two?"

Haley's eyes widened, and her lips spread into a devilish grin. "They're great. After that night on the dance floor, ooh-wee did we have some smokin'-hot sexin'. We got to talkin', and he really opened up about what he likes and asked me what I like, and well . . . let's just say the dam got to burstin' and it's been really smokin' hot ever since."

"That's just excellent," Elizabeth said, really happy for Haley. "Have to keep those fires of lust burning."

"I'll say." Haley fanned her face with the game program. "And as far as you and Gavin, honey, if you want him, then you have to be honest with him. Tell him how you feel."

"I don't think that'll work for me."

"Why not?" Shawnelle asked.

"Our situation is complicated."

"Bullshit. You're just scared."

She laughed. "That, too. But I'll think about it. It might just take a little time."

She focused her attention on the game, and that got Shawnelle and Haley off her back about Gavin. She checked his stats, and his batting average *had* plummeted to the basement during the few days she'd been out of town. As soon as she'd gotten back, though, he'd been hitting at almost every at bat.

Interesting.

She seriously doubted there was any correlation, though.

Elizabeth didn't believe in luck. The players she managed had success in their respective fields because they were good at what they did. Luck played no part in it. If Gavin sucked, it was because there was a glitch in his swing. If he started to play better when she came back from Saint Louis, it was purely coincidental, because she was no one's lucky charm.

"We're going for manis and pedis after the game. You interested?" Shawnelle asked.

Girl stuff? With girls? So not Elizabeth's thing. Then again, she liked these women, and that was a first for her. She had no girlfriends, could never relate to women at all. But there was just something about Shawnelle and Haley that made her feel comfortable.

"Sure. I'll buy lunch."

"You are so on, honey. We'll leave the men in the dust and have ourselves a ladies' afternoon out." Shawnelle whipped out her cell phone. "I'll text Dedrick, and he can pass the word on to Tommy and Gavin."

"I know this great spa," Haley said. "I'll call and make us appointments."

Elizabeth smiled. "Sounds absolutely perfect."

She did text Gavin and let him know what she'd be doing, even though Shawnelle told her Dedrick would pass the word along. She just felt better about telling him herself. By the time they arrived at the day spa, he'd texted her back and told her to have a good time.

She intended to.

The spa was heavenly, private, and deliciously decorated in creams and beiges. They were whisked away and pampered by their own personal attendants. They were seated next to each other for their pedicures and manicures, and Haley had them laughing hysterically with stories of her backwoods life back home and the girls she'd gone to school with, who thought the hottest thing to do was to get pregnant before you graduated high school.

"I'm telling' ya, it was like a contest with these girls to see who could get knocked up first. Those poor guys didn't know what hit 'em. The smart ones dumped the girls as soon as possible and offered up child support. The dumb guys married the hos."

Elizabeth was appalled. "That was their long-term plan? Babies and marriage?"

Haley nodded. "Yup. And they were mad when I said that's not what I wanted. I was dating Tommy by then, and he was older than me. They thought I should get pregnant so he'd marry me. He loved me and wanted to marry me anyway, but we didn't want to get pregnant. I went to Planned Parenthood and got me some birth control. No babies for me for a long damn time. I want a degree first, and want to be self-supporting. No way do I want kids for a while."

"I knew there was a reason I liked you, Haley," Shawnelle said.

"You have a brain. That's how I did it. I went to college, fell in love, got married, had a career, then had my babies. And I still have a career."

"I don't know how you manage it all," Elizabeth said to Shawnelle. "You're an attorney. Your husband plays Major League Baseball, and here you are supporting him, plus you have two children under the age of six."

Shawnelle smiled. "I have a wonderful, supporting family. We both do. His mother is watching the kids right now, so I can be here for a couple weeks and enjoy a little vacation. When I head back to Saint Louis, it's back to work for me. And when Dedrick travels and I have to work, my mom and his mom and my aunt pitch in to help with the kids. I couldn't do it without them. We're very lucky he got drafted in the city where our families are from."

"You're very lucky to have such a great family."

"Believe me, I know. They've allowed me to have it all. The man, the kids, and the career."

"Tommy's family is great," Haley said. "My family sucks. Not sure what we'll do when we have kids. I know Tommy's mother will move heaven and earth to be wherever we are so she can be near our kids, so I know she'll be there to help. But that's a long time in the future, so I'm not even thinkin' about it."

"What about you, Elizabeth?" Shawnelle asked. "Any thoughts about marriage and kids?"

Elizabeth turned her gaze to her toenails, which were being painted a beautiful shade of pink. "Wow, look at our toes. Aren't they pretty?"

"Avoider."

She grinned at Shawnelle. "Expert at it, as a matter of fact."

After the spa, Elizabeth took them to a trendy bar and restaurant. It had gotten late, and they were all thirsty and starving. They ordered food and margaritas, though the margaritas turned out to be way more fun than the food. By the time their lunch—though it was closer to dinner—arrived, they were on their second pitcher of margaritas, and Elizabeth was feeling every one of them. Her skin tingled, her lips were numb, and she was laughing at everything the women said.

But her burrito tasted heavenly, and she managed at least a few bites of it, even if she'd lost her appetite since she was now drinking her lunch. Or dinner.

The waitress brought another pitcher of margaritas, and Elizabeth turned to Haley.

"Okay, tell us about the sex, Haley."

Haley's eyes widened, and she grinned. "It is so awesome now that we're talkin' about it. Who knew all we had to do was communicate what we both liked and wanted? Tommy thought I was shy, and I thought he was sexually ignorant. Once we broke the ice, it turned out he's a sexual animal in bed, and I sure as hell have no problem telling him how I want it. And he has no problem giving me *exactly* what I ask for."

"Woo-hoo!" Shawnelle said, lifting her glass. "A toast to great sex and a man who knows what to do with his cock."

Elizabeth giggled and raised her glass. "I'll drink to that."

"So tell us about your sex life, Elizabeth. You're typically closed up about Gavin."

She took a long swallow of her margarita, then refilled her glass. "Mmmm. It's good. Really good. He has great hands. A very talented tongue. And one hell of an awesome cock. His stamina is out of this world. I'm not sure I'm going to know what to do with myself when we're not together anymore. I was in a sexual drought for so long it's like I can't get enough now. I've easily fallen into this pattern of sharing the beach house with him, sleeping with him, fucking him."

Haley rested her chin in her hands and blinked, a dreamy expression on her face. "Sounds nice."

"Why does it have to end?" Shawnelle asked.

Elizabeth shrugged and lifted her glass. " 'Cuz. It does. We're just playing house, you know? It's not serious."

"It isn't? Who says?"

"We do. I do. I don't know. It just isn't."

"It's serious for you, doll, isn't it? And it has been for years."

Elizabeth laughed and took a drink. "Well, yeah, but he doesn't know that. And he never will."

Haley wrinkled her nose and lifted her empty glass. Elizabeth tried to focus on filling it, even though there seemed to be two glasses in front of her.

It was entirely possible she was drunk.

"I think you should tell him how you feel about him," Haley said.

"Oh, no. That would be bad. If I told him how I felt, he'd have power over me. I can't give him the power."

"Bullshit." Shawnelle said, pointing her finger at Elizabeth. "See, this is the problem with men and women and relationshits. Shit. Relasinsips. Dammit. Relationships. There, I got it. Lies and games and positioning. You should try honesty. Communication." She tilted her head at Haley. "Look how well communication worked for Haley. She's having great sex now."

"I'm already having great sex."

Shawnelle snorted. "You know what I mean, missy. Don't try to double-talk me. I'm a lawyer."

"Yeah, but you're a drunk lawyer."

"True that." Shawnelle emptied her glass and refilled it.

Elizabeth signaled the waitress for another pitcher, then pulled out her phone to call Gavin. He answered on the first ring.

"Hey. Having fun?"

"Yup. Really drunk here though. Think you can swing by Bernards and pick up three toasted women and give us all a ride home?"

He laughed. "On my way. Don't drive."

She saluted the phone. "Yes, sir."

"I'm serious. I'll be there in about twenty minutes."

"Thanks, Gavin. Love you."

She closed the phone and lifted her gaze to Shawnelle and Haley. "I called Gavin. He's going to give us all a ride home. We're drunk, you know."

Haley's eyes widened. "We are?"

Elizabeth nodded. "We totally are."

Haley covered her mouth with her hands. "That's so funny."

"Hey, drunk girl," Shawnelle said, patting Elizabeth's hand.

"What?"

"You just told Gavin you loved him on the phone."

She frowned. "Did not."

"Yup. You did. I heard you," Haley said.

"I did?"

Shawnelle nodded. "You so did."

Elizabeth snorted. "That's fucking hysterical. I'll bet he passed out from shock. Good thing the waitress is bringing another pitcher. Our ride might be delayed."

"You're not worried?" Haley asked.

"About what?"

"About telling Gavin you loved him."

She waved her hand. "Honey, I'm drunk. Anything you say when you're drunk is bullshit and doesn't mean anything. He won't think anything of it."

Shawnelle gave her a sideways look. "Uh-huh."

Elizabeth grinned when the waitress came, so damn glad she was drunk and she would forget what she said to Gavin. "Oh, look, ladies, it's margaritas!"

ELEVEN

DRUNK WAS AN UNDERSTATEMENT. GAVIN WAS CERTAIN the manager of Bernards was going to kiss him when he walked out with Elizabeth, Shawnelle, and Haley.

In fact, he heard their voices as soon as he walked in the front door. They were laughing. Loud. They were doing everything in high-pitched voices. Talking. Yelling. Squealing. Cussing.

He wondered if he and his friends were that obnoxious when they were drunk.

Probably.

Elizabeth squealed and flung her arms around him when she saw him, then pressed kisses all over his face.

Definitely drunk. Which probably accounted for the "love you" she'd said on the phone. Drunken declarations of love never counted, so he'd brushed it off as meaningless.

He extricated what seemed to be eight arms from him, poured the women into his car, buckled them in, and drove Shawnelle and

Haley home first. He'd already given Tommy and Dedrick a heads up, so they were waiting for him outside when he pulled up at the hotel where they were both staying.

"Woman, you got no sense," Deed said with a smile and a shake of his head.

"Yeah, but you love me anyway." Shawnelle laughed as Dedrick pulled her out of the car.

Tommy just scooped Haley up and carried her, since she'd passed out on the ride over.

"Thanks, man," Dedrick said over his shoulder.

"No problem."

He climbed back inside and headed to the beach house, forced to listen to Elizabeth's off-key singing along to the radio the entire way.

He turned the volume down, deciding talk was a better option.

"So you had fun?"

She grinned. "We had a lot of fun. We had a few drinks, you know."

Yeah, he knew. The tequila smell filled his car. "Really. Just a few?"

She giggled and kicked her shoes off. "Okay, a lot."

She started singing again, leaned forward to turn the volume up on the radio.

It was a good thing he really liked Elizabeth, because she couldn't sing for shit.

He pulled into the driveway, but before he could get his seatbelt off, she'd thrown the door open and bounded out, her shoes and purse forgotten. She went around the side of the house and disappeared into the dark.

Good lord. He grabbed her purse and shoes, went in through the front door, dumped her stuff, and headed out back.

She was on the deck, stripping her clothes off. She was down to her bra and panties, and it was making his dick hard seeing her on his deck like that. He brought his focus up to her face.

"What are you doing, honey?"

"Getting naked."

"I see that. Why?"

She turned to him and gave him a wicked grin. "I want to go skinny dipping in the ocean."

He couldn't help but smile at her. She was a really cute drunk. Dumb and senseless, but cute. "I don't think swimming drunk in the ocean is a really good idea."

"By myself, of course not. But you'll be with me to keep me from drowning." She unhooked her bra and waved it at him, then dropped it on the floor.

She made a good point. So did her nipples.

"So? Are you going to get naked and go skinny dipping with me?"

"Do you know how cold the ocean is at night?"

"Suck it up. I'll warm your cock and balls when we get back inside. Then you can fuck me."

She shimmied out of her panties and stood naked in front of him, her hands on her hips.

He sighed and pulled off his shirt and dropped his shorts. Her gaze rocketed to his cock, already semi-hard at the thought of taking her to bed later.

He should be ashamed of himself, thinking of taking advantage of her in her drunken state.

Then again, the cold water should sober her up a little.

She laughed and turned, making a beeline for the water. He ran after her, easily overtaking her. He got to the water before she did and dove in, waiting for her. She leaped in, the waves crashing into her and knocking her over.

Gavin was there to pull her up, and she came up sputtering and laughing.

"Holy shit, that's cold."

"Told ya."

She splashed him with water, then grabbed him as another wave rushed over them. Her legs wrapped around his, and he dug into the sandy bottom to hold them both steady as the water battered at them.

She laughed as they stood waist high in the water and took a beating.

"You think this is fun? It's freezing out here. My balls are the size of walnuts."

She kissed him. "I told you I'd warm them up when we got back inside. This is living, Gavin."

"This is freezing, Elizabeth. Your nipples are frozen and poking my chest."

She rubbed them against him, tilted her head back, and dragged her hair against the water. "It feels great."

"You're numb and feel nothing. I'm going to make you pay for this."

"Ha. You will not." She pushed away from him and floated on top of the waves.

But she was obviously enjoying herself, laughing and acting like a kid. He liked seeing her this way, unguarded and free, even if it took several pitchers of margaritas to get her to relax.

And she was obviously warmed by tequila. He was not. He was freezing and had had enough. He scooped her up in his arms.

"Okay, ocean mermaid, time to head into a warm shower before my dick freezes and falls off."

She lifted her head and focused slightly bleary eyes on him. "If you insist."

He carried her out of the water and into the house, where he deposited her wet, dripping body on his bathroom floor. He turned on the shower and tried not to shiver as the water heated, then directed her inside and followed her.

Hot water had never felt so good. Her body was chilled, but she leaned against the wall and grinned while he washed the sea out of her hair, rinsed it, and put that conditioner stuff on it. Then he soaped up her body.

She was at least pliant, turning whichever way he told her to.

"You ready to get out? Think you can dry yourself and make it to bed while I wash?"

Instead, she took his soap in her hands and lifted her gaze to his. "I'm not ready to get out yet. Turn around and let me wash you."

He wasn't going to argue. He gave her his back, and she rubbed soap all over him. There was something about her hands on his body—even if it was just his back—that got him hard. Maybe it was the closeness of being in the shower together or the heat and steam from the water or the fact that his teeth weren't chattering anymore.

And maybe it was just Elizabeth, who replaced her hands on his back with her breasts as she moved into him and wound her arms around him to rub the soap across his chest and stomach, her breasts soaping his back as she slid back and forth.

When her hands snaked lower, he looked down to watch rivers of soap streaming toward his very hard cock.

"Turn around, Gavin."

He took the soap from her hands, put it on the shelf, and let the shower spray rinse him. Then he turned and grabbed the spray nozzle, lifting it from the holder to rinse all the soap from her breasts, using his hands to smooth the bubbles from her nipples.

She giggled. "That tickles."

He directed the spray over her belly and between her legs. She lifted her gaze to his. "That doesn't tickle. It feels good."

"Do you get yourself off with shower spray?"

She nodded. "It's an easy orgasm. Fast and hard when I'm in a hurry."

His cock twitched. He replaced the sprayer, then turned and

slipped his hand between her legs. She gasped. "Fast and hard, huh? Is that how you like it?"

She gasped and reached for his shoulders as he rubbed her pussy. "Sometimes when I really need to come."

He put his other arm around her, then slipped two fingers into her pussy, continuing to rub her clit with his hand. "Do you really need to come, Elizabeth?"

"It's all I've been thinking about since we've been in here, since I've been touching you."

He pulled his fingers out and pushed her against the wall, dropped to his knees and lifted one of her legs, draping it over his shoulder so he could spread her wide for him.

She had the most beautiful pussy he'd ever seen. Plump, juicy lips and a pretty tuft of red hair covering her sex. She was glistening wet, and he couldn't wait to taste her. He cupped her butt cheeks and drew her to his mouth, sliding his tongue over her pussy lips.

"Oh, God, Gavin. Yes, that's so good."

He licked her clit, put his mouth over her, and sucked the bud, rolling his tongue over it. She pushed her pelvis against him, silently asking for more. He moved his tongue all over her, from her clit to her pussy, licking her all over.

The water cascaded down her belly and over her sex, washing into his mouth as he devoured her. He wondered if that added to the sensation. He hoped so, because he wanted her going crazy as he made her come. He slipped his finger inside her, pumped it in and out, swirled his tongue over her clit, and felt her pussy grip his finger. He added another and another, and each time her pussy tightened, her moans grew louder and her hands slapped the wall.

"Dammit, Gavin," she cried.

He kept the focus of his tongue around her clit, licking her with relentless strokes while fucking her pussy harder with his fingers.

"Oh, God, I'm coming. Suck my clit."

He latched on to her clit and gave it a hard suck as her pussy constricted around his finger, and she shook with the force of her climax. She cried out, her fingers digging into his hair as she held on.

He rose, lifted her leg over his hip, and drove into her while she was still climaxing. She screamed, and he kissed her, drinking in her cries as he pumped up into her still convulsing pussy.

God, she was tight, still coming as he took her into another climax. Her eyes flew open, and she dug her nails into his shoulders and bit his lip, moaning as she came.

Fuck. Fuck. It was so good feeling her squeeze his cock as she came again. He felt his own orgasm rushing toward him, and he held on to her ass, rocking against her as he burst inside her. He kissed her deeply, his tongue winding with hers, his groans mixing with hers as his climax hit him with a devastating force that nearly buckled him and left him sweating and panting.

He leaned his forehead against the cool tile wall of the shower. Elizabeth was limp against him as he withdrew and rinsed them both, then turned off the shower. He guided her out of the shower and dried her hair and body.

She was done for, her eyes no more than slits. He lifted her and carried her to bed, tucked her under the covers. He climbed in with her, pulled the covers up, and slid up behind her. She wiggled her butt against his crotch and mumbled a few contented words.

That's exactly what he was.

Content. With Elizabeth.

And didn't that have danger signals pinging in his head?

TWELVE

ELIZABETH NURSED A CUP OF COFFEE AND THE LARG-
est glass of orange juice ever.

Whose brilliant idea had it been to have margaritas?

Hers, probably.

Ugh. This was a good time for a self-reminder on the evils of
alcohol and why she very rarely overimbibed.

Weren't girlfriends supposed to watch over you and prevent you
from doing stupid shit like this? As she recalled, Shawnelle and
Haley, her partners in crime, had gone along for the ride with her.
At least she took comfort in the fact they were probably suffering
just as badly as she was this morning.

She took out her phone to check for messages. There was a text
from Gavin.

> *Early game today. Didn't want to wake you. Don't feel like you have
> to be there. Will understand if the mermaid is hung over. Have had
> your car brought back to you, too, in case you need it. Cul8tr. G*

Mermaid? She frowned, trying to remember . . .

Oh. The dip in the ocean last night. She smiled, remembering how he'd indulged her idiotic idea to go skinny dipping. Bet his cock and balls hadn't appreciated that chilly dip. Then again, she had no problem at all recalling their steamy shower sex, so obviously he hadn't suffered any ill effects from the icy ocean swim.

She read over his text message again. And again. Then realized she was mooning over his message as if it were a love note. How very stupidly high-schoolish of her. Disgusted, she tossed her phone on the table and picked up her orange juice, taking several tentative sips.

Her stomach, though a little queasy, decided it would accept the orange juice, so she drank more, then picked up her coffee cup and took several caffeine-laden swallows.

She went into the kitchen and fixed a couple of eggs and some toast. After eating she felt immensely better, though she looked like hell. Going to bed with her hair wet and uncombed was a disaster. She took another shower, did her hair, and put on some makeup. She drank another cup of coffee and opened her laptop to do some work. She made a few calls and lost track of time.

Her phone rang while she was typing out a letter. It was Shawnelle.

"Hey, why aren't you here?" Shawnelle asked.

"Where is here?"

"The game, dumb-ass."

"Oh. I'm working today."

"Bullshit. You're hung over and making Haley and I suffer here in the heat by ourselves."

"No, actually I feel fine. And I was doing some work and just lost track of time."

"Well, your boy isn't doing so well today. He needs his lucky charm. Get your ass out here."

Elizabeth laughed. "I'm not his lucky charm. He can play just fine without me."

"No, he can't. It's bottom of the fourth, and he's oh for everything. Besides, I need sympathy. I feel like hell."

She rolled her eyes. "Fine. I'll be there in a half hour."

She dressed and headed out to the ball field, found Shawnelle and Haley hiding under floppy hats and dark sunglasses.

"Feeling good today?" she asked as she took the spot they made between them.

"You should know," Haley grumbled. "This is all your fault."

"Don't blame me. I didn't put that glass in your hand. Nor did I drink those three pitchers by myself."

Shawnelle groaned and laid her head in her hands. "Don't remind me."

"So how are they doing?" Elizabeth asked.

"They're down by two runs in the sixth," Haley said. "We figured maybe your presence could light up Gavin, who isn't batting for shit today."

Elizabeth snorted. "Probably because he was up late tending to his drunken house partner."

"Girlfriend," Shawnelle said.

"What?"

"You're his girlfriend. Not house partner. Not roommate. Girlfriend."

"I'm not his girlfriend."

"Really. Then what are you?"

"His agent."

Haley snorted. "You're sleepin' with him. Do you do that with all your clients?"

"Of course not."

"Then you're not *just* his agent, are you?"

"You two make my head hurt. Give it a rest, will you? Gavin and I are just having some fun together. It's nothing."

"I might be wearing dark sunglasses, but trust me, my eyeballs are rolling clear out the back of my head," Shawnelle said. "Are you really that far into denial?"

"Yes. Now watch the game because that's what I came here to do."

In fact, in her rush out the door she'd forgotten to bring her laptop with her, so she was going to be forced to give the game her full attention. Dammit.

The Rivers were up to bat, and Gavin stood in the on deck circle, waiting for his turn at bat. He swung the bat a few times to warm up, then scanned the crowd, saw her, and his lips lifted.

And her body warmed. She smiled back.

You have it so bad for him, Elizabeth.

It was really pathetic how wound up she was around Gavin. And how badly she was going to be hurt by him when he decided he was bored with her and kicked her to the curb.

It was Gavin's turn at bat. There were two runners on base with one out. Elizabeth clasped her hands together and leaned forward as the first pitch sailed by and was called a ball. Elizabeth held her breath on the second pitch. Gavin swung and it fouled off to the right. One ball, one strike. She swallowed, wishing she'd stopped to get a cold drink before she sat down. The third pitch was high, also a ball.

Gavin swung on the next pitch and it dropped into short center. Elizabeth stood and screamed. Gavin dug in and made it to first base. The runner on second base scored, and the runner on first base had to stay at second.

But Gavin had batted a run in. Elizabeth, Shawnelle, and Haley hugged and squealed as Gavin got a good lead off first and looked like he might run on this pitcher.

Dedrick was up to bat.

"Oh, God, they're going to try a double steal, aren't they?"

"Likely," Shawnelle said. "Dedrick will take a strike if it means Gavin and Jose can advance."

"Or Dedrick could just hit a home run and put up three more runs on the scoreboard."

Shawnelle grinned. "Well, yeah, that would be nice. But I'll take a double steal, and then my baby can drive those two runs home. Either way works for me."

"Me, too."

The pitcher kept his focus on Gavin, tossing a few pitches to first base to keep Gavin from leading off too far from the base. Gavin was quick, though, and made it back to safety without a problem. As soon as the pitcher turned his attention back to Dedrick, concentrating on winding up the pitch, Gavin and Jose were off, digging into the dirt and running like hell. The pitcher turned and fired off the ball to second base.

Elizabeth held her breath for the entire ninety feet. Jose slid into third, Gavin into second. Both were safe and the crowd erupted in cheers. Elizabeth, Shawnelle, and Haley screamed, jumped up and down, and hugged each other again.

She wanted to cry and didn't think she'd ever been more excited about watching a preseason baseball game before.

This was going to ruin her reputation as a cool and unaffected agent.

And when Dedrick hit a line drive into the left field corner and both runs came home, she was certain she'd have no voice left by the end of the game, because she screamed nonstop until Dedrick got to second base, a wide grin on his face.

It was now three to two in favor of the Rivers, and by the time the inning ended two more runs had scored.

The Rivers ended up winning six to three. Elizabeth was exhausted from the sun, the screaming, and her hangover. She knew Gavin would be busy, so she headed back to the beach house to finish working. Unfortunately, once she hit the sofa, she passed right out.

When she woke, it was dark in the house. Disoriented, she reached for the lamp on the table next to the sofa, grabbed her phone to check the time.

It was eight p.m. She'd slept three hours. She sifted her fingers through her hair, stood, and went into the kitchen to fix herself a glass of iced tea. She took the glass out onto the deck, expecting to find Gavin sitting out there.

He wasn't. Surprised, she headed into the bedroom and bath, thinking he might be sleeping or showering, but he wasn't there, either.

Huh. Maybe he went out with the guys after the game.

She shrugged and went back out on the deck to sip her tea. She checked her phone, but there were no messages from Gavin.

Okay, so he didn't owe her anything. He didn't report to her. They weren't a couple. Hadn't she been telling everyone that?

Still, he always left her messages letting her know where he was going and where he was going to be. So why nothing now? She kind of expected him to come home after the game. Okay, she didn't really expect him to, but it might have been nice if he'd let her know if he were going somewhere else, just so she wouldn't worry about him.

She went back inside and picked up her laptop to do some work, but she kept staring at her phone, disgusted with herself for her own weakness.

Dammit. She'd known this was going to happen, that it was going to come to this if she let her heart get wrapped up in Gavin. Now she was checking her phone every five minutes, hoping he'd toss her a crumb.

She was spending entirely too much of her time on Gavin and not nearly enough on herself, which is what she normally did. Her career was vital to her happiness. Not a man. She knew what focusing on a man—on love—could do to a woman. It could make a woman lose all sense of herself, could change her career-driven focus and skew her priorities.

It was time she altered her trajectory and stopped worrying about Gavin other than as one of her clients. She needed to think about what was best for his career, because what was best for his career would be what was best for *her* career. And what was best for his career was definitely not her.

Everyone already thought of her as his girlfriend, which was going to screw up his image once the season started. Gavin Riley off the market was a death sentence for his PR.

Gavin had a reputation as a hotshot first baseman and a sexy, product-endorsing single guy who played the field.

He hadn't been playing the field lately. He'd been playing with her. Just her. No one else but her.

She was not good for his image. Lots of young, sexy women throwing themselves at him were very good for his image.

Fun and games were over. It was time to get back to business. Her business. The thing she most loved and needed to make a priority in her life.

Her work would never hurt her. And with the way things were going with losing Mick and now Steve Lincoln, playing house with Gavin was the last thing she should be doing.

Spending time on her clients should be a priority. Getting Blane McReynolds signed with Tampa Bay in the first round of the draft needed to be a priority.

She hadn't been focusing on her work because she'd been too busy playing with Gavin.

That had to stop. Now.

She searched the airlines online and found a flight back to Saint Louis early tomorrow morning. She could drive down to Miami, stay at one of the airport hotels, and be ready for her flight in the morning.

Which meant she'd have to pack and get out of here in a hurry, just in case Gavin was on his way back to the house. She didn't want to face him, didn't want to have a conversation with him about her leaving.

She packed up, changed clothes, and tossed her bags in the car. As she hovered near the front door, she decided at the last second to jot down a note for him. No text message because that was too immediate. When he got home, he'd see the note.

She pressed the lock on the door and pulled it shut, climbed into her car and clenched the steering wheel in her hands.

"You're doing the right thing. Career first. Always first."

Never let a man have power over you, Elizabeth.

"Damn straight, Mama," she said as she backed out of the driveway.

It's too bad her mother never had the strength to take her own advice.

* * *

Gavin,

Have to head back to the office. The draft is coming up soon and I need to focus on a few deals. Plus, it's time I get back to work. It's been fun.

E

Fun? That was it? What the hell was this bullshit blow-off note?

Gavin crumpled up Elizabeth's note and tossed it across the room, pissed at himself for even being angry that she had left.

He had no idea what the hell set her off running this time, but he was tired of wondering. Or caring.

She was right. It had been fun. That's all it had been.

He went to the fridge and grabbed a beer, irritated that the team owner had forced them all into a three-fucking-hour meeting right after the game that had sucked up his entire night. And he'd left his phone in his locker, so he hadn't been able to call or text Elizabeth to let her know because he was a moronic slave to technology and he didn't know anyone's phone number by heart other than his parents', and that only because they'd had the same phone number for forty years.

Obviously, it wouldn't have mattered since she'd just decided to leave.

Again.

Fine. He didn't need her in his life. The regular season was about to gear up, and he needed to be ready for it. Baseball was all he needed to be thinking about right now. It was time to focus on the game.

Not on Elizabeth.

THIRTEEN

ELIZABETH STARED OUT OVER DOWNTOWN SAINT LOUIS
from her office on the twenty-seventh floor. The sun shone brightly
over the Mississippi River. Tugboats sailed down the muddy river,
and the sun glinted off the silver Gateway Arch, nearly blind-
ing her.

It was about damn time the sun came out after two weeks of
nonstop rain. Just in time for baseball season's opening week, too.
At least that would make some people happy.

Not her. But some people.

Bright and sunny outside. Dark and moody inside.

With a sigh she pushed off the credenza and paced her office,
staring at the clock on her laptop just waiting for the call from her
prospective client, NFL pro Jamarcus Daniels.

Rumor had it Jamarcus's agent was in a financial free fall, and
Jamarcus was ready to bail on him, which meant every sports agent
out there had been courting Jamarcus for the past week, including

Elizabeth. She'd flown to Cleveland and met with him and his wife, wined them, dined them, talked terms, and offered representation. She had a really good feeling about this guy. He seemed honest and genuine, and his wife was very sweet. Elizabeth laid it all out there for him, told him what she could do for his career and advised him not to wait too long before making the change. Rod Franklin, his current agent, was in deep trouble financially due to some risky investment strategies. He was losing clients left and right, and the sharks were circling.

Elizabeth should know since she was one of the sharks hoping to grab some of Rod's clients.

Showing weakness could destroy a sports agent, and Rod was bleeding heavily. His time in the industry was over, and he knew it. The best he could hope for was being able to pay his taxes on time in the coming year, because he was sure as hell going to lose every one of his clients.

Not her problem. Business was business, and only the strong survived.

She sat at her desk and checked her e-mail, excited to see an e-mail from Jamarcus.

"Son of a bitch."

He thanked her for meeting with him, said a lot of nice things about her, then said he'd signed with the Davis Agency.

Fuck!

She shoved her laptop and stood, kicked her chair across the room, crossed her arms and stared out the window again.

Another loss to the Davis Agency. What the fuck was Don Davis offering to these guys as incentive to sign with him anyway? That was two she'd lost to him.

Three if she counted Mick, who was also with Davis now.

Mick. She wondered if Mick had something to do with all of

this. As mad as he'd been at her over the whole Tara affair, she wouldn't put it past him to try and sabotage her agency.

Mick was a draw, a huge name, and a lot of athletes followed who was repped by what agent. Successful sports stars got great deals because of who their agent was. Smart players knew who those agents were.

Elizabeth had many big names on her client roster, but there was no doubt Mick firing her had hurt her—continued to hurt her—as evidenced by losing Steve and Jamarcus to the Davis Agency.

Dammit. She hated being suspicious of Mick, but being suspicious had kept her on top of her game for the past ten years. She hadn't become successful by being blind. She was almost certain that Mick and Don Davis were working together behind her back.

She picked up her phone and pressed the button for her assistant, Colleen.

"Yes?"

"Get me the list of the Davis Agency clients, Colleen."

"You got it."

She turned around and glared out the window, missing Florida and the fun she'd had there.

She missed Gavin, too. Then again this was like it had always been before, so she was used to it. She'd kept her distance from Gavin to protect her heart, and she'd let her guard down, allowed herself to get close to him, and gotten used to having him around.

Big mistake, and it wouldn't happen again. It was best to keep her relationship with Gavin professional.

She hadn't heard a word from him since she'd left him that note.

Not that she'd expected to. He had probably grown tired of her being there with him and just couldn't figure out how to ask her to leave. Good thing she was smart and insightful and knew when it was time to pack up and go.

She inhaled, sighed, and returned to her desk and her paperwork, burying herself in her work so she didn't have to think.

Her assistant buzzed in about an hour later.

"Tyler Anderson is on the phone," Colleen said.

Elizabeth's brows raised. Tyler Anderson was a premier hockey player for the Saint Louis Ice. And *not* one of her clients. "Thanks, Colleen."

She picked up her phone. "This is Elizabeth Darnell."

"Ms. Darnell, this is Tyler Anderson. I play for the Saint Louis Ice hockey team."

"I know who you are, Tyler. What can I do for you?"

"First, you can call me Ty. Second, my agent is an ass."

Elizabeth grinned, adrenaline pumping through her system as she took a seat at her desk and brought up Ty Anderson's stats and bio. "I take it then that you're interested in changing agents and working with me?"

"Yeah. Eddie Wolkowski said you're a good agent and that we should talk."

She made a mental note to send Eddie, one of her clients and another player on the Ice, a bottle of his favorite whiskey. "That's nice of him to say."

"Can we arrange a meeting?"

She clicked open her calendar. "At your convenience."

"I want to get this done soon. I already gave my agent the boot."

She made arrangements to meet with Ty, then hung up and swung around in her chair.

Finally, things were starting to look up. Ty was a star player, and even better, as she discovered when Colleen had brought her the list of Davis Agency clients, Ty Anderson was with the Davis Agency. It would be an absolute boon to steal him away from Don Davis since

Davis had been doing his damned best to bleed her dry over the past six months.

It was about time she started getting some payback.

OPENING WEEK OF THE SEASON NEVER FAILED TO MAKE Gavin feel like a kid. It wouldn't matter how many years he played baseball, he'd still be six years old, and the sights and sounds and smells of the home stadium would still fill him with the excitement he'd felt when his dad had brought him to his first Rivers game. He'd been wide-eyed and taken it all in, from the sheer size of the stadium to the smell of hot dogs and popcorn to the deafening screams of all the fans. He'd fallen in love with baseball that first day, and the thrill had never left him. It didn't matter if he was sitting in the seats watching a game or standing at first base ready to field a ball. The love of the game was in his blood, and he'd never tire of it.

Putting on the uniform was an honor, one he didn't take lightly. He knew how hard players worked to make it to the major leagues, knew how few did and how easily that privilege could be lost, and he savored every minute he was allowed to play, because it could all go away with one big injury or a loss of mojo.

So far so good, though. The preseason had ended pretty well for the Rivers, even though Gavin hadn't batted as well as he thought he should. His game hadn't been consistent. He'd been all over the place and not all of it had been good. He'd lost his focus somewhere mid preseason, and he hoped to get it back now that the season had started.

"You gonna just stare into your locker all night, or do you think you might get off your ass and play some baseball?"

Gavin lifted his gaze toward Dedrick. "I'm channeling my mojo."

Dedrick leaned against the locker, his glove under his arm.

"Maybe your mojo is somewhere up your ass, and that's why you can't find it."

Gavin snorted. "Likely."

"Or maybe your pretty redheaded girlfriend ran off with it when she stopped coming to the preseason games."

Gavin didn't want to think about Elizabeth. "No woman has ever had my mojo." He grabbed his cup. "I got all the mojo I need right here."

Dedrick laughed. "Yeah, that's what we all say, 'til some woman brings us to our knees."

"Just because it happened to you, doesn't mean it's going to happen to me, brother." Gavin stood and followed Dedrick down the long hallway toward the dugout. "You ready?"

Dedrick touched his glove to Gavin's. "Hell yeah. Ready for this season to get under way. You?"

"You know it."

"Then let's play some ball and kick Milwaukee's ass."

"SO GAVIN RILEY IS ONE OF YOUR CLIENTS, RIGHT?"

Elizabeth sat in the owner's box with Ty, her new client. He wanted to see the game, she wanted to impress him, so she got him seats in the owner's box since she and Clyde Ross, owner of the Rivers, were close.

She made it a point to be on friendly terms with all the team owners. Not too close, but close enough that negotiations would go her way and her clients would get a good deal. Owners trusted her because they knew she wasn't out to screw them over. She didn't give them drug- or steroid-addled players or players who were interested only in becoming the next action movie star. She represented players who were serious about their sport. Which was why she'd spent several days in close meetings with Ty Anderson before she signed him on. She checked out his background and his playing history, wanted to make sure there were no skeletons in his closet, then she hit him with some tough questions and let him know she'd tolerate no bullshit. He had to be serious about playing hockey and staying in the sport. Money was great and all, but as she told all her clients, it wasn't just about the money. They had to love their sport.

By the time she'd spent several days with Ty, she was convinced he lived, breathed, and ate hockey, which was just what she loved in a client. They'd signed the papers yesterday.

"Yes, Gavin is one of my clients."

"He's damn good at first base. I played first base when I was a kid. Football, too. Tight end."

Elizabeth lifted her glass of wine and took a sip, studying Ty. "A little schizophrenic about your sports, were you?"

Ty laughed, a deep, booming sound that matched the man. "Hey, I had to play them all before I figured out what I wanted to do. Hockey seemed to fit me. Probably because I was always getting into fights."

"I can so see that about you." She was going to make a fortune off him and product endorsements. Don Davis might be able to sign players to a team contract, but he didn't know shit about promoting a player through the media.

Women's tongues were going to be dragging on the ground when they discovered Ty. Elizabeth had to get him a cologne or deodorant ad. Something that would feature him in print media. He had steely bluish gray eyes that simply penetrated when he looked at you, a square jaw, the kind of rough stubble that made a woman want his face rubbing across the tender parts of her skin, and he was tall and just utterly built like a man.

He was rough around the edges and a little crude, but he wasn't rude. He was the kind of man who knew he was a man and made no apologies about it. If Elizabeth wasn't stupidly hung up on Gavin, she could easily drool over Ty.

But despite appreciating his utter masculinity and fabulous good looks, the man didn't hit her hot buttons in the least.

She intended for many women to fall madly in love with Ty. She just wasn't going to be one of them.

"Elizabeth. So glad you called me today."

She rose to great Clyde, who kissed her cheek and gave her a hug. At sixty-four, Clyde was robust and an avid golfer. She played a few rounds with him whenever the weather was good and she had a free day on her calendar.

"Hello, Clyde. Thank you for allowing us to join you in the box tonight. I know opening day brings a crowd."

"Nonsense," he said, his brown eyes bright with excitement. "Always room for you in here."

Elizabeth introduced Ty to Clyde. Clyde beamed. "You're the center for the Ice. I go to many of the games."

"Thank you, Mr. Ross. It's an honor to meet you. I attend as many of the Rivers games as I can. You have a great team."

Ty was an awesome ass kisser. A point in his favor.

"I'll make sure you have season tickets and good seats, then. Bring some friends with you and talk us up."

"Yes, sir."

Clyde and Ty struck up a conversation about their respective sports, which left Elizabeth free to visit with some of the other people in the box, including Clyde's wife, Helen, who had showed up late with their daughter Aubry. Aubry was a cute, petite blonde with the brains to match her beauty. She was in med school at Washington University and didn't often have time to pop in and see a game.

"How's medical school?" Elizabeth asked.

Aubry rolled her eyes. "Torture. Pure hell. I love it."

Elizabeth laughed. "Of course you do. You were born to be a doctor. It'll all be worth it when it's over."

Aubry blew out a breath and pushed her glasses up the bridge of her nose. "At this point I don't see a light at the end of the tunnel, but I know someday it'll be over and I'll be delivering babies."

Elizabeth grinned. She'd always loved Aubry, could remember meeting her when she was in high school. It made her feel old, as if time had passed her by and maybe she'd missed out on marriage and having a family. Not that she'd ever wanted those things.

One couldn't have everything, could they? Elizabeth had long ago decided that her career would be the number-one priority in her life and nothing else would get in the way. No man, no marriage, no children. Sacrifices would have to be made because she couldn't have it all. No one could.

But lately . . .

Well, there was no point in thinking about that. She'd made her choices: she had a successful career, and she was happy.

Mostly.

She turned her attention to the game, to Gavin digging in at first base. He looked good. More than good, actually. Tanned and muscular, his fine ass stretched his uniform as he bent to scoop up a grounder and run to touch the base before the runner got there. He threw the ball, his muscled forearms glistening in the waning sunlight.

She inhaled, let out a small sigh and sat, enraptured, through the rest of the game. Since she'd gotten to know Shawnelle and Haley, she paid particular attention to Dedrick and Tommy. Dedrick played third base, and Tommy was a relief pitcher, right now set up to pitch in the middle innings if needed. He didn't get to see a whole lot of action. But Haley had told them they were grooming Tommy to be a starter.

Gavin had gone one for four on the night, which wasn't his best, but he did knock in a run. The nail-biter came in the ninth when the bases were loaded and Dedrick was up. The game was tied so if he didn't bring a run in, they were going to extra innings.

Elizabeth leaned forward in her seat, her fingers clasped together as Dedrick stared down Milwaukee's closer. Dedrick dug his toe into the dirt, leaned in, and swung. It skidded along the third-base line, and Elizabeth held her breath, certain it was going to slide outside the foul line.

It didn't. It stayed fair, and the runners took off from first and second. She leaped from her chair and squealed with delight as Jose charged around third base toward home while the right fielder scrambled for the ball. As soon as Jose touched home plate, the game was over. They only needed that one run to win the game.

The stadium erupted into chaos. The Rivers had won.

"That was a great game," Ty said, turning to her with a grin.

"It was, wasn't it?"

"Thanks for bringing me. I'm new to the city and haven't had much of a chance to get out to meet too many people. Since the move to the U.S. after the trade to the Ice, I've been busy finding a place to live and playing hockey. And then changing agents, of course. It's nice to get out and do something for a change."

"But you like the team change?"

"Of course. I was the one who wanted the change. Davis resisted."

Elizabeth leaned against the wall and crossed her arms. "Why?"

Ty shrugged. "No clue. He just said I should stay with Toronto, that change was never good."

Elizabeth laughed. "Your stats were abysmal in Toronto. Since the trade, you've been kicking ass on the ice. And with the Ice. Sometimes change is exactly what a player needs."

"That's what I thought, too. But hey, that's why I've got you and not him. He and I never saw eye to eye on my career. You and me mesh."

She grinned. "Yes, we do. And I'm glad you're happy. Now you can relax, play excellent hockey, and enjoy life in Saint Louis. The guys on your team are great. You should get to know them."

"I have. A few of us are making plans to go out this weekend."

"Settle in and make this your home. From what I hear from the team owner, you're going to be here awhile. He likes you and your style of play."

"Hey, Ty, want a tour of our fine facility here?"

Ty perked up at Clyde's suggestion. "Love one. Come on, Elizabeth."

She shook her head, not wanting to go anywhere near the locker room. "I've seen the place, but you go ahead."

"Come with us, Elizabeth. Afterward, you and Ty can come with Helen and Aubry and me. I'm buying dinner."

Crap. Schmoozing the owner was on the top of her list of things to do, and she never turned down an opportunity to hang out with him. "What a nice offer. We'd love to, wouldn't we, Ty?"

"I'd consider it an honor. Thank you."

Clyde took them on the standard tour of the ballpark, from the executive offices all the way down to the players' locker room. Elizabeth opted to wait outside the locker room with Helen and Aubry while the guys went inside, but she was certain Ty would get a kick out of meeting some of the players.

Elizabeth preferred not to see Gavin. In fact she hoped like hell she could avoid it.

"That guy is gorgeous," Aubry said.

"Which guy? Oh, Ty?"

"Yes. Makes me wish I had a nanosecond of free time to date. The only men I get to hang around with are the other medical students."

"Well, you do have a lot in common with them."

"True. My mother tells me I'm destined to marry one. She's probably right."

"Or a baseball player."

She rolled her eyes. "The last person I would ever marry is a baseball player. I've been surrounded by them my entire life. I think I'll stick with doctors. Baseball players have entirely too much ego."

Elizabeth laughed. "And doctors don't?"

"Okay. Good point. But I think I'll take my chances with doctors. Their egos I can handle. Baseball players on the other hand? Ugh."

"You're right about that, Aubry. We're horrible."

Aubry's eyes widened. "Gavin. You know I didn't mean you."

Shit. Elizabeth turned around. Gavin stood outside the locker room door with Ty.

Gavin grinned at Aubry, didn't even look at her. "Just teasing you, Bree." He leaned over and kissed her cheek.

Aubry blew out a breath. "You scared me, dammit. You know some of those guys really have inflated opinions of themselves. I might hurt some feelings."

Gavin hugged her against him. "Not me. I don't have feelings."

She laughed and so did Helen. "Gavin, you played well tonight."

Gavin shrugged. "Not as good as I'd like to, but thank you, Helen. Clyde said to tell you he'd be out in a minute. He's giving an inspirational speech."

Helen rolled her eyes. "Oh, Lord. I'm starving. We could be waiting an hour. Do go move him along, Gavin."

"Yes, ma'am."

Gavin stepped back inside the locker room. In five minutes, Clyde was out. With Gavin.

Damn. Elizabeth had hoped he wouldn't come back outside.

"Finally," Helen said. "I was about to faint. Gavin, are you coming to dinner with us?"

"Apparently. Clyde insisted."

"Excellent. Let's go, then. The limo is outside."

Well, what a big, happy group this was. Gavin skirted a look in her direction as Ty grabbed her arm and escorted her to the limo. She wondered if Gavin thought Ty was her date for the evening. He didn't seem pleased by that.

Elizabeth, on the other hand, was wholly pleased by the idea that Gavin looked a little less than his usual overconfident self.

They ate at an elegant restaurant downtown that afforded them privacy and a superb view of the riverfront. Clyde ordered champagne and toasted the Rivers new season.

"Gavin, was your family there tonight?"

"Not tonight. You know my family runs a bar in south Saint Louis, so they packed the crowds in for opening night."

Clyde smiled and nodded. "Well done. I like your parents. I hope to see them at our opening month picnic."

"You will. Mick should be in town for that, too."

"Excellent. I'm sure he's on cloud nine after his Super Bowl win."

Gavin grinned. "Yeah, he was pretty stoked about winning the Super Bowl, but I think he's more excited about planning his wedding to Tara."

Elizabeth kept her gaze averted, not wanting to listen in or get involved at all when discussions turned to Mick.

"Now, Ty, tell me about yourself. Getting all settled in?"

"Yes, sir. I've got a temporary place I'm staying in right now. Just waiting for the season to be over with this month, then I'm going house hunting."

"I'll put you in touch with an excellent Realtor we know," Helen said. "She'll be happy to help you."

Ty nodded. "Thank you. I'd like that. Elizabeth has been helpful. It's obvious she knows the area."

She smiled. "I've got a few clients here."

Ty grinned at her. "And now you have one more."

Gavin coughed. Elizabeth ignored him, glad he was sitting at the other end of the table entertaining Aubry, who was shooting interested glances toward Ty.

This whole dinner would be comical if Elizabeth wasn't acutely aware of Gavin's gaze on her the entire time. And okay, maybe she had been shamelessly flirting with Ty, who cast her knowing smirks as if he knew exactly what she was doing because she'd treated him completely professionally from the get-go. Until tonight. So she was being blatantly obvious, and Ty wasn't the clueless type.

Damn men.

Ty leaned in and whispered in her ear. "How badly do you want this guy?"

She turned her face to him. "I have no idea what you're talking about."

"I mean, do you want me to kiss you, or would just holding your hand be enough?"

"Neither. I'm not playing games here, Ty."

"Oh, I think you're definitely playing games, Elizabeth." He ran his finger up her bare arm. "And don't look, but the fish is biting."

She didn't look, but felt Gavin's gaze on her. Instead, she lifted her gaze to Ty. "Stop that."

"You don't want me to stop. You want him to watch. You want him to get jealous."

"No, I don't. Gavin is a client."

"So?"

"So, I keep my professional life and my private life separate."

Ty's generous lips lifted as he raised his glass and took a drink. "Apparently not."

"You're a smug son of a bitch, you know that?"

"So I've been told. But your boyfriend over there doesn't care that I'm smug, only that I'm paying attention to you."

"He's not my—" She rolled her eyes and gave up, happy when the food arrived and her argument with Ty ended. Not that it kept him from talking to her, which he did—rather incessantly throughout dinner. And since she'd found him to be mostly quiet during their previous meetings, she chalked it up to him trying to irritate Gavin.

The competitive nature of men and its relationship to women was one she'd never be able to understand. Add men in sports to the equation, and the competitiveness quadrupled. Ty had done everything but haul her onto his lap, and only because he did manage to take time out from his blatant flirting to eat his steak.

Gavin, on the other hand, seemed content to keep Aubry company. He had her laughing and engaged in conversation, so maybe Ty was totally off base, because not once did Elizabeth see Gavin glancing her way.

"He's not even looking at me."

"Not when you're looking at him," Ty explained. "But as soon as you turn away, he's looking. Trust me. I've got this under control. I know when to turn up the heat. And you know I won't mind if you want to use me to make your boy toy jealous."

Trust him? Ha. At this point she'd like to kick him with her pointy-toed shoe. She somehow made it through dinner and the limo ride back to the stadium, thanked Clyde and Helen when they dropped her off at her car, declined Ty's offer to accompany her and make sure she was safely escorted back to her condo. She opened her car door, slid in, and laid her head against the steering wheel.

What an epic disaster. She hadn't expected to run into Gavin tonight when she'd brought Ty to the game. It was a big damn stadium. She'd thought sliding Ty into the owner's box would be a piece of cake. They'd watch the game, slip out, and Gavin would have never known she was there.

Except his SUV was rolling toward her right now.

No. She had nothing to say to him. She started her car up and put it in gear, made a right turn, and headed for the ballpark exit, Gavin's headlights right behind her. She pulled out of the park, conscious of him following her as she pulled onto the highway.

Okay, so she knew he'd take the same highway going home. No big deal, right? But he stayed right behind her the entire time. Surely he didn't intend to follow her, did he? What did they possibly have to say to each other? Unless he was trying to find out if she had a tryst with Ty?

A tryst? She laughed out loud.

Yeah, and you watch too many Lifetime television movies, Elizabeth.

She was being ridiculous. If Gavin was at all interested in what she was doing or who she was seeing, he'd have called her after she abruptly left his beach house a few weeks ago.

He hadn't. Which meant he wasn't interested. They were over.

Ignoring the hurt, she took the highway exit.

So did he.

Butterflies took up residence in her stomach and stayed there as she pulled into her driveway.

Gavin didn't, instead driving past her condo entrance as she got out. She waited, wondering if he was going to pull up to the security gate.

He didn't. She watched him drive to the end of the street and turn back onto the highway, headed in the direction of his house.

Well, son of a bitch.

FOURTEEN

ELIZABETH WATCHED GAVIN'S CAR DISAPPEAR.

What the hell had that been all about? Was he just fucking with her, trying to freak her out?

She went inside, checked her mail, then tossed it on the kitchen table. She walked back and forth in front of her living room window, certain at any minute she'd see Gavin pull up.

He didn't.

Dammit. She grabbed her keys, got in her car and headed out onto the highway.

By the time she'd made it out to the dark road where Gavin lived, she had second thoughts. What the hell was she doing? What was her plan? To knock on his door and ask him why he'd followed her? She could have called him.

Well, she was here now, heading up the long driveway to Castle Grayskull. The imposing two-story dark brick behemoth stood hidden behind thick, imposing trees that didn't seem at all welcoming.

It looked eerie and foreboding with vines crawling up the front and sides of the exterior.

She shuddered, hating this house and its isolation. She had no idea why Gavin liked this place. It was a mausoleum. When he'd bought it several years ago and showed it to her, she'd pronounced it the house of a vampire and had never come back.

He'd laughed at her. He'd probably laugh at her again tonight when she knocked on his door, affronted that he'd followed her.

Tough. They had a few things to get straight.

As she pulled in front of the house and turned the ignition off, she almost decided to turn around and head back to her place. With a sigh of resignation and just enough righteous indignation left to see this through, she got out, smoothed her skirt, and marched up to the front door. She lifted the hideous gargoyle knocker and rapped three times. It wouldn't surprise her at all to hear screams coming from the other side since this house was straight out of a horror movie.

The door opened—with a creak, no less—and Gavin stood there, a surprised, wide-eyed look on his face. She helped herself to a scan of the rest of him, since he wore no shirt and a pair of ratty sweats, and he was barefoot. Everything that was female about her went into overdrive, and she had to resist the urge to leap into his arms and lick him senseless.

"Liz, what are you doing here?"

"Followed you, just like you followed me."

He shrugged and opened the door wide. "Come on in, since you're here."

She stepped inside, shadows flicking their menacing greeting from the wall sconces in the entryway. It was cold in this place. She grabbed her jacket and pulled it tighter around her and followed Gavin into the living room.

Dark burgundy paint on the walls only added to the opposing atmosphere.

"Still gloomy in this place."

His lips curled. "I like this house."

"It suits you."

"You want something to drink?"

"I'll have whatever you're having." She looked at his glass.

He went to the bar off in the corner of the living room and poured her a whiskey, added a couple of ice cubes, and refilled his own drink.

"You going to sit down or just glare at me?"

She plopped onto the sofa. He handed her the whiskey and sat in the chair next to the sofa. She sipped the whiskey, grimacing. Not her drink of choice, but as it burned its way down to her stomach, it at least helped warm her up a little.

"It's freezing in here."

"Bitch, bitch, bitch." He grabbed a remote off the table in front of him and clicked a button. The fireplace roared to life, heat blazing forth and providing instant warmth.

"Thanks."

"Not like Florida here, is it?"

He just had to mention Florida, didn't he? "Not quite. It was bad here while you were down there. Rained for weeks."

"Yeah, I saw you were getting bad weather."

They were talking about the weather. Is that what their relationship had been reduced to? They used to be comfortable with each other before sex had gotten in the way.

"Why did you come here, Liz?"

"Why did you follow me to my condo?"

"Just wanted to make sure you got there safely since it was late."

She took a giant swallow of whiskey. "I'm a big girl, Gavin. I travel all over by myself without a bodyguard and make it home without an escort all the time."

"I'm sure you do. But if you're somewhere with me, I'm going to make sure you get back home okay."

"I wasn't 'with you' tonight."

"Semantics. You were driving home alone, and it was on the way to my place anyway, so I just made a couple of extra turns to be sure you got home safely."

"Why?"

He shrugged. "Don't know. I guess it's the nature of our relationship. I feel responsible for you."

"We don't have a relationship, Gavin, so you don't need to feel responsible for me."

He dragged his fingers through his hair. She wanted to run her fingers through the thick dark strands, remembered how soft his hair was, hated that she'd made him off-limits.

He lifted his gaze to her. "Why *don't* we have a relationship, Elizabeth? What happened in Florida? Why did you leave?"

She shrugged. "Seemed time."

"Time for what? Time for you to write me some bullshit note and run like hell?"

"You didn't call me."

"What?"

She'd said it so low she knew he hadn't heard her. "Nothing."

He came over and sat on the sofa next to her. "Tell me what you said."

She shook her head. This had been a mistake. "Nothing."

"Elizabeth." He tipped her chin and forced her to look at him. "Talk to me."

"I got scared, okay? You didn't come home and didn't call that night. I had no idea where you were and what you were doing. And I started thinking about being in a relationship with a guy. I'd never done that before. All the expectations. God, I hate expectations. I didn't want to be that woman."

She stood, went to the oversized window, and stared out at the tree limbs blowing in the wind, reaching toward the window, seemingly mocking her, laughing at her.

She heard Gavin approach. He put his hands on her, and she inhaled, breathing in his scent, so crisp, like the wild outdoors battering the window.

A storm was blowing in.

"What expectations? You didn't want to be what woman? I don't understand."

She crossed her arms, hating that she was here having this conversation with him. "I know you don't understand, Gavin. Because it doesn't make any sense. I don't make sense. This doesn't make sense. I need to go."

She turned to leave but he grasped her arms.

"Don't go. I want to talk to you about that night. After the game I got stuck in a meeting and left my phone in my locker. And since I'm a moron and don't know phone numbers because they're programmed into my cell, I couldn't call you. When I got back, you were already gone. I tried calling you after the meeting to tell you I was on my way back. You didn't pick up."

"I know."

"Why?"

Because she'd been hurt and felt stupid for staying as long as she had. Because she'd given him the power to hurt her and make her vulnerable for caring about him. Because she already loved him and it devastated her. She'd spent years guarding her heart around him, and it had been working just fine. Laying her heart open around him had been dangerous. She'd had to run.

"It can't work between us, Gavin. You know that."

He arched a brow. "I don't know that. I thought we were having a pretty good time together. You just got bent out of shape because I didn't call saying I'd be late for dinner."

Her lips twitched. Damn him. She didn't want to cave on this. She wanted to remain firm and distant. But his impish green eyes and his hair falling across his brow were melting her, not to mention the warmth of his hands squeezing her shoulders.

She'd missed him over the past few weeks, more than she wanted to admit. Her body missed his touch. She missed looking at him and sleeping next to him. And despite her resolve to shove him back in the "client only" corner, they'd crossed the bridge into something else, and she wasn't going to be able to shove him back into where he had been before.

Shit.

"I might have overreacted."

"Just a little. And so did I. Admittedly, I was pissed off when I came back to the house and you were gone. I should have called you again. And again. Instead, I let the radio silence continue because I was hurt you up and left me."

"You were?"

"Hell yeah. I liked having you in Florida with me. A warm body to share my bed at night, a sexy, independent woman who has her own career and doesn't look to me to see to her every need? It's every man's dream."

Her heart did flip-flops. "I hardly qualify as every man's dream, Gavin. You said it yourself. I'm a pain in the ass."

"Yeah, you are. But for some reason I like you, Lizzie. Despite your attempts to piss me off."

He pushed her jacket off her shoulders. It was warm in the room now, and she was comfortable in her sleeveless top. He skimmed his hands down her arms, and he drew her against him.

"I missed holding you."

"I'm sure you haven't been lonely without me."

He stopped and pulled her back. "There hasn't been anyone

since I was with you. Believe that. All I did after you left was play ball and brood a lot."

She stared at him, unable to believe the bad boy of baseball would go almost a month without a woman. She wanted to believe him, but the men in her life had never been honest with her.

Gavin, however, had never lied to her. Why would he now?

"The brooding part I can definitely believe."

He smiled and grazed his knuckles across her cheek, then leaned in and brushed his lips across hers. "Hey, I've been busy. It's not like I go out and randomly pick up women."

She craved more of his mouth on hers. "Neither do I."

His lips lifted. "You don't randomly pick up women?"

She laughed. "No. That's not what I meant. I don't randomly pick up men."

"Not even Ty Anderson?"

She laid her palms on his bare chest, loving the feel of his skin. "He's a new client and nothing more. Wanted to see a game tonight."

"He seemed to want to see more of you."

She lifted her gaze to his. "Jealous?"

His gaze narrowed. "Hell yes."

When he kissed her this time, his lips were firm and possessive. He wrapped his arms around her and crushed her to him. His tongue slid inside her mouth and sucked on hers, demanding she surrender.

No problem there. She'd missed him so damn much. Being in his arms still felt like a dream to her. Being with Gavin felt forbidden, as if he was something she wasn't supposed to have. And no matter how many sweet things he said to her about how he missed her and how it felt right between them, she knew what they had was always going to be temporary, for so many different reasons. So every moment they had together felt stolen, and she was going to enjoy every second.

He swept his arms down her back and cupped her ass, bringing her closer to his erection. She whimpered, needing him inside her right now, feeling a burst of primal hunger and a desperate need to be satisfied.

He backed her up against the wall next to the windows and tore her top from the waistband of her skirt. She kicked off her shoes and held up her arms while he lifted her blouse over her head.

Lightning flashed outside. She felt the electricity inside, too, when Gavin swept his hands over the bare flesh of her belly, then around her back as he unzipped her skirt and pushed it to the floor. She brushed the skirt to the side and reached for his sweats, pushing them down his hips. He stepped out of them, and she couldn't help but look down and admire the power of his body.

His eyes were heavy lidded with passion, which fed her own need. She thrust her fingers into his hair and pulled him toward her for a kiss that blazed as hot and furious as the growing storm outside. Thunder rolled outside and rain lashed the windows. Lightning lit up the living room like daylight and the power flickered.

Gavin pulled back only long enough to sweep his hand over her bra-clad breasts while she was illuminated by the lightning.

Elizabeth took a few moments to catch her breath, to watch Gavin's face as the lightning bathed it in on-and-off shadow. She gasped when he released her bra clasp and held on to the cups to pull her to him, then bent and sucked a taut bud between his lips.

The power of the storm outside only intensified her arousal, made her grab his hair and draw him closer to her breasts. Watching him lick and suck and bite her nipples made her clit and pussy tingle, made her want to feel him inside her pounding away.

God, she really needed him to fuck her, wanted to come so badly she could touch herself right now and go off like the lightning arc-ing across the dark skies.

"Gavin, fuck me."

He lifted his head and bent to remove her panties, sliding his hands slowly down her hips, her thighs, her calves. She shivered at the feel of his fingers on her skin. And when he kissed his way up her legs, she parted them, knowing where he was going and wanting him there so desperately.

"Lean against the wall, Elizabeth."

She leaned back and spread her legs. Gavin kissed her thighs, cupped her butt cheeks, and put his mouth where she needed it—right on her pussy. Seeing his lips on her clit made her shudder. Feeling his tongue rolling over the bud made her legs weak. She palmed the wall for support, closed her eyes, and let the sensations wash over her.

It had been so long since she'd had a climax, she came with a wild, surprising rush, letting out a cry and tightening her hold on Gavin's hair. He rose and slid his cock inside her while she was still coming, intensifying her already insane orgasm.

Elizabeth laid her hands on his shoulders and dug her fingers into his skin, focusing her gaze on his eyes. She couldn't even come down off the high of her climax, because he thrust into her, rolling his hips over her already sensitized sex and taking her right back to a fevered state. She wound her fingers around the nape of his neck and drew his lips to hers.

He kissed her, and thunder rolled outside, shaking the founda-tion and the walls, making her crazy as the storm intensified inside her again, too. Gavin didn't stop, just continued to pummel her with the slow, steady slide of his shaft in and out of her. It was the sweet-est torture, and the way he kissed her was maddening, taking her breath away with his lips and his tongue, nipping at her, licking at her, demanding she give him all she had.

It was a total bombardment of her body, her senses, her heart, and she shook her head, finally pulling her lips from his as he pummeled her beyond reason, his chest scraping her nipples, his pelvis rocking against her clit, and his mouth nuzzling her neck.

"Gavin."

He didn't answer, just dragged his tongue from her neck to her shoulder and bit down on her.

She shuddered, felt the rising storm of another climax building inside her, felt her pussy tightening around his cock. He stilled, and she felt him swelling impossibly thick inside her. She knew he was ready to come inside her. And when he gripped her buttocks and lifted her, she wrapped her legs around him and let go.

He let out a guttural cry and slammed her against the wall, found her mouth and drove his tongue inside. She moaned into his mouth when she climaxed, drinking in his groans as he came with her.

They sank to the floor together, Gavin holding on to her with his hands and pulling her on top of him. He held her, stroked her back, and swept her hair away from her face, but he didn't let her go, though she was certain she had to be heavy. After a while, she lifted her head, afraid he'd fallen asleep. His clear gaze rocketed to hers.

"I thought you were sleeping," she said.

"No. Just enjoying touching you."

"Are we going to stay like this the rest of the night?"

"I thought about it. I like listening to the storm."

She shook her head and pushed up to sit on him.

"I like this view even better." He grabbed her hips and lifted his, rocking against her.

She laughed, pushed against him, and stood. "I need to go."

He sat up and watched her get dressed. "Why?"

She grabbed her panties and bra. "Why what?"

"Why do you have to go?"

"Because I have my own place."

"I know that. But why can't you sleep here with me?"

She stepped into her panties. "In the dungeon?"

"Ha-ha. Seriously."

She shrugged. "I don't know. I'm thinking we should maybe keep things light and easy."

He stood, and she found it utterly, deliciously disconcerting that he seemed content to stand there naked. "So, you just want to get together and fuck on occasion, and then go our separate ways."

She fastened her bra and lifted her gaze to his. "Something like that. It's less complicated that way."

He came toward her and pulled her into his arms. "You could hire a prostitute to fuck you. Or find any number of willing guys."

She laughed. "Contrary to what you might think, there aren't a bunch of men lined up waiting to fuck me."

His lips curled in a smug smile. "So . . . just me?"

"Just you."

"Stay with me. Sleep with me."

She shuddered as his hand moved over her back, his fingertips rested just above her butt. "I can't."

"You won't. You're afraid."

She arched a brow. "I'm not afraid, Gavin. I've slept with you before."

"And then you ran out on me. You're afraid to get close to me."

She laughed. "Are you serious? We just got pretty damned close."

"That's not what I mean and you know it."

She snatched her skirt and climbed into it. "This is ridiculous. I'm not having this conversation with you."

And he still stood there naked. Arguing with her. Naked. Damn him anyway. She grabbed her blouse and pulled it over her head, then slipped into her shoes and searched for her purse and keys.

"You do realize I'm not going to let you drive in the rain."

She rolled her eyes. "You're not my father. You don't control me."

"I'm not trying to control you, Elizabeth. But there's one hell of a storm out there. If you'd pull your head out of your ass and think logically you'd realize you shouldn't be out there driving in it."

Ignoring the punctuating thunder and bright flash of lightning that was trying to prove his point, she dug into her purse for her keys. "I've driven in rain before. I've lived in this city for a while now. I can handle it."

He didn't say anything so she pulled the door open and was immediately blasted by a harsh, cold wind and flash of rain that soaked her. Shivering, she stepped outside and tried to pull the door closed, but the wind battering her prevented it.

"Goddamn it, Gavin, would you help me out here?"

"Sure." He came over, jerked her by the arm and pulled her inside, then shut the door and locked it. "You proved your point. Don't be an idiot."

She dropped her purse and keys and swiped her soaked hair out of her eyes. "I forgot my jacket anyway."

His lips curled. "Yeah, that would have helped a lot." He took her hand. "Come on, honey. Let's get you upstairs and into a hot shower."

He led her upstairs and turned on the shower. And okay, even though Castle Grayskull was a giant medieval mausoleum, the bathroom was modern and roomy and, oh, thank God, had a heater and a spacious shower with multiple jets. Gavin stripped her of her soaking wet clothes and threw her in the shower, soaped her up with this great-smelling honey soap, and even washed her hair for her.

Afterward, while she dried off and blow-dried her hair, he went downstairs and made her hot chocolate with real whipped cream. She slipped into the fluffy bathrobe he left out for her, and they crawled into his bed. He'd turned on the fireplace in his bedroom and it was warm and toasty, so the last of her chills had dissipated.

She sat cross-legged in the middle of his bed sipping hot chocolate, feeling foolish for her childish tantrum earlier.

"Why do you continue to put up with me, Gavin?"

He shrugged and took the cup from her, sipping the hot chocolate. "You're a challenge, Lizzie. I do like a challenge."

"I'm a giant problem for you."

He handed her cup back. "Yeah."

She laid the cup on the nightstand, took off the robe, and slid under the covers with him. He turned off the lights and opened the drapes. The storm had died down now, and the only thing left was the low thunder and occasional lightning. The rain had lightened to just a patter against the French doors of the balcony.

He pulled her against him, and she laid her head against his chest and stared outside.

"I think you're worth fighting for, Elizabeth. Even if I'm fighting you for you."

She didn't know what to say to that.

No one had ever fought for her before.

She didn't think she was worth it.

FIFTEEN

"THAT WAS ONE HELL OF A HOME RUN IN ATLANTA THE other night, son. The entire bar erupted in cheers. We sold a lot of beer after you hit that grand slam."

Gavin grinned as he helped his dad loosen some nuts on the lawn mower. "Thanks, Dad. It was a big hit."

He'd come over after his weeklong road trip to help his dad with some repairs. His father was sweating over the lawn mower, trying to remove the wheels.

"Dad, let me do that."

"I got it. Just get that one in the back, and then we can get these wheels off."

Gavin dug in and cranked the wrench, muttering a litany of curses in his head when the rusty bastard wouldn't budge. Finally, it gave and he got the nut moving. Wiping the sweat from his brow, he said, "Dad, why don't you just get a new mower? This beast has to be older than me."

"Hey, don't be tossing out the old shit. It still works. Just needs a tune-up."

"It needs a burial. You could get a riding mower. Or one of those that are self-propelled."

His father's face turned nearly purple as he pushed the wrench. Gavin held his breath, waiting for his dad to collapse right there trying to get the rusty bastard to let go.

"Goddamn this old thing needs some WD-40."

"It needs the junkyard."

His dad got up slowly from his position on the ground and hunted around in the garage. "You kids just want to toss everything out as soon as it doesn't work anymore. You just need to give it a loving hand."

"No, Jimmy. You need to know when something has given up the ghost and needs to be traded in for a newer model."

Gavin looked up in thanks at his mother. "Amen to that, Mom. Tell him he needs to get a new lawn mower."

His mother rolled her eyes. "As if I could tell him anything. In matters of the outside and the garage, he is king of the world."

"Damn right." His father looked at Gavin. "We'll get her fixed."

Gavin cast a pleading look at his mother.

She laughed. "Gavin, come in and get the iced tea I made. You and your father look like you could use a drink."

He could kiss his mother right now. "Sure. Be right back, Dad."

His father waved him off. Gavin followed his mom into the kitchen and took a seat at the kitchen table.

"What is his deal?"

She shrugged. "I have no idea. He's always been fond of fixing things, but lately he's got some bug up his butt about retooling the lawn mower and the weed whacker, and he even found an old window air conditioner in the attic and has been futzing around with that, though I have no idea why."

"You have central air."

"Exactly." She threw her hands in the air. "Maybe he's planning to air-condition the garage. I don't have a clue."

He took the tea his mother offered. "He's bored. That's got to be it."

"If he's bored, I have a whole list of projects that need to be done around here, starting with a new fence. He ignores those and fiddles with stupid things."

"Well, those projects aren't fun, Mom."

She laughed. "I guess. And I don't know how he could be bored. There's the bar."

"Jenna probably manages the bar single-handedly these days. And we have great cooks and waitresses. Dad probably feels like he's in the way."

"Hmmm. You know, you could be right about that. I don't know what to do about it, though."

"Just tell Jenna to give him more work to do at the bar. Anything to keep him from tearing things apart here. Or find something here that interests him."

She inhaled, then sighed. "I suppose so." She took a drink of tea and studied him.

"What?"

"It's nice to have you here."

He knew what that meant. Something was on her mind. "Go ahead. Spill it."

She took a seat at the table. "Mick came by and said he ran into you and Elizabeth."

Somehow he knew this was going to come up. "And?"

"You could have told me you and Elizabeth were dating."

"Do I ever discuss women I'm dating with you?"

"Elizabeth isn't just one of the many women who parade in and out of your life, Gavin. She's . . . Elizabeth. She's practically family."

"I don't really know what's going on with me and Liz yet, so there wasn't a point in mentioning it. Mick said you were pissed at her."

She narrowed her gaze. "He did, did he?"

"Yeah."

"About what happened with Tara and Nathan?"

"Yeah."

"Elizabeth apologized?"

"She did."

"Mick said she corrected her error."

"Yeah, she did."

"Then why would I be angry with her? She made a mistake. We all make mistakes. Michael fired her for it. I would think losing a prominent client like Michael would teach her not to manipulate a client again."

"I think she learned a valuable lesson from it."

"Michael should be the last one to throw stones."

Gavin shrugged. "He holds a grudge, and he's protective of Tara and Nathan."

"Understandable. But Elizabeth did some very good things for him and for his career. He needs to get past it."

"Yeah, tell him that. He laid into me about seeing Liz and told me I should dump her."

His mother's eyes widened. "He did not."

"Not in so many words, but he made his feelings clear."

She sighed. "I don't know why you two have always gotten into it. So competitive all the time. I'll talk to him."

He laid his hand over hers. "Thanks, Mom, but I don't need you to fight my battles. It's like you said. He'll have to get over it. I'll see Elizabeth for as long as whatever it is we have together lasts. If Mick doesn't like it, that's too bad. He's going to have to deal with it."

"How does Tara feel about you seeing her?"

Gavin shrugged. "I have no idea. Haven't seen her since I got back from Florida."

"Maybe you should tell her. If Elizabeth's going to be in your life in a romantic way, she's bound to run into Tara. You should pave the way and prepare her—prepare both of them—so it's not a shock when it happens."

"I'm sure Mick's already told Tara I'm seeing Liz."

His mother folded her arms. "And maybe he hasn't."

He nodded. "You have a point. I'll talk to her."

He'd try to make sure Elizabeth and Tara didn't run into each other, which was easier than trying to explain to Tara why he was dating a woman she hated.

They both jumped at the sound of metal against metal coming from the garage.

"Now what?" Gavin asked.

She shook her head. "I have no idea. Did your father tell you he's thinking of redoing the roof?"

Gavin rolled his eyes and slid his empty glass across the table. "Thanks for the tea, Mom. Guess I'll head out there and figure out what he's up to."

"SO I HAVE THIS THING TONIGHT."

Elizabeth rolled over in bed, her nails dragging down his chest, his abs, and slid under the covers to grasp his semi-hard cock.

"You have a thing? What thing?"

They'd spent the afternoon in bed. It was rare for him to have a day off, and they took full advantage of it. Elizabeth had met him at his house, and they'd shed clothes like they were on fire, fallen into bed, and spent the past few hours there. He was utterly exhausted.

Not that his cock had noticed, because it grew stiff under her stroking hand.

It was damned hard to concentrate on what he was trying to say to her when she was fondling his balls.

"Yeah. A thing. At my parents' house."

"Oh." She let go of his dick and sat up in bed. "Okay. I'll take a shower and get out of here."

He grabbed her hand. "No. Wait."

He pulled her back down on the bed. "It's Mick's birthday. Party at my parents' house. My mom wants you to come."

She looked horrified, like he'd just asked her to kill a chicken.

"I don't think so, Gavin."

"I told her you wouldn't want to come . . . for obvious reasons."

"Uh, yeah."

He scratched his nose. "She's kind of insisting. Said it's time for you and Mick to bury the hatchet."

She let out a laugh. "Yeah, he'll bury the hatchet all right. In my back."

She stood and stretched; her pretty nipples puckered as her back arched toward him. "Look, Gavin, tell your mother I appreciate the invitation and the sentiment behind it, but no way in hell am I ruining your brother's birthday party by showing up there."

He leaned back against the headboard and crossed his arms behind his head. "Not even if I ask you to come?"

"Why would you do that? You know how it will go. Mick will be pissed."

"We don't know that."

She rolled her eyes. "Yes, we do know that. I'm going to get dressed, and then I'm going home. You need to take a shower and head on over to your parents' house."

An hour later he stood at his parents' front door, not at all happy he didn't have Elizabeth with him. He'd tried to argue with her and did everything short of kidnapping her and tossing her into his SUV to get her to come with him, but she'd refused.

Not that he could blame her. This wouldn't have been a pleasant event for her.

And that pissed him off. Like it or not, he was seeing Elizabeth, and his brother was just going to have to start dealing with that.

Which meant that he and Elizabeth were a package deal. No Elizabeth, no him. He pivoted and stepped off the porch, wincing when the front door opened.

"Gavin."

Shit. He turned and smiled at his future sister-in-law. "Hey, Tara."

"You're leaving? You just got here."

"Yeah. I'm leaving."

She pulled the front door closed and stepped outside.

Damn, she was a beauty, her blonde hair pulled back in a long ponytail, her brown eyes clear and guileless. She was the sweetest woman he'd ever met.

Mick didn't deserve her.

"What's wrong, Gavin?"

He took her hands in his. "My brother and I aren't seeing eye to eye right now, and it's probably not a good idea for me to go inside."

She crossed her arms. "What did he do?"

Gavin laughed. "He didn't do anything. It's me. I'm seeing Elizabeth."

"Oh. And Mick has a problem with that?"

"You don't?"

She laughed. "Do you like her?"

"Yeah, I kind of do. Don't really know why since she tries my patience, but I'm no picnic, either. So I guess we kind of fit, at least for now. Mom wanted me to bring her tonight."

"And you didn't want to because of Mick."

"Well, I asked Elizabeth to come. She begged off because of . . .

well, because of everything that went down before. She didn't want to ruin Mick's party."

Tara drummed her fingers on her arms. "Mick needs to learn to let go. What happened is in the past. Elizabeth fixed it and apologized. My God, he fired her. What more does he want from her? A kidney?"

Gavin laughed. "I think I might have asked him the same thing."

"Go get her and bring her over here. If Mom wants her here, then she should be here."

"I can try, but I'm not sure she'll come."

"At least try. You won't get any objection from me, Gavin."

"You're a better person than most people I know, Tara."

She kissed him on the cheek. "You just keep reminding your brother how wonderful I am, okay?"

He laughed. "I'll do that."

"I'll go talk to Mick."

"I'VE CHANGED MY MIND. I'M NOT GOING IN, GAVIN. THIS has disaster written all over it. Why don't you just line me up in front of a firing squad instead?"

"Aren't you being just a little overly dramatic?"

"No, I'm being realistic. They all hate me."

Gavin rolled his eyes and got out of the car. They'd been sitting in the driveway for fifteen minutes. He was hungry. He came around to Elizabeth's side and opened the door. "Get out now. If you don't, I'll throw you over my shoulder and carry you inside."

She leveled him with a mutinous glare. "You wouldn't."

"Are you challenging me? Because you know I will."

"Damn you, Gavin Riley." She got out of the car and stood there. "I can't believe I agreed to this."

He took her hand and dragged her stiff body to the front door. "At least try to smile and pretend to be pleasant."

The front door opened, and his mother greeted them. "I thought you two would never get here." She folded Elizabeth in her arms. "Lizzie. It's been way too long."

Elizabeth's stiff stance melted when Gavin's mother hugged her. She put her arms around Gavin's mother like a life preserver on a sinking ship. "I've missed you, Kathleen."

Gavin never got over how cute the two redheads looked whenever they embraced. They could be mother and daughter, which is probably why his mom had always gravitated toward Liz. Of course Liz was so sweet whenever she was around his mother, something Gavin never could fathom. Her entire personality changed when she was with his family. She loved his father equally as well.

Of course now that he knew her history, he realized maybe she just liked having a warm family to come home to since she'd lacked one of her own.

His mother held on to Elizabeth's hand as they walked toward the house. "Shame on you for staying away so long. We missed you at the holidays."

"I didn't think I'd be welcome. I screwed up so badly with Mick."

"Bah. You made a mistake. Who among us hasn't? You made up for it. All is forgiven."

"I'm so sorry, Kathleen. My career gets the best of me sometimes . . ."

Gavin didn't hear what else Elizabeth said because when they walked into the house the noise level in there was deafening. People were spread out everywhere. And his mother had run off somewhere with Liz, so Gavin went to find Mick or his dad.

They were both in the kitchen, his father with a beer in his hand and Mick with a bottled water. Nathan was there, too, and they were laughing and talking sports, of course.

"Happy birthday, old man," Gavin said to Mick.

Mick greeted him with a guarded smile. "Hey, thanks."

They shook hands. Gavin was still irritated after their last meeting.

Their father noticed the lack of familial hugging.

"Hey, Nathan, great to see you again."

"Hi, Gavin." Nathan offered up a wide grin.

He seemed to have grown a foot since Gavin had seen him last, and had filled out some muscle, too.

"You look great. Doing some workouts?"

"Yeah. Football keeps me busy. And working with Dad . . . Mick . . . Dad has really helped a lot."

Gavin shifted his gaze to Mick, whose eyes filled with pride when Nathan called him Dad.

Son of a bitch. His big brother was a father to a teenager now. Things sure had changed a lot. "I'm sure it has. I'll bet you're happy your mom and Mick are getting married."

"I am. I couldn't ask for a better father. He's what I always wanted in a dad."

"And you're the son I always dreamed about having."

Gavin's dad cleared his throat, looking a little teary-eyed, too. "Okay, fellas, before we all break down and start sobbing and end up in a group hug, let's get back to talking about baseball."

"I'll leave you all to talk about me while I'm not here," Gavin said. "I need to go find Elizabeth. Mom ran off with her."

"So you actually brought her here."

Gavin stopped. "Yeah, I did."

"I can't believe you, man. You're still seeing her?"

Gavin's gaze skirted to Nathan, who cast a frown in their direction. "Let's not do this now."

"Why? This affects Nathan, too."

"Mick. You need to be polite to your brother," their father said.

"Oh, I need to be courteous to Gavin. What about how he treats me? Where's the respect?"

Right. Because it had always been about Mick. What was best for Mick. Be careful what you say to Mick. Don't upset Mick. Mick has a problem, so we need to be extra nice to Mick. Look up to Mick. Be like Mick. Stand in Mick's shadow.

Shit.

His whole life had been about Mick.

But not anymore.

He turned and walked out of the kitchen.

"Hey, we're not done."

"Michael!"

Gavin's father must have gotten Mick's attention, because Mick didn't follow his brother down the hall.

Fine with Gavin, because in his current mood there was no telling what would happen between the two of them. And birthday or not, he'd had just enough of his brother telling him how to live his life. He hadn't asked for advice on who to choose to date, and he sure as hell wasn't taking unsolicited advice from Mick.

Now he just had to go find Elizabeth before any more trouble stirred up.

Like her running into Tara.

ELIZABETH LOVED KATHLEEN. SHE WAS THE CLOSEST thing to a mother she had, and Kathleen had always made her feel welcome in the Riley home.

That of course changed when Elizabeth screwed up and Mick fired her.

Losing Kathleen and Jimmy Riley had been harder on her than losing Mick as a client.

She'd missed spending the holidays with the Rileys. Over the past few years it had become habit for her to spend Thanksgiving and Christmas at the Riley home.

Last year had been brutal. She'd spent the holidays alone.

She'd never felt more alone, had never realized how much she'd come to think of Mick and Gavin's family as her family until she didn't have them anymore.

Stupid. And what had she gone and done? Started sleeping with Gavin, which would only end up permanently severing her relationship with the Riley family when things ended with Gavin.

Kathleen had pulled her upstairs, away from the crowds, and took her into the master bedroom, sat her in one of the two old chairs nestled into the corner of the crowded room.

"Now that it's just the two of us, why don't you tell me what's going on?"

"You mean what went on with Mick?"

Kathleen waved her hand. "No. I think what happened there is clear. You made a critical business error, and you paid a very dear price for it. You lost Michael's business. I trust you're smart enough to have learned something from that."

"Yes, ma'am." Kathleen had the ability to say very little and mean a lot when she said it. Elizabeth felt about two inches tall at the moment. "I'm very sorry I hurt Mick, Tara, and Nathan."

Kathleen took her hand. "I know you are. But you had to suffer the consequences for what you did, didn't you?"

"Yes, I did. Mick wasn't only my client. He was my friend. And I lost his friendship, too."

"Well, I hope not forever. My son is a stubborn mule, but he'll come around soon."

"I hope so. I need to make amends with him. And with Tara."

Kathleen nodded. "That you do. But I mean what's going on with you and Gavin?"

She swallowed. "Oh. That."

Kathleen leveled very wise eyes on her. "Yes. That. I never realized you and Gavin had a thing for each other."

Oh, Lord. "Well, it just sort of happened. We're casually dating, really. It's nothing serious, Kathleen."

"Really."

"Yes."

"So you don't care about him."

She laid her head in her hands, then turned it to the side. "You'd make a great prosecutor, you know that? You really know how to put a girl on the spot."

Kathleen laughed and patted her hand. "Come on. You know I'm joking with you. It just took me by surprise is all. You're like a daughter to me. I was shocked to find out you and Gavin were together."

"It kind of hit me by surprise, too."

"Not me. I saw it the first night I met you. I knew you were in love with Gavin."

Elizabeth whirled around and saw Tara leaning in the doorway, Gavin's sister, Jenna, next to her.

"What?"

"Come in, you two. Did you know that Elizabeth and Gavin were dating?"

Tara took a seat on the edge of the bed. "I didn't until Gavin told me. But like I said, it doesn't surprise me. I saw the sparks that night in the bar when I first came to town and met all of you."

"Sparks? What sparks?"

Tara turned her gaze on Elizabeth. Elizabeth expected animosity, hatred even. But what she saw was just . . . interest. "I saw the way you looked at him. I could see right away that you were in love with him."

She remembered Tara mentioning it before, but she'd brushed her off, thought she'd minimized it. She thought she'd hid it so well. "In love—oh. No, really. I'm not."

Jenna snorted. "You're in love with Gavin?" She twirled some of the many earrings in her ear and flopped belly-first on the bed. "Now this is getting interesting."

"I'm not in love with Gavin."

Tara laughed. "Yes, you are. And I'll bet you have been for some time."

"Is this true, Elizabeth?" Kathleen asked. "Are you in love with Gavin?"

She looked from Kathleen to Jenna to Tara, and for the first time in her life she had no idea what to do. The room closed in on her, and she found it hard to breathe. This was why she didn't have female friends. With guys she could bullshit her way out of anything.

Women were tougher. They bore down on her with their steely gazes, and there was no way out. Dizziness made her breathing quicken, and she sucked in air faster and faster, which only made it hotter in there.

"I don't feel very good," she said, raising a shaky hand to her sweaty brow.

"Oh, shit, Mom, she looks kind of white," Jenna said. "I don't know, but it looks like she's going to pass out."

"Someone get her head down. I'll get a cold cloth." Tara's voice sounded like it was far away, as if she was talking from a tunnel. The room had started to turn, and Elizabeth's fingers felt numb. She tried to suck in air faster because she couldn't breathe.

"Jenna, close the door. Elizabeth, bend over and put your head between your knees."

"I can't breathe." She wrapped her arms around her stomach, feeling sick.

"Elizabeth. Pay attention."

She tried to lift her head, but all she could think about was breathing. All she could think about was gasping for air. And she might just fall out of the chair.

Cool hands pressed onto the back of her neck and shoved her forward. She felt something icy cold and wet on her neck.

"Breathe slow and easy honey. Not so fast. That's what's making you dizzy."

Kathleen's calm voice penetrated. Elizabeth did as requested, and it helped. The pins and needles feeling in her hands and feet started to subside, and eventually the numbness in her face started to go away.

"That's it. Focus on each breath. Not so fast. Keep it slow."

She did, keeping her eyes shut so the room would stop spinning.

"Now lift your head. Think you can do that without feeling dizzy?"

"I have no idea."

"Try. Just try. If you still feel dizzy, we'll lay you down on the bed."

She opened her eyes and looked down at her feet, then slowly lifted her head. Still a little dizzy, but not the roller-coaster ride she was on a few minutes ago.

Tara swiped her hair away from Elizabeth's face. "Better now?"

Elizabeth nodded. "Yes."

"Here," Kathleen said, holding a glass of water in front of her. "Take a couple of sips."

She took the glass, but Kathleen held it for her while she sipped the water. She tilted her head back and tried for a smile. "Thank you."

Elizabeth directed her gaze to Tara, then to Jenna, who kneeled in front of her. "Thank you both, too. I'm so embarrassed."

Tara grinned. "Nothing like a good old panic attack, is there?"

"Is that what it was? I've never had one before." She blew out a breath, then inhaled again, this time not doing it like she was running a breathing race. "Scared the hell out of me."

"So the topic of my son brings out panic in you?"

She looked over at Kathleen. "Oh. No, not at all. Yes. Maybe. I don't know. I wasn't prepared to answer questions about how I feel about him."

"Obviously," Jenna said with a smirk. "Who knew my brother incited such panic in women?"

Elizabeth managed a laugh. "No, really, it's not him. It's me."

"I'm sorry," Tara said. "I didn't mean to back you into a corner about Gavin."

Elizabeth leaned back in the chair. "You have nothing to be sorry about. I'm the one who should be apologizing to you. Until the day I die, probably."

"It's okay, really."

Elizabeth wasn't sure it would ever be okay with Tara. "I really am sorry, Tara. I was so wrong, so focused on my career and Mick's career that I was blinded. I hurt you and Nathan without thought. I would never use a child like that. I don't know what I was thinking, and there's no excuse for what I did."

Tara leaned forward and grabbed her hands. "Apology accepted. Let it go, Liz. I have. And Nathan holds no grudge."

She shuddered out a sigh. "Thank you. You're very generous and much nicer than I probably would be."

Tara laughed. "Well, don't go fainting on me every time you see me. That would be a start."

Elizabeth managed a smile. "It's a bit disconcerting that you knew how I felt all along."

"Well, you were kind of obvious. Your feelings for Gavin are written all over your face."

She put her palms over her cheeks, the flame of embarrassment heating her. "They are?"

Tara gave her a sympathetic smile. "Yes, they are."

"So, you're in love with Gavin. Wow. I didn't see it," Jenna said. "You two have known each other for years. So is this a recent thing or have you been carrying a torch for a while?"

"For a long time, is my guess," Tara said.

"Is she right?" Kathleen asked.

Elizabeth nodded.

"Does Gavin know?"

Elizabeth shook her head. "No. God, no. And I don't want him to know."

Kathleen frowned. "Why not?"

She looked down at her hands. "This is hard to explain."

"Because a guy has to fall in love with you because it's what he wants, not out of obligation."

Elizabeth lifted her head and nodded at Tara. "Yes."

"Which means, Mom, that we need to butt out and let Elizabeth and Gavin handle their relationship the way they see fit," Jenna said.

"All right. But I have to tell you, Lizzie, that I love you and I love my son. And I don't want either of you hurt."

Elizabeth reached for Kathleen's hand. "I love you, too. And I don't want to hurt him. I just don't know how this is going to play out. I don't know what we are to each other yet. So I'm asking you to give us some time to figure it all out."

She turned to Tara. "And give Mick some space, too. He's still mad at me, and he has a right to be. And he and Gavin are at odds over it. I'm strong and I can take it. I just don't want them fighting because of me."

Tara shrugged. "I've already decided to step away from that battle."

Kathleen nodded. "Probably a good choice. Sometimes brothers need to find their own solutions to their problems. And when a woman—or women—are involved, it's best to steer clear. They'll find a way through this. They always have before."

Elizabeth hoped that was true. She'd walk away from Gavin before she drove a wedge in his relationship with Mick.

She just hoped it wouldn't come to that.

SIXTEEN

GAVIN SEARCHED THE WHOLE DAMN HOUSE FOR ELIZA-
beth, wondering if maybe Mick had found her and stuffed her in the
trunk of a car.

Okay, he wouldn't do that. Or at least he didn't think his brother
would go that far.

As he made his third pass through the house, he saw Elizabeth coming down the stairs with his mother and Jenna—and Tara, of all people.

They were all smiling, chatting away, seemingly at ease with
each other.

That he hadn't expected.

"Hey, I've been looking everywhere for you," he said as she
reached the bottom of the steps. "What have you been doing?"

"It's a secret women's society. We're plotting the demise of the
male species," Jenna said.

"Smart-ass." He kissed the cheek Jenna presented to him, then
she walked away.

Tara came up to him and hugged him. "Girl talk. You don't have to monopolize all of Elizabeth's time, do you?"

He looked to Elizabeth, who seemed just fine. "I guess not."

"Then I suppose you can have her back. Your mother and Jenna and I have to go get Mick's cake ready. Did you and your dad grill the meat?"

"Yeah," he said, unable to take his eyes off Elizabeth, wanting to make sure she was all right. "It's on the counter in the kitchen."

Elizabeth looked at Gavin's mother. "Do you need help?"

"No," Kathleen said. "You catch up with Gavin. We have it under control."

They walked off, and Gavin led her out the front door so they could have some privacy.

"What's going on? Why were you upstairs with Jenna, Tara, and my mom?"

She shrugged. "Nothing. We were just talking."

"Did Tara grill you or give you a hard time?"

Her lips quirked. "No. We talked. It was good. It cleared the air. We're fine now." She laid her hand on his arm. "Really, it's okay."

"You sure?"

"Positive."

"Okay."

"So can we go inside and help out instead of skulking around avoiding everyone?"

He put his arm around her shoulder. "I guess so."

She slid her arm around his waist. "Really, Gavin. I can take care of myself. Even with Mick."

Who was at the front door with Tara when they opened it. Elizabeth gave him her biggest smile.

"Happy birthday, Mick."

Gavin could tell Tara had talked to him. "Thanks. Glad you could make it."

Elizabeth's lips curled. "No, you're not, but thanks for being civil about it. I'll try to stay out of your way." She let go of Gavin. "I'm going into the kitchen to help your mom."

"Me, too." Tara leaned up and kissed Mick. "Behave."

"When have I not behaved?"

Tara rolled her eyes, then switched her gaze at Gavin. "You, too."

Tara left and Gavin stood there with Mick. "Thanks for not jumping on Elizabeth."

Mick shrugged. "I don't have anything to say to her as long as she doesn't fuck with my family. She's already done enough of that."

There was a lot Gavin wanted to say in reply, but it was Mick's birthday, and his mother would probably smack him on the head if he punched the birthday boy. Which was probably why Mick figured he could get away with saying whatever he wanted.

The free pass would only last so long. Like today was the only day.

"I think we should see what Dad's up to," Gavin suggested, swallowing his anger.

"That's probably a good idea."

Dad was neutral territory. He was outside, surrounded by the smoke of the barbecue pit and a handful of Gavin and Mick's uncles. Gavin heard the tail end of a story about this year's Super Bowl game, about one of Mick's outstanding plays and how there was standing room only at the bar that Sunday.

Mick groaned. "Like Uncle Robert and Uncle Matt haven't heard that story a hundred times already."

"Heard? Hell, they were at the bar that night. We all were. Doesn't mean Dad isn't going to tell it over and over again."

There were a handful of neighbors surrounding Dad, and they'd all been at the bar that night, too. So had Gavin, who'd seen all the plays, heard all the cheers, and still had to listen to the replay.

Not that he was jealous. Winning the Super Bowl had been a damn big deal for his brother. He didn't begrudge him the glory at all. If the shoe had been on the other foot, Gavin would be reveling in the glory and milking it for as long as he could.

"Mick, my boy, come on over and tell the guys about the winning touchdown pass."

"Again," Gavin murmured.

Mick rolled his eyes. "They don't want to hear it."

"Probably not, but Dad wants you to tell them. Maybe if you're lucky, they'll take up a collection for you not to tell it."

Mick snorted and headed into the throng. Gavin stayed back and sipped his beer, listening to the story he'd heard many times before.

"Your season is looking good so far."

Gavin hadn't heard Tara's son, Nathan, come up behind him. The kid was always so quiet. Of course a fifteen-year-old amidst the boisterous Riley clan could get swallowed up like a small fish in a shark tank.

"Thanks, Nathan. How are you doing?"

"Pretty good."

Gavin knew there was something Nathan wanted to talk to him about.

"Is there something on your mind?"

Nathan glanced over to where Mick was mimicking the throw of a football.

"Yeah, kinda."

"Go ahead. We're family now. Tell me what you're thinking."

Nathan paused for a second, then said, "It's about your girl-friend."

"Elizabeth."

"Yeah."

"Are you mad at her?" Gavin asked.

"No. But Mick still is. And he thinks I should be, but I'm not."

Gavin swiveled on the steps to face Nathan. "No one should tell you how you should feel, Nathan. Not your mom or Mick or me. If you're pissed off about what Elizabeth did to manipulate the media that day, that's your right. If you're over it, that's your right, too. If Mick is still angry about it, that's his problem to deal with."

"I guess so."

"You don't have to feel whatever he feels about anything. He'll still care about you. It's kind of like when two people love each other, but they're on different sides in politics."

"You mean when one's a Democrat and one's a Republican."

"Exactly. They don't have to agree to still love each other, right? Even though they might not agree on some serious fundamental issues."

"We talked about that in my government class. That it's our right to stand up for what we believe in, even if we're in disagreement with the people closest to us."

"Exactly. Your grandparents oppose each other politically."

Nathan's brows popped up. "Really?"

"Yup. But they love each other like nobody's business. And I've never seen two people who can argue so fiercely, especially around election time. It'll make your ears burn. But pick on one, and the other will defend them to the death. It's kind of like that with how you feel about something. Just because you love Mick doesn't mean you have to agree with everything he believes."

Nathan stared at Mick, then nodded. "That makes sense. Thanks."

"You're welcome."

"I kind of like Elizabeth. She came up to me today, and we sat down, and she told me how she screwed up and how sorry she was. I think that takes some guts."

"Yeah, I guess it does."

Nathan tilted his head up at Gavin. "I think she's really trying, Gavin."

Gavin bumped his shoulder against Nathan's. "I think she is, too, Nathan. Maybe your dad will figure that out someday soon."

ELIZABETH WAS DRAINED. PHYSICALLY, MENTALLY, AND emotionally exhausted.

First the meltdown in front of Jenna, Kathleen, and Tara, and oh, God, could that have been a more horrifying moment? And then she'd sat down and had a heart-to-heart with a fifteen-year-old boy, who'd handled her apology with a maturity she hadn't expected.

And to top it off she'd had to spend the rest of the night doing her best to dodge Mick, which wasn't easy considering it had been his birthday party.

She wanted to strip down, crawl under the covers, and end this day.

Gavin had brought her home and had gone to take a shower. He had worked up a sweat with an impromptu game of football with his brother and his soon-to-be nephew, along with the various cousins.

While he did that, she opened a bottle of wine and poured herself a glass. She headed upstairs, stripped off her clothes, and fell face-first onto the bed.

She was almost asleep when she felt strong hands sliding down her back, followed by warm lips pressed against the nape of her neck.

"I'll give you an hour to stop that."

He didn't speak, just conducted a very sensual assault over her shoulders with his hands, massaging the tension away from her shoulder blades, the middle of her back, her lower back, and lingering at her butt—which made her giggle. He compressed the spots that needed it and used whisper-light touches on the places that weren't so tense. He followed his fingers with the barest touch of his lips as he mapped a trail from her back to her butt to her thighs to her calves, then lifted her feet and kneaded the arches.

She moaned as he massaged her feet, a weak spot since she spent all her time in heels.

"God, that feels good. Please don't stop."

He pressed his thumb on the arch of her foot, and he surprised her when his tongue wrapped around her toe. She gasped, the dual sensation of comfort and sensuality shooting right to her pussy. Wet, hot flames of arousal licked at her, made her lift her butt in the air and slide her hand between her legs to massage the ache in her clit.

"Stop," he said. "I'll get there in a minute."

She laughed. "I can't wait. I want to come."

"You don't have much patience, do you?" he asked, then slid her big toe in his mouth and sucked it.

Oh, damn. She lost all track of what she was about to do with her fingers, mesmerized by his talented tongue and mouth. And when he slid his tongue across the bottom of her foot, she jerked her foot away.

"That tickles."

"We can't have that." He licked his way over her ankle, up her calf, and lifted her leg, then laid it down on the bed, kissing the back of one knee, then the other, parting her legs to crawl between them. He pressed his lips to the backs of her thighs and where her butt cheeks met her legs, then massaged her buttocks.

She moaned again when he started rubbing her lower back, especially the one spot that . . .

"Ohhh . . ."

"Really."

"Yeah."

"It's because you insist on wearing those four-inch heels. Bad for your back."

"Yes, Doctor. Whatever you say, Doctor. Just keep rubbing there."

"You sure you want me to rub here? Or maybe here instead."

He let his fingers drift lower over her ass again, then between her legs to tease her pussy.

"Well, that's nice, too. Rub there instead."

He did, using three fingers to part her pussy lips and spread her juices over her clit. She followed his hand by lifting her butt and rubbing against him like a cat craving attention.

Hell, she might even be purring. She knew she made some kind of noises but had no idea what they were. She was lost in sensation, her mind focused only on his touch and the feel of his body as he moved over her and slipped his cock inside her, then reached under her to continue to sweep his fingers over her clit.

He swelled inside her, thickening, stretching her, taking her to the limit and back again. She fisted the sheets and buried her head in the covers, shutting out everything but his breathing as he whispered dark words in her ear. She turned her face to the side, catching only a glimpse of his tightened features as her lips met his in a fevered kiss when he thrust deeply inside her.

Pressed to the mattress, she was powerless, giving up total control to him as he whipped her into a fevered state. Tension turned her muscles to steel as she fought the explosion that hovered so close. She wanted to prolong this ecstasy, where every stroke of his cock was bliss and every whispered word he uttered was sweet heaven.

"Let go, Elizabeth. Let me feel you come."

She shook her head, holding on for just a few seconds longer as he wound her tighter into a ball of the sweetest pleasure imaginable.

But when he bit down on the nape of her neck, she was awash in heat that she couldn't survive, and she climaxed, crying out and meeting his lips as he ground against her, his balls slapping against her clit. He groaned and spilled inside her. He was glued to her, shuddering against her, and she wanted this to go on forever, just the two of them connected like this.

Gavin dropped down on top of her and rolled to the side, bringing her with him, stroking her breasts as she came down off the high.

She always gave so much to him in sex, so much of herself. She laid herself open and gave him everything, held nothing back. She had never been like that with other men.

She had never loved other men.

She wondered if he realized how much she gave him, or if he thought she was simply like every other woman he'd been with.

She'd never ask. She didn't want to know. There was only right now between them. She'd never tell him how she felt. He had too much power as it was.

And every day that passed he gathered more.

She sighed and snuggled against him. He stroked her hair in the darkness, and she allowed a single tear to slip down her cheeks.

Little by little she was losing herself in Gavin.

She was never going to win this game.

SEVENTEEN

IF THIS WERE A ROCK CONCERT INSTEAD OF A WEDNES-
day afternoon baseball game in Milwaukee, the girl with the huge
tits in the second row along the first-base line would be lifting up
her shirt and flashing her goods at Gavin.

Instead, she'd held up signs proclaiming her love for him, her
boobs bouncing up and down as she held the sign over her head.

He loved fans, especially the out-of-town ones since the visiting
team was typically booed.

But this woman was having a wet-panty party in her seat for
Gavin, and he was loving every minute of it, despite the ribbing he
was taking from his teammates in the dugout.

"Dude, you should definitely get her number."

"She's done everything but fling herself on top of the roof of the
dugout."

"I'll bet you a hundred bucks she'll be waiting for you outside
after the game."

No way was he taking that bet. He'd seen plenty of groupies before, and blondie up there was a class-A fan girl. He was flattered, but he knew better than to indulge the fantasies of the crazies. She probably kept a room filled with his photos and an ice pick under her pillow.

After the game he and a few of the guys headed downstairs to the hotel restaurant for dinner and drinks to console themselves after a tough loss. Sometimes it was easier to lose a game by six runs than to drop a close game. This one had been a nail-biter until the bitter end, and they'd had guys on first and third in the top of the ninth, but they couldn't bring them home.

"Bats were cold today," Dedrick said. "Or at least mine was."

"Wasn't just you," Gavin said, lifting his glass of beer and taking a couple long swallows. "I couldn't hit for shit."

Tommy took a drink and sat his mug on the table, grimacing. "Pitching didn't help much, either. Bailey couldn't hold those two runners in the third, I couldn't help him out in the fifth. I didn't last but two innings. My relief sucked. Must be a full moon or somethin'."

Gavin lifted his glass. "To a better game tomorrow."

They clinked glasses.

"Couldn't get any worse than today," Dedrick muttered.

"Well, yeah, it could," Gavin said. "But it won't. Tomorrow we kick their ass."

They drank beer, ate burgers, and moaned about the game some more. Dedrick and Tommy called it a night and went back to their rooms. Gavin hung out in the bar, too restless to pace the confines of his hotel room. There was a night game on, Atlanta and Tampa Bay, so he sat at the bar and watched the game, switching to soda after having one more beer.

A knockout brunette pulled up a barstool next to his since the bar was pretty full. She ordered a drink, pulled out her phone, and started punching buttons.

Gavin judged her to be in her mid-twenties, no doubt in town on business since she had her hair pulled up like Elizabeth styled hers and she wore a suit and some fancy shoes, same as Elizabeth.

She frowned at whatever nonsense was happening on her phone.

"Problem?"

She glanced up and offered a smile. She had nice brown eyes.

"Client canceled our meeting."

Gavin nodded. "Hate when that happens."

She laughed. "Me, too. You in town for business?"

"You could say that."

She held out her hand. "Judith Stafford. I'm a marketing rep for Lincoln Aluminum. And you are?"

He shook her hand. "Gavin Riley."

"Nice to meet you, Gavin. Who do you work for?"

"The Saint Louis Rivers baseball team."

Her brows rose. "Oh. You're a baseball player. No game tonight?"

"No. We played Milwaukee this afternoon."

She let out a soft laugh. "I'm so sorry. Not a big sports fan, obviously. I should probably be drooling or squealing or something, shouldn't I?"

He liked this woman. "Not required, really. Not everyone is a fan."

She half turned in her seat, enough to showcase a set of spectacular legs. "So did your team win or lose today?" she asked.

"We lost."

"I see. So you're in the bar drowning your sorrows."

"My teammates and I were earlier. Now I'm just having a soda and watching another game. I'm not big on spending the night in a cramped hotel room. I hate day games."

She nodded. "Worst part of travel is the hotel rooms. I usually go to the mall to kill time, or do the same thing you do—either hang out in the restaurant or the bar. It's a shame you already had dinner, or I'd invite you out and we could see the city."

"I don't get to see too much of any city when we play. It's usually just in and out, and again, a lot of hotel rooms."

"Sounds like my business, though I do get to eat in plenty of lo-cal restaurants. Schmoozing clients, you know."

"So you travel a lot?"

She nodded. "Around the country. I'm director of sales, so I'm on the road probably three-quarters of the year."

"Yikes. How does your husband feel about that?"

Her lips lifted. "That's why I don't have one, at least not yet. Maybe when I find a man willing to put up with the craziness that is my job, I'll cut the travel back some. And then again, maybe not."

"You need to marry a baseball player. They'd understand that travel schedule, plus you wouldn't be leaving a guy at home all the time. At least not until the off season."

She smiled, showing white, even teeth. "Is that a marriage pro-posal?"

He choked on his drink. "You move fast, Miss Stafford."

She picked up her own drink and took a sip, then crossed her legs. Gavin had been around enough women to know that was a sign of interest.

She was drop-dead gorgeous, she smelled good, and she was throwing off signals that a guy would have to be blind not to notice. She was smart and fun to talk to, and if he played his cards right, he could have Judith Stafford in his bed tonight.

The problem was, a certain feisty redhead kept entering his mind. She was the only one he wanted to take to bed, the only one he wanted to think about.

What the fuck was wrong with him anyway?

"And what about you, Gavin Riley? How does your wife feel about you traveling all the time?"

"No wife."

Her eyes positively sparkled now.

"But there is a woman I'm seeing. I've been seeing a lot of her the past couple of months, actually. She's on the road a lot, like you, so she understands the whole travel thing."

And just like that, the light went off in her eyes. She uncrossed her legs and slid them under the barstool. A sure sign that screamed hands off, even though her smile was still friendly.

Friendly and polite, but she was making it clear that their fun conversation was over.

"She's a lucky woman. And I think I'm going to head upstairs, get out of my professional clothes, and watch some television. Nice to meet you, Gavin."

"Nice to meet you, too, Judith."

After she left, Gavin finished his soda and paid his bar tab, then headed up to his room. He took out his cell phone and scrolled through the names, smiling when one came up.

He had a sudden urge to talk to Elizabeth.

THERE WAS NOTHING THAT FIRED UP ELIZABETH'S COM-petitive spirit more than a roomful of other sports agents.

The conference on networking, negotiations, and social media was right up her alley. Everyone in her industry was here, and this was her chance to get caught up, to fill two days and nights with nothing but what drove her.

She and her fellow sports agents didn't get together all that often other than maybe seeing each other at the drafts and banquets, and they were usually too busy with their clients to say more than a brief hello. Of course there were her peers from the agency she worked at, but they were still competitors. Her goal was to be the top of the upper echelon, even within her own company. And so far she was doing just that.

Plus it was a great learning experience. She was on top of social media, had a Twitter presence and her own Facebook page where she listed the goings-on of all her clients. She wanted prospective clients to know what she was doing and who was on her client roster. Young players today were all online, and if they wanted to find a sports agent, that's where they looked. She was no dummy. She knew how to play the game. It was all digital. College players weren't going to drag out the Yellow Pages to look for an agent.

But there were valuable workshops to attend on salary caps for rookies, improving your negotiation skills, waging the war on arbitration, and dealing with labor relations. There was so much more to being a sports agent than just signing and keeping great players. Often it was like maneuvering in a minefield, and a good agent stayed on her toes and made sure he or she kept abreast of all the current legal and contractual ramifications.

Of course her agency had great lawyers to sort out the legal aspects of a player's rights and contract. But Elizabeth wanted to be as knowledgeable as possible, so these annual meetings were essential.

"Soaking it all in, Elizabeth?"

She gritted her teeth, turned, and put on a professional smile for her arch nemesis, Don Davis. "Don. How nice to see you."

He flashed his oh-so-white-and-no-doubt-capped teeth, adjusted the cuffs of his perfectly tailored shirt under his impeccable dark and ostentatious suit that went with his very expensive tie. His slicked back black hair made her think of some mobster out to threaten her to pay up in three days or she'd be found in a dark alley missing a few fingers. Or maybe he resembled a high-class pimp. She couldn't decide. Even his tan looked expensive. And spray-on.

"I'm surprised you're here, Elizabeth, being as cutting-edge as you are. I would think you knew all there was to know about agenting. Of course you have suffered a couple of setbacks recently, haven't you? So maybe a refresher is in order."

Prick. How she'd love to dig one of her stilettos deep into his balls. "Oh, I've more than made up for anything I might have allegedly lost, Don. But thank you for your concern."

"Always need to stay on your toes. And look over your shoulder."

She offered up a smug smile. "So should you."

He gave her a condescending laugh. "I don't have anything to worry about. I keep my clients happy."

She patted his arm. "You keep thinking that, Don. Lovely talking to you, as always."

She brushed past him, not interested in playing the game of one-upmanship with him. He'd taken more than enough of her time already, as well as her clients. He could be as smug as he wanted to be, but payback was a bitch and Elizabeth had a long memory for those who had screwed her over. Granted, Mick had fired her, and he had a right to select another agent. But did he have to go with the one person Elizabeth hated the most?

Mick had done that on purpose.

"Elizabeth!"

She heard her name and turned, searched across the crowded hotel lobby and waved at Victoria Baldwin, one of the few other female sports agents she knew. She waved at Tori and they headed toward each other.

"Ugh. This place is a nightmare of testosterone," Tori said. "I'm barely surviving with my uterus intact."

Elizabeth laughed. "I know exactly what you mean. Do you have time for lunch?"

Tori pulled out her phone and punched a few buttons, checked her calendar, then lifted her gaze back to Elizabeth. "Yes. The next workshop I want to attend isn't until one. I'm starving and my feet are killing me." She looped her arm around Elizabeth's. "What I wouldn't give to do this conference in my sweatpants and bunny slippers."

Elizabeth arched a brow. "Somehow I can't see you trading in your Louboutins for pink bunny slippers."

Since the lunch crowd hadn't yet piled in, they were seated right away at a table. Tori fell into her chair and kicked off her shoes. "Oh, honey, you'd be surprised how schlumpy I am when I work at home. I was serious about the fluffy slippers. You, on the other hand, probably live in heels."

Elizabeth offered a sly smile. "I do love my heels. Probably because I'm always on the defense and have to prove that I'm a woman."

"Isn't that the truth?" Tori smoothed back tendrils of her mink brown hair and tucked them behind her ear.

The woman was absolutely gorgeous. In her early forties, she'd sacrificed a husband and family for her career. When she came on the scene as a green college graduate, Elizabeth had done her best to emulate Victoria Baldwin's drive for success. Even though Tori worked for a competing agency, she'd taken Elizabeth under her wing and shared many secrets about being a woman working in a predominantly male field.

Elizabeth adored her.

"God forbid we should dress comfortably around these sharks. We have to work three times as hard as they do to be taken half as seriously. It's a jungle and getting worse all the time. But in sports agenting and attracting the young up and comers, at least the boobs come in handy."

Elizabeth snorted. "And you certainly have those."

Tori accepted the glass of iced tea the waiter brought. They ordered their lunch, then Tori leaned forward. "Look, honey, I've got almost ten years on you, age wise, so I've got to use whatever is in my arsenal to secure the talent, you know?"

"Tori, you're also one of the most savvy agents I know. You paved the way for women to get into this business. You showed us how to bully our way in and force the men to accept us, showed us that sports was a field we could master and that it wasn't owned by the men."

Tori shrugged. "Thanks, Liz, but it's still a battle. A lot of the young guys still want to sign with a man."

Elizabeth narrowed her gaze. "Oh, come on, Tori. You must need a nap because that's the biggest line of bullshit there is, and you're the one who taught me that. Athletes want to sign with an agent who's going to get them the best deal. And we'll get them the best deal. Besides, we're prettier and we smell better. And then there are the boobs."

Tori laughed. "You're absolutely right. I'm just having a hellish day. I should be having a cocktail instead of an iced tea."

"I can fix that." Elizabeth signaled for the waiter, and they ordered martinis. "We'll drink to women agents kicking ass. I've had a particularly hellish few months myself."

"I heard that asshole Don Davis took some clients from you."

"Well, one was my own damn fault because I was blind and stupid. The other followed because of Mick's name, I'm pretty sure."

"Hmmm." Tori tapped a long, manicured nail on the table, accepted the cocktail the waiter provided, and took a sip. "Do tell. What did you do to screw up?"

"I got too greedy with Mick Riley, and I messed with his now-fiancée who was his girlfriend at the time. I didn't think she was good for him, and I tried to intercede."

"Oh. Bad move, princess. Never mess with a client and his woman."

Elizabeth raised her glass. "Amen to that. Lesson learned the hard way. I figured out I don't know everything. Imagine that."

Tori laughed. "Well, our egos do get the best of us sometimes, and we like to think we can walk on water, cure cancer, negotiate the best contract for our client, and do it in killer high heels."

"When will we learn we can't have it all?"

"Why can't we?"

Elizabeth shot Tori a direct look. "Do you? Do you really have everything you've ever wanted?"

"Of course. I have a career I love, tons of money, a great apartment in New York, incredible clothes, amazing friends, and I take ridiculous vacations. What more could I want?"

"So you don't feel like you sacrificed a husband and kids to get what you wanted?"

"No. I date fabulous men all the time, have great sex, and then I boot them out the door when I get bored with them. And I don't have a single maternal bone in my body. My younger sister has three beautiful children whom I adore and can visit in Connecticut whenever I feel the need to cuddle little ones. Believe me, that cures me of any feelings I might have ever had that I was missing something. And men have about a six month shelf life in my world."

Elizabeth laughed. "So you're perfectly content."

"Perfectly. But it sounds like you're not. Biological clock ticking?"

"I never thought so before. I was always happy with my life."

Tori took a swallow of her martini. "That must mean there's a man in it who's making you think of husband and babies."

"Oh, hell no."

Tori laughed. "Liar. It's written all over your face. My God, Elizabeth. You're in love."

"I am not. I'm in lust."

"Lust never makes you think of babies, Liz. Maybe you'd better reevaluate this relationship you're in."

"I'm not in a relationship."

"Again. Liar. Written all over that beautiful face of yours. Time to sit back and figure out what you really want out of life. Maybe a career as a sports agent isn't it."

"God, Tori. Sometimes I hate you."

Tori smiled at her over the rim of her glass. "No, you don't. You love me because I never lie to you like you lie to yourself."

Shit. She was going to have to work harder at keeping her facial expressions in check, or the next thing she knew Gavin would find out how she felt.

And that could never, ever happen.

ELIZABETH FELT BOTH PENSIVE AND REENERGIZED after her lunch with Tori.

How could she have ever thought that she didn't like women or that she put more value on her relationships with men than with women? She could have never had a conversation with a man like she'd had with Tori today. No man could understand the drive and ambition and sheer willpower it had taken to rise to the top like Tori did. Nor could any man ever understand the yearnings Elizabeth had. Yet with one look at her face, Tori got it. She may not have the same cravings Elizabeth had, but she identified.

There was nothing like a little female empowerment to spark the creative juices, as well as a cold slap of reality across her face to make her realize that maybe she couldn't have it all.

She loved her career, had loved it since the moment she'd stepped foot through the agency doors as a green newbie not knowing what the hell she was doing but knowing this was the only thing she'd ever wanted to do with her life.

She'd loved sports, had always loved them. She loved contract law and marketing, and the marriage of all three meant being a sports agent was a win on all counts. She couldn't see herself doing anything else for the rest of her life.

Until the night she'd slept with Gavin. And every night since, she'd felt a tug in her priorities. Her wants and needs were starting to shift, and she was beginning to think of other things besides her career.

And she wasn't certain if that was a good thing or a bad thing.

All she knew was she'd been at this conference for three days and she was missing Gavin. He was on the road, too, and had texted her and called her.

Like it or not, they were in a relationship, for whatever that was worth.

It was starting to feel like it was worth a lot.

And that scared the hell out of her because her world was tilting on its axis.

EIGHTEEN

GAVIN HAD A BOUQUET OF FLOWERS IN HIS HAND WHEN he went to Elizabeth's condo. It had been almost a week since he'd seen her, and he missed her so much he ached inside.

Now he stood at her door with flowers in his hand. How ridiculous was that? He wasn't a flowers kind of guy. A bottle of Jack Daniel's, maybe, especially if there was going to be some hard partying involved. But flowers? Not unless it was Mother's Day and he was going to see his mom.

He thought about going back to his car and tossing the flowers in the backseat. She'd laugh.

Fuck it. He rang the doorbell.

She answered a few seconds later, a bright smile on her face.

God, she looked good in a black sundress with tiny yellow print on the fabric. High heels of course. And her hair was down.

She glanced at the bouquet and her smile brightened. She lifted her gaze to his. "You brought me flowers."

"Yeah."

She grabbed his free hand and pulled him inside, shut the door, wrapped her hand around the nape of his neck, and put her lips on his, sending him into a quick buzz of arousal. All he'd done for the past week was think about her—her smell, her taste, the way her lips and her body moved against him. He thought about her smile, her laugh, the way they argued with each other, and how much she irritated him.

She tasted like mint and wine, and he sucked in a breath at the same time he was gut punched by how much he'd missed her. He swept his arm around her and pulled her close, his body and his mind swamped with sensation and emotion.

When she pulled back, she licked her lips and took the flowers from his hand, laid them on the table next to the door and wound both her arms around him.

"I probably shouldn't tell you this, but all I've done is think about you."

He liked hearing it. "Why shouldn't you tell me? I've thought about you, too. I think you probably have about fifty text messages from me."

She shuddered out a sigh. "I know. I saved them all. I feel like a teenager. How pathetic am I?"

"I should probably just dump my balls into your hand."

"I should hand over my feminist card because they're going to kick me out of the club."

He laughed, swept her into his arms, and carried her up the stairs to her bedroom. It was still early enough that sunlight streamed in through the gauzy curtains at her windows. He stood her in front of them and admired the halo of light around her hair.

God, he was poetic now. If he didn't fuck her soon, he might cry like a girl.

"I know you dressed all pretty for me, and you look great, but I'm going to strip your dress off and get you naked and messy."

She moved closer, wriggled against him. "Oooh. Can't wait."

He pulled the straps of the dress down her arms and reached behind to unzip it. It floated to the floor and she stepped out of it.

It was a good thing he was a young guy with a strong heart, because she wore a black and yellow bra with matching panties. Christ, even her shoes matched. She fell onto the bed and spread her legs, leaving those dangerous heels on.

Gavin stepped forward and skimmed his hands along her calves and thighs, lifting her legs to get a look at her shoes.

"You buy underwear to match your shoes now?"

She giggled. "Sometimes."

"You never fail to surprise me, woman."

"I hope not."

He swept his hands down her legs, so smooth and soft, then laid them back on the bed, spreading them apart so he could stand between them. She planted her heels in the side slat of the bed and lifted her hips to him.

He slid his thumb over the bright yellow and black silk of her panties, found her clit. She hissed as he brushed his thumb back and forth over the hard bud; she let out a soft cry when he tucked his fingers under the lace to touch her soft flesh. When he moistened his fingers with her juices and circled her clit, her hand shot around his wrist.

"There. Right there. Don't stop."

He rubbed the bud back and forth, and she arched against him, dancing against his finger.

"Gavin, I need to come. I've held off all week just waiting for you."

There was such power in a woman demanding to be pleasured. But he wanted to taste her, wanted to peel off her panties and bury his face between her legs. That's how he wanted her to come.

He pulled his fingers away and she whimpered, but when he drew her panties down her legs, her eyes blazed emerald fire.

She lifted up on her elbows and widened her legs for him, panting as he shouldered his way between them.

"Yes. Lick me. Make me come."

She reached for his head and slid her fingers in his hair, pulling him down to her pussy.

Oh, yeah. She really needed it. Her desperation made his dick pound, because that meant she'd waited for him, that she needed him. The ego boost made him want to slide his cock inside her, made his need to come almost as strong as hers.

But Elizabeth was going to come first.

He swiped his tongue along her soft flesh, inhaling the sweet aroma of her arousal, licking every secret fold as he made his way to the tight button that would rocket her into a climax. She tensed, lifted her butt off the mattress, and shoved her pussy against his face.

"Please," she murmured. Her back arched, and her knuckles were white with strain.

He swept his arms under her legs and lifted her pussy, then drove his tongue inside her, fucking her with long strokes, using every part of his face to rub against her. When he felt her shaking, when he knew she was close, he swept his tongue across her pussy lips and up to her clit, then covered it with his lips and sucked, sending her over the edge.

She came with a wild cry, bucking against his face and tearing at the sheets. He loved watching her come apart, her sweet flavor filling his mouth, and knowing he could give her this release. And when she finally settled, he crawled up her body, peppering it with light kisses, giving her time to catch her breath.

He leaned over her, and she took a big breath, sighed, then grinned up at him.

"That might have been worth waiting a week for."

He arched a brow. "We're not done."

* * *

GOOD GOD. WHAT A WELCOME-HOME PRESENT. ELIZA-
beth was certain she'd just had the best orgasm of her life.

Then again, every orgasm Gavin gave her always seemed like
the very best she'd ever had.

He was the best she'd ever had. No surprise there. Maybe being
in love with someone upped the climax factor. She'd always heard
sex was better with someone you loved. She'd just never believed it.

Now she did.

One orgasm down, and his hair brushed her belly. She slid her
hands in the lush softness of it. She loved his hair, could never tire
of running her fingers through it.

He bent over her and licked her breasts around the lacy cups of
her bra.

"Mmm, that's nice," she murmured.

And when he surged forward and took the strap of her bra between his teeth and dragged it over her shoulder, she felt herself
melting, desire screaming to life.

If that wasn't the sexiest damn thing, especially when he grabbed
the other bra strap and did the same thing, then reached underneath
her, popped the clasp like a champion, and pulled the bra from her
body—again with his teeth.

Yowza.

He moved to her neck and kissed her there, then dragged his
tongue across her throat, down her collarbone, and to her breasts.
He licked her nipples, sucked them, took her breasts in his hands
and used his fingers, his thumbs, his mouth on them until every
nerve ending in her body screamed to the heavens.

Dear God, she had goose bumps.

She felt . . . worshipped.

He left her only long enough to strip off his clothes, then came back to the bed and sat. He dragged her to a sitting position on his lap, his cock hard as he pulled her on top of him. She wound her legs around him, and his cock naturally fit right where her pussy was—how convenient was that?

"Slide on me. Fuck me," he said, his voice raspy and hoarse, as if he'd been holding back and just couldn't anymore.

She liked that, didn't want to be the only one on the brink.

She put her hands on his shoulders and slid onto his cock, watching it disappear inside her inch by inch.

It was always at this moment that she stilled. That moment when he was all the way inside her, thickening, pulsing, right before he started to move within her. Every nerve ending was completely in tune with his, and she could come right now. But she calmed her body, forced it to wait for the big moment, because it was going to be even better if she just had the patience to wait it out.

And then he began to move, and so did she. He moved backward and she slid forward, a seesaw of thrust and slide. His hand was on her ass and she held on to his shoulders as they fucked in tandem, a perfect rhythm. She watched where they were connected, leaning back far enough to see his cock slide in and out of her. A voyeur's view of fucking—of them fucking, which only ratcheted up the sensations.

And when she lifted her gaze to his, saw the lines of tension on his face, the focus and the hunger that matched hers, she dug her nails into his shoulders and rocked forward with a furious thrust, slamming her body onto his cock. His gaze narrowed, and he pushed back against her, driving into her deeply, giving back what she'd given him. She gasped, leaned back, and he powered into her again, harder this time.

She dug her heels into his buttocks, then reached down and rubbed her clit.

"Fuck," he said, watching as she got herself off.

She felt the tightening, the pulses that thundered through every nerve ending, and knew she was going to come.

"Yeah, baby, that's it, come on me."

"Oh, Gavin," she whimpered, then fell, her orgasm squeezing his cock with waves of pleasure that catapulted her into waves of ecstasy. He took her mouth as he drove deep inside her, and she savored the moment of her climax with his lips on hers and the depth of emotion that carried her to a place she'd never been before, to a wholeness she'd never felt with any other man.

After, he held her, the two of them still connected, still wrapped up in each other as if neither one of them wanted to let go.

He kissed her shoulder and her neck, nibbled on her ear, which made her laugh.

"I'm hungry," he finally said.

"How about pizza?"

He leaned back. "You're cooking me pizza?"

"Ha. Fat chance. I'm ordering pizza."

They dressed and went downstairs, ordered pizza and ate. Halfway through the meal Elizabeth remembered the flowers Gavin had brought her. She jumped up and grabbed them from the entryway and brought them into the kitchen where they were sitting.

"They're really lovely, Gavin. Thank you for these."

"You're welcome."

She dragged a crystal vase down from on top of the refrigerator and put the flowers in water, then set them on top of her kitchen table.

GAVIN LIKED WATCHING ELIZABETH AT HOME. HE'D been here a couple of times for client parties, but she'd been "on" then. Now she was relaxed, wasn't entertaining clients.

They finished the pizza and moved into the living room.

She had an enormous condo, and as they settled on the couch, Gavin remembered his surprise the first time he'd seen her big-screen television and several game consoles.

"Drink?" she asked.

"Whiskey is good."

She went over to the bar on one of the side walls and fixed him a drink, refilled her wine from the wine bar in there, then brought both over, sliding her game remote to the side.

"Playing Major League Baseball on your Xbox?"

She gave him a shrug. "PlayStation has a better game, actually. And I like to see what's out there and where my players are being showcased."

He grabbed a seat and picked up a controller. "Bullshit. You're a competitive bitch and you like to win."

She laughed. "You know way too much about me."

In no time at all they were deep in a game, nudging each other and calling out obscenities when one would get a hit or score a run.

Elizabeth was laughing so hard she struck out—twice.

"Dammit. You're deliberately sabotaging my game."

"Not my fault you suck at baseball."

She kicked him. "I do not suck at baseball. I'll have you know my team has gone to the World Series three times."

"Obviously, you cheat."

She lifted her chin. "I never cheat. I'm just that good."

He tossed the controller on the table and went after her. She shrieked and tried to get away, but he grabbed her and threw her facedown on the sofa, covering her body with his. "That good, huh?"

She let her controller drop to the ground. "Mmm hmmm. That good."

"Show me how good you are."

"Tell me what you want."

His body covering hers, all hard muscle yet not overpowering, caused her nipples to pucker, especially when she felt his cock begin to harden against her butt.

She was that easy to arouse. Her pussy dampened at the thought of Gavin taking her like this on her sofa. Right now.

"Anything?"

Oh, God. Yes. "Anything."

He jerked her dress up. She hadn't bothered to put her panties back on.

"What if I want to fuck your ass, Elizabeth?"

Her clit quivered. She rubbed it against the couch.

"Does that excite you?"

"Yes."

"Have you ever been fucked in the ass before?"

"No."

He reached between them and spread her ass cheeks, his finger dancing between them. Just that light touch excited her.

She'd give him anything.

"Do you want me to fuck your ass?"

She could hardly breathe. Excitement drilled her, aroused her, made her want to rub her clit right now and come. "Yes. Fuck it."

"Where's your lube?"

"Upstairs. Left-side drawer."

"I'll be right back. Get on your knees on the floor."

While he was gone, she slid onto the floor and spread her legs, waiting, her heart pounding in anticipation. She slid her hand between her legs and started rubbing her clit, unable to resist slipping two fingers inside her pussy to fuck herself.

God, she was so turned on just thinking of Gavin pumping his cock in her ass she could come in a minute or two.

Gavin came down the stairs and stood there, watching her.

"God, you're beautiful. Are you fucking yourself?"

"Yes. I couldn't wait."

"Don't come yet. Not until I'm in your ass."

"Hurry."

He moved behind her and dropped his pants. She kept up the rhythm of her fingers on her clit, the tension and excitement mounting.

Gavin spread her ass cheeks and applied lube over her anus, then rubbed his fingers back and forth over her hole, teasing her, sliding a finger partially inside her. The pressure was intense, exciting, and nothing like what she expected. She wanted him to fuck her.

"Gavin. That feels so good."

"I'm going to make you come hard tonight with my cock in your ass."

She shuddered and bent all the way over. "Shove your finger inside me. All the way. Let me feel it."

He slid his finger in, and she convulsed, pulled her own fingers out of her pussy. It would have been so easy to come right then. The sensation of having his finger in her ass and her fingers in her pussy was tremendous.

Double fucked. She wanted to be double fucked. Her fingers and his cock.

She was going to come so hard.

"Do it. Fuck me. Now."

He poured more lube on her ass, then she heard the tearing of a condom wrapper. Gavin leaned over her back to whisper in her ear.

"I'll go slow and easy. If it hurts too much, tell me and I'll stop. You control this, okay?"

"Yes."

She felt his cock head at the entrance to her anus. He probed, pushed past the muscled entrance. It burned, but oh, it was a sweet burn as she continued to lightly rub her fingers over her clit. She took some of the lube that had dripped down her pussy and swiped it over the tortured nub, taking herself right to the edge again. And as he pushed his cock inside her, she shoved her fingers in her pussy again.

She felt him pulse as he stilled, letting her get used to his thickness. But she wanted to feel him move inside her.

"Gavin, fuck me."

"Your ass is so tight, Elizabeth. It's squeezing my cock. Do you know how good it's going to be when we both come?"

She strummed her clit faster, fucked her pussy with three fingers. She was moaning, sweating, out of her mind with a primal hunger that left her senseless. She'd never felt so full before. His cock was thick and hot in her ass as he eased in and out, thrusting against her with a gentle rhythm.

But as her orgasm tunneled ever closer, she didn't want slow and easy.

"Harder. Fuck me hard, Gavin. Make it hurt."

"You sure that's what you want?"

"Yes! Now fuck me and come in me."

He reared back and slammed his cock into her ass. She screamed and thrust her fingers deep into her pussy and drove the heel of her hand against her clit. As he glued his hips against her buttocks, she felt her oncoming climax and bucked back against him.

"I'm coming, Gavin."

"And I'm going to come in your ass right . . . now."

He powered his cock inside her and then burst, yelling out with his orgasm. She tilted her head back and cried out as she climaxed, convulsing on his cock as they both came apart at the same time, both of them shuddering against each other.

It was wild, out of control, nearly unbearable in its intimacy as he took her to a place she'd never been, the sensations jackknifing through her like fire searing every nerve ending. She couldn't think, couldn't even breathe as she collapsed in utter exhaustion.

It had been an amazing experience being this close to him, giving him something she'd never given another man. And he'd been right there with her the entire time—holding her, kissing her, his hands all over her body.

And now that it was over, Gavin leaned over and kissed her back, withdrew, then lifted her up as if she were a weightless feather. He carried her upstairs and deposited her in the bathroom and turned the shower on. He was so tender with her, washing every inch of her body, then helping to dry her off. She put on a T-shirt and panties, and they climbed into bed and watched a movie together. When she woke, it was one in the morning, and Gavin was sprawled on his stomach, one foot hanging off the bed.

She wanted him in her bed every night.

Every night forever.

Why couldn't she just tell him that? Why couldn't she tell him she loved him?

She knew why. Because things were light and fun between them right now. Oh, sure, he told her he missed her, and he did spend all his time with her. And as far as she knew, he wasn't seeing anyone else.

But love? That was a whole different animal.

And permanence? She just didn't see it between her and Gavin.

She snuggled up against him, and he rolled over onto his side and pulled her against him, wrapping his arm around her.

They belonged together. She knew it.

But did he?

She was too afraid to ask him.

Sometimes it was best to not say anything at all.

NINETEEN

THE SHRILL RING OF HIS PHONE MADE GAVIN WISH HE had turned it on vibrate. He rolled over and shoved his head under the pillow. Still, the sound wouldn't go away.

Goddamn it. What the fuck time was it anyway?

"Gavin, your phone is ringing."

He heard Elizabeth's muffled voice next to him.

"I'm ignoring it. They'll go away."

"It's rung three times already. Might be important."

"It's probably some drunk dialing the wrong fucking number." He was tired, he was snuggled up against his warm woman, and he didn't want to be bothered.

"Or it could be important."

He sighed, threw the pillow off his head, and fumbled around in the dark, trying to gather his bearings and find the damn phone, finally locating it on the nightstand.

Elizabeth's nightstand. Oh, yeah. He was at her condo.

He blinked his eyes and tried to open them enough to read the missed-call register.

He shook off the dregs of sleep when he read the name.

"Fuck. It's Jenna."

Elizabeth turned on the light while Gavin dialed. She slipped beside him and rubbed his back.

She looked as concerned as he felt.

His stomach clenched. Something was wrong.

"Hey." Jenna answered on the first ring.

"What's wrong?"

"It's Dad. They think he had a heart attack."

Gavin swung his legs over the side of the bed, his heart sinking to his stomach. A hundred kinds of dread filled his head. "How bad is it?"

Elizabeth was right behind him, her body a lifeline. He was drowning.

"Don't know yet. He's at Barnes Hospital."

Swallowing panic, he said, "I'll be right there."

"Okay."

Her voice sounded shaky. "Did you get hold of Mick?"

"He's on the way, too."

"How's Mom?"

"A mess, but trying to pretend she isn't."

"Are *you* okay?"

"I'm fine, Gavin. Just get here."

"I'll be there in twenty minutes."

He clicked off the phone. Elizabeth was already off the bed, grabbing Gavin's clothes.

He lifted his gaze to her. "They think my dad had a heart attack."

Her eyes filled with tears. She came to him and sat on the bed, wrapped her arms around him. "Oh, God, Gavin. I'm so sorry."

He took a few seconds to absorb her warmth, her comfort. Then he pulled back.

"How bad is it?"

"They don't know yet. Everyone's been notified. I'm going to meet them there."

He got up and pulled on his clothes. Elizabeth sat on the edge of the bed, staring down at her clasped hands. "If there's anything you need me to do, anyone you need me to call, just let me know."

"Lizzie."

She lifted her gaze to his. "Yes?"

"I need you. Come with me?"

Silvery tears drifted down her face. "Yes. Of course." She leaped up and went to get dressed.

GAVIN HATED HOSPITALS, HAD SEEN HIS SHARE OF them—at least the emergency room part of them—for injuries over the years. To Gavin they signaled the possible end of his career.

Right now a hospital meant something entirely different. He didn't want to think about what might be going on with his dad. His father was a rock, the lifeblood of the Riley family. James Riley had always been invincible and indestructible. He was the strongest man Gavin had ever known. Nothing could topple him.

He was only sixty-five. Too young for a heart attack, right? Sure, his dad had put on a little weight over the years, and his mom's cooking wasn't exactly on the low-fat side of things. And maybe exercise wasn't his father's favorite thing. He liked to put his feet up and watch sports when he was home. Though he hustled plenty at the bar. And he played basketball with them when they came to visit. And he was always outside doing things.

Okay, maybe Jenna did a lot of the hustling these days behind the bar. Dad was slowing down more and more, hanging out with the customers, chatting them up, doing a lot of the PR work. They'd hired cooks and waitresses so Mom and Dad didn't have to do so much of the labor intensive work anymore. And Mom still taught dance classes part-time, so she was always running around and staying busy. When she was at the bar, she supervised a lot of the staff and kept her fingers in the cooking. Dad . . .

Shit.

Elizabeth grasped his hand as they got out of the car and headed through the ER doors at the hospital. He shifted his gaze to hers, and her smile strengthened him. Walking in with her beside him helped. He didn't want to do this alone.

"He's going to be all right. You have to believe that. If you go in there with the look of doom you have on your face now, it isn't going to help."

He nodded. "You're right."

He lifted his chin and forced the fear away.

The doors slid open, and the disinfectant smell hit him first. Then the crowd of people with their expressions of worry, exhaustion, and utter despair made him wish he could turn around, go home, and pretend this wasn't happening.

Elizabeth tugged his hand and went to the information counter.

"We're here for James Riley," she said.

The woman typed something on her computer. "He's in Room 14A. Cell phones must be turned off. Go through the doors to your left. Press the button on your right and give the patient's name. They'll buzz you through, and you can ask for directions to his room at the desk there."

"Thank you," she said and pulled Gavin along. They got through the security door and to another desk.

What would he have done if Elizabeth hadn't been there leading him through this crazy maze of doors and hallways that zigzagged this way and that? They finally found the room. Mick and Tara,

Jenna and his mom were standing outside. Elizabeth let go of his hand as he stepped up to his family.

"Doctor's in with him right now," his mother said as he pulled her into a tight hug.

He nodded. "Any more news?"

Mick shook his head. "We're waiting to hear from the doctor."

Mick glanced over Gavin's shoulder at Elizabeth, frowned, and wrapped his arm around Tara.

"What's she doing here?"

Gavin's mother shot Mick a look. "Not now, Michael. Focus on your father."

Gavin reached for Elizabeth's hand and twined his fingers with hers.

"I can go sit in the waiting room."

Gavin pinned her with his gaze. "I need you here with me."

She nodded. "I'm here for you as long as you want me."

The doctor finally came out. "We're going to run some tests. It'll be a while before I can tell you anything for sure."

"Was it a heart attack?" Gavin's mother asked.

Gavin and Mick put their arms around their mother.

The doctor nodded. "Yes. We're going to examine the extent of the damage next. Once we run more tests, we'll know. Why don't you all go to the waiting lounge, and I'll have someone come and get you after we're finished."

"Can I see my dad before you take him for the tests? I just got here."

"That's fine. Only for a few seconds."

Gavin pushed through the sliding glass door, his heart dropping as he saw his dad, pale and hooked up to a bunch of beeping machines. His eyes were closed.

Gavin had never once in his life seen his father look so frail. He fought back tears and put on a smile as he walked in and took his father's hand.

"Hey, Dad."

His father's eyes blinked open. "Hey, kiddo. Guess maybe I took on one too many home-improvement projects."

Gavin slumped in relief. His father's trademark sense of humor was still intact. "I blame the lawn mower."

His dad laughed. "Damn thing. I'll beat it yet."

"That's the spirit. You're going to be fine."

"Yeah, I am. Don't you forget it. I'm not leaving you yet."

"Didn't think you were." If he fell apart in front of his father, it would be the worst thing that could happen.

"Stay strong for your mother. She needs you and your brother most of all."

Gavin lifted his chin and nodded. "You got it, Dad. Don't worry about anything."

A nurse came in. "We need to prep your father now."

He squeezed his dad's fingers. "Buck up. We'll see you soon."

His dad squeezed back. "I will."

Gavin stepped into the hall and waited. When they wheeled his dad out, his mom gave him a kiss, then they all watched as he was taken down the hall. When his mother broke and fell against Mick's chest, Tara and Jenna comforted her.

Gavin felt . . . lost.

They moved to a waiting area one of the staff directed them to, a room with a television and magazines. They sat in silence, all of them no doubt absorbed in their own thoughts. That lasted for about fifteen minutes before Gavin stood and started pacing the room.

"Mind not doing that in front of the television?" Mick asked.

"Since the TV is in the middle of the room, that's kind of hard unless I leave the room."

Mick gave him a pointed look.

"Tough shit," Gavin said. "Deal with it."

Mick stood.

So did their mother. "Boys, please. I have enough to deal with."

Tara stood and pulled Mick back into a chair, whispered to him. He looked pissed. Gavin didn't give a shit.

Elizabeth stood and linked her fingers with Gavin. "I'd love a cup of coffee. Go with me?"

He knew she was trying to defuse the brewing fight between Mick and him, which was probably a wise move. He didn't feel like putting up with his brother right now.

Instead, he turned to Elizabeth and nodded. "We'll be right back."

No one acknowledged his comment, so he walked out the door with Elizabeth. She led him through the maze until they found a vending machine where they bought two coffees. They found a waiting area that was deserted, so they sat and sipped their coffee in the quiet.

"This is terrible coffee," she said.

"Yeah," he replied, though he hadn't even noticed the taste of the coffee. It was a caffeine jolt, so that was good enough. Not that he even needed the caffeine. He was wide awake and would stay that way as long as it took to . . .

To what? To cure his father? How long did it take to cure a heart attack? Was there even a "cure," or did you just change your lifestyle and move on from there?

Shit. So much he didn't know. He leaned over and laid his forearms on his knees.

Elizabeth rubbed his back.

"That feels good."

"You're doing a lot of thinking."

"How can you tell? Are my brains leaking out my ears?"

She let out a soft laugh. "No. But you go really quiet when you do a lot of thinking. Want to talk about it?"

He sat up and faced her. "I don't know anything about heart attacks. What's going to happen now? Does he modify his diet and do more exercise, and then he'll be fine? Or does he have to have surgery?"

"I imagine that depends on the severity of the blockage. If it's not too bad, a change in diet and exercise might help him."

"And if it's more than that?"

"Then they'll need to do more."

"Like?"

"Angioplasty. Maybe a bypass surgery."

He leaned back in the chair, took a long swallow of the toxic-tasting coffee, and studied her. "Since when did you become an expert on all things cardiac related?"

Her lips lifted. "Don't tell anyone, but I'm a reality-medical-show junkie. I know just enough to be dangerous. Medical diagnoses intrigue me, so I watch every medical show I can when I have a spare minute."

"Get the fuck outta town."

"No, I'm serious."

He stared at her, wondering what else he didn't know about her. "There are facets to you that continue to surprise me."

She took a sip of coffee. "Good. I hate being predictable."

"You are anything but predictable, Lizzie."

He leaned over and brushed his lips against hers. "Thank you for being here with me tonight. I couldn't have made it without you."

"No place I'd rather be, for as long as you need me."

Her words made him lean back, look at her. Really look at her. There was something in her eyes . . .

"Gavin."

Gavin lifted his gaze to Jenna. He stood and so did Elizabeth.

"Doctor's back. He said for us to meet him in one of their family discussion rooms, and he's going to talk to us in about ten minutes."

They followed Jenna to the room and sat. And waited. Ten minutes turned into thirty. Gavin's skin crawled, and he was ready to climb the walls. He squeezed Elizabeth's hand on one side and his mother's on the other.

Finally, the doctor came in.

"I'm Dr. Miles Spinelli, one of the cardiac surgeons here. Mrs. Riley, your husband has a blockage in three arteries."

His mother squeezed Gavin's hand. Hard.

"What does that mean?" she asked.

"It means he's going to need triple-bypass surgery."

"Oh, God."

Tears fell down her face. Gavin wrapped his arm around his mother, and Mick held her, too. Mick held Jenna's hand, and they all sat and listened while the doctor described the bypass surgery and what it would entail for their dad. The doctors were going to strip veins from his leg and use those to bypass the clogged arteries in his heart. It was a complicated and dangerous surgery, but the doctor indicated it was done frequently with a high success rate. He would have to spend about five days in the hospital after surgery, and after that would be sent home with strict dietary and exercise instructions. The recovery would be slow and would require some lifestyle changes.

"The important thing is, he's alive. He survived the heart attack. Many don't. Now we'll get him moved up to a room in the cardiac care unit, monitor him over the next twenty-four hours, and get him ready for surgery on Monday."

Everyone stood as the doctor left.

"Well. He dodged a bullet," Mick said.

Gavin's mother looked pale, her tear-streaked face more than

Gavin could handle. If his father had always been a rock, his mother had been Mount Everest. She held the family together, and if she fell apart, the rest of them would, too.

Right now she looked as fragile as a cracked egg.

Jenna took both of Mom's hands in hers.

"He's alive, Mom," Jenna said. "Remember that. He's still with us. He's going to make it through this just fine."

"That's true," Gavin said. "Dad's one of the toughest guys I've ever known. He's going to fight."

She nodded, glanced at each of them. "I'm so glad I have all of you." Then she shifted her gaze to Tara and Elizabeth. "And the two of you, too. I don't know what I'd do without you all in my life. You give me such strength. I'm going to need all of you to get through this—to get Jimmy through this."

"We'll all be here for you, Mom," Gavin said. "Whatever you need."

She swept her palm across his cheek, then kissed him and hugged him.

"I'm going to go see your father now before they get his room ready."

Gavin exhaled, dragged his fingers through his hair. He didn't even know what time it was, what time they'd gone to sleep last night, or what time Jenna had called. It felt like there was a boulder tied around his neck, dragging him down.

"Someone needs to convince Mom to go home and get some sleep."

"I'll take her," Jenna said. "She'll probably want to stay up here with Dad tonight, so she'll need a shower and a change of clothes. I'll make her something to eat."

Mick nodded. "We can do shifts up here with her so she's not alone."

"I don't know that they'll allow more than one family member at a time in there," Elizabeth said. "ICU usually only permits one or two. CCU might be different. You might want to check."

Mick narrowed his gaze at her. "And now you're an expert on hospitals? You just know everything, don't you?"

Tara laid her hand on his arm. "Mick . . ."

He shrugged it away. "What's she doing here anyway, Gavin? Just because you're fucking her doesn't mean she's family."

Tired, wired on bad coffee, and worried about his dad, Gavin didn't need this right now. But he understood Mick probably felt the same tension. "Whatever beef you have with Elizabeth doesn't belong in the halls of a hospital. Dad wouldn't want this, and Mom sure as hell doesn't need it. Let it go."

"It's okay. I can go. I don't want to be the cause of family tension when you all need to be rallying around your mother."

Gavin swiveled and grasped her arm as she turned to leave. "You're here because I asked you to come with me. You have as much right to be here as anyone else."

"Gavin, really, it's all right. Your brother doesn't want me here. I'll go."

"Nonsense, Elizabeth. I want you here. You'll stay."

Gavin turned at his mother's words. She stood outside the door to his father's room, looking small and lost, but her eyes burned fire as she looked at Mick.

"Michael, this is the last time I want to hear you say an unwelcoming word to Elizabeth. Is that understood?"

Mick gave a curt nod.

"I need all of you here. I need all the support I can get right now, and that includes Elizabeth, who I consider family. It's times like this that forgiveness is more important than anything. Come here, Elizabeth."

Elizabeth walked slowly over to Gavin's mother, who wrapped her arm around her.

"You've been family a long time. Remember the talk we had. You're always welcome around us. Gavin will need you now more than ever."

She lifted her gaze to his mother. "I'll do whatever I can to help all of you."

She kissed the top of Elizabeth's head. "Thank you."

"Mom, let me take you home so you can take a shower and get some clean clothes," Jenna said. "I figure you'll want to stay with Dad."

She nodded. "I'll wait until he gets settled in a room. The nurse said that might take several hours, and I don't want to leave him alone in there. You can run me home after he gets moved. The rest of you, go home and get some rest and something to eat. When Jenna and I are ready to leave, I'll call and one of you can come up here and sit with your dad."

It was hard to leave his dad—and his mom—but Elizabeth pulled him away, and they headed back to her place so he could pick up his SUV. She grabbed a change of clothes and followed him to his house.

He let her inside, wanting nothing more than to just crash and sleep for like twelve hours. Or maybe twenty-four.

"I'm going to fix you something to eat."

He raked his fingers through his hair, not even able to think. "I'm just going to sleep."

"You need to eat something first because if your mom calls you won't eat then."

He sat at the table, too tired to argue with her. She had scrambled eggs, bacon, and toast on a plate in a hurry. He downed the glass of orange juice and dove into the food, not realizing how hungry he was until he'd cleaned his plate.

"I was starving."

She scooped the last of her eggs onto her fork. "Obviously. Would you like more?"

"No, this was enough. Thanks for cooking for me."

"You're welcome. Not quite the gourmet cook you are, but I can manage the basics."

He leaned over and kissed her. "You cook just fine. Now let me help you with the dishes."

She laughed. "I can handle those. I'm sure you want to take a shower, maybe change clothes."

He pulled her against him. "What I really need is to sleep. At least a couple of hours."

She took his hand and led him upstairs to his bedroom. He felt like he was on autopilot, like none of this had really happened.

He sat on the edge of his bed and kicked off his shoes, stared down at his feet.

Elizabeth sat next to him, silent but there.

"He's not old enough for this, Lizzie."

She rubbed his back. "I know."

"He's so strong, always out there playing ball with us or tinkering around with something or working at the bar. I thought he'd live forever."

"He's still here, Gavin. He's going to be fine."

He stood and moved to the window. It was daylight now. Hell, he didn't know what time it was. He barely even registered what day it was. Sunday? He had a game today.

"I need to call Coach, let him know what's going on. I have a game this afternoon."

"Already taken care of."

He turned to her.

"I called him when you were in with your dad. They have you covered. Coach said not to worry about a thing."

He nodded. "Thanks."

"It's okay to fall apart, Gavin."

He blinked, looked at her. "What?"

"You don't have to be the big, strong man. Not in front of me. I've known you too long for that."

"I don't know what you're talking about."

She came up behind him. "You're crushed about this. You're father could have died."

The ache was a constant, but he was glad she was there to help him through it. He wrapped his arm around her.

"There's nothing scarier than the possibility of losing someone you love."

Where was she going with this? He frowned, looked down at her. Tears shimmered in her eyes.

She had no family, none that counted anyway.

Except his.

He pulled her around to face him. "It's okay to love them like they're yours, Lizzie."

Her bottom lip trembled.

His tough Elizabeth, never one to show weakness to anyone. She had to be everyone's rock. Who was hers?

"Baby, I'm okay," he said.

"You sure?"

"Yes."

He drew her against him, and she let out a hiccup of a sob, and he realized she was the one who needed to fall apart.

"It's okay. Let it go."

She shuddered, then gasped, clutching the back of his shirt as she wrapped her arms around him and released into a full cry.

Oh, damn. It was gut-wrenching hearing her sob out her heartache over his dad. Tears pricked his eyes as he held on to her while she wept. He stroked her hair, kissed her head, held tight to her, and let her cry it out. And with every tear she shed, he realized that the shell she kept around herself all these years was nothing but a façade to protect herself.

This was the real Elizabeth.

She had a heart. She had feelings. She cared.

She cared about his family, about him. She cared about his father, his mother. She even cared about Mick, and she'd made a mistake, a mistake she'd paid heavily for.

And she'd had no one to lean on when she fell.

She sniffed, pulled back, and tilted her head to look at him. Despite the tear-streaked face, she'd put the shell back on, because she was smiling again.

"I think I'm supposed to be taking care of you."

He swept his thumb across her cheek, wiping away the remnant of a tear. "You did."

"I'm sorry, Gavin. I didn't mean to fall apart like that." She tried to pull back, but he wouldn't let her, held her there in his arms.

"You're entitled to care about my father."

"Of course I care about your father."

She was trying to brush it off as something less than what it was to her. He wasn't going to let it go that easy. "Sometimes the world falls apart. Sometimes your world falls apart. And it's okay for you to let people in and let them see you crumble."

She lifted her chin, her barriers back in place. "You didn't crumble."

"Didn't I? You've been leading me around for hours now. I wouldn't have been able to find my way to the hospital, let alone my dad's room, without you guiding me. I was in a haze, Lizzie. I couldn't have done it without you helping me."

She blinked, droplets clinging to the spikes of her lashes. Her eyes were wide pools of sea green, mesmerizing him. Her lips parted, and he suddenly wanted to offer her comfort and maybe take some for himself.

He brushed his lips against hers. Without question she kissed him back, her soft hands at his back switching to her nails digging in as the quiet kiss turned more demanding.

Passion flared, and need arose. Hunger flashed between them, and Gavin pushed her onto the bed. Elizabeth pulled off her top, kicked off her sandals, and scooted back on the bed, already drawing her Capris down her hips while he tore his shirt over his head and reached for the button and zipper of his jeans.

She had her bra and panties off by the time he was naked. He climbed onto the bed and grabbed her, needing the feel of her skin against his. It had only been hours since they'd made love, but his need for Elizabeth was like a hunger that hadn't even come close to being satisfied. Only she could give him what he needed. He needed to get lost inside her, to shut out what had happened at least for a little while, to feel nothing but pleasure, nothing but her heart beating against his, his cock swelling inside her, her heat surrounding him.

She held out her arms, and he came to her, already hard. He slid inside her and put his mouth on her mouth, driving away everything but her touch, her taste, her skin against his. Her moans and the way she lifted against him were all he needed right now.

She wrapped her legs around him, and he drove against her, lifting up on his hands to look down at her as her gaze met his. Her lips parted, her lids partially closed as he shifted and ground against her, making sure to rock his body against her clit. He wanted to take her there, to make her come so she'd shatter around him.

She scored her nails down his arms, the sensation rocketing to his balls. He shifted and drove deeper inside her, reaching for one of her legs so he could push her knee against her chest, needing to be deeper inside her.

"Kiss me," she whispered.

He dropped down on top of her, slipped one hand underneath

her, and pressed his lips to hers. His balls tightened as he felt the rushing train of his climax approaching. Her tongue wound with his, and all he could think of was being alive. The only thing that mattered at this moment was being here with Elizabeth, being one with her, losing himself within her, inside her as she moaned against his lips. Her pussy convulsed around him, and then she was coming and so was he. He tightened his hold on her and let go, groaning as he came with hard thrusts, burying his face in her neck and knowing there was no one he could let go with like this but Elizabeth.

After, he kissed her neck and her earlobe, and tunneled his fingers in her hair before lifting up to look at her.

"Thank you."

She smoothed her fingers over his brow. "You're welcome."

Instead of jumping out of bed to grab a shower and change of clothes, he pulled her against him, stroked her hair, and kissed the back of her neck.

"Do you need to go? Do you have work to do?" he asked.

"Nothing that can't wait." She turned to face him, pulled the covers up over them both, and laid her head on his chest. "Sleep, Gavin."

He was out as soon as he closed his eyes.

TWENTY

ELIZABETH HAD BEEN GLUED TO GAVIN'S SIDE FOR THE past two weeks. She'd told him there was nothing so pressing with her work that it couldn't be rescheduled or handled by phone and laptop.

The Rivers understood his dilemma with his father and had pulled someone up from the minor leagues to take his place at first base. There was no way Gavin was going to leave his father's side right now.

The surgery went fine, thank God. Seeing his father after had just about done him in. Hooked up to oxygen and IVs and beeping machines, his formerly robust, rock of a father had been reduced to something Gavin hadn't wanted to admit.

His father was human. Vulnerable. He could die. Mortality wasn't something Gavin ever wanted to think about, especially where his parents were concerned. It wasn't time yet. It wouldn't be time for a while. A long while.

He spent every second he could at the hospital, helping his mother out until she told him he was becoming annoying, which was okay because he knew how stressed she was. Between him, Mick, Tara, and Jenna, they made sure she was never alone. One of them always stood by her. His dad slept a lot after the surgery, or at least he tried to. When he wasn't sleeping, he was either being poked and prodded by the nursing staff or hauled off somewhere for some test.

How the hell were patients supposed to recover in the hospital when the staff never let them sleep?

They'd dragged his dad's ass out of bed the day after surgery, something that surprised the hell out of Gavin. He and Mick even questioned the nursing staff about it, and Mick went on the hunt for the cardiac surgeon, certain the nurses were out of their goddamned minds. But the staff assured them the sooner they got his dad out of the bed and walking around, the quicker he would recover.

Four days post surgery, his father was walking up and down the halls, no longer connected to tubes or IVs, and eating solid food again, something his dad was damned happy about. He'd been anxious to go home. The doctor had said maybe the next day if he continued to be a pain in the ass and a medical miracle, and performed as well as he had been. His dad said he'd run around the damn nurse's station if that's what it took to get him discharged.

That made Gavin smile. His dad cranky and impatient? Yeah, that sounded normal to him.

True to his word, his father had walked the entire floor. They'd discharged him the next day.

Maybe his mother could get some sleep at home.

They'd been home for three days, all of them going in and out all day long. Jenna, Tara, and Elizabeth had made a grocery store run the day they'd brought his dad home so Mom wouldn't have to worry about having food in the house. Since Dad wouldn't be able to take the stairs for a while, they'd set up the downstairs guest room as their master bedroom for the time being, something Dad hated but he'd just have to deal with. At least he was home, and he was happy about that.

Not that Mom was going to let him prop his feet up in his favorite chair and veg. She had him up twice a day for walks around the house and in the backyard, the best he could do the first week. She was like a drill sergeant. She had his schedule mapped out and knew what to feed him, knew what his exercise schedule was down to the hour and minute of the day, knew what pills he was supposed to take and when his doctors' appointments were. And she at least allowed her kids to help.

Jenna had gone back to manning the bar since they'd enlisted aunts, uncles, and cousins to take over while they were standing vigil at the hospital. The bar didn't run itself, though, and Jenna was itching to get back to work.

Gavin, not so much.

Gavin sat in the living room with his dad, Mick, and Elizabeth. Tara had taken Mom to the grocery store to pick up a few things.

They were watching a baseball game. A Rivers game to be exact. It was a doubleheader against San Francisco.

"The first baseman they brought up from the minors is pretty good."

Gavin acknowledged his father's comment, trying not to pay attention to the hotshot twenty-one-year-old scooping up the grounder and dashing to first base for the out.

"He's decent."

Elizabeth squeezed his shoulder. She sat on the edge of the chair with him.

"Might be time for you to get back to work before they replace you with someone younger."

Gavin laughed. "I'm hardly out to pasture at twenty-nine, Dad.

I've got a lock-solid contract. The kid there is a temp. They'll shoot him back to the minors as soon as I come back."

His dad reached for his glass of water. "I'm doing fine here, kid. You need to get back to work."

"I'll get back to work soon enough. No hurry, Dad. And don't worry about my job. It's secure. I have a great agent, here." He patted Lizzie's hand and stared up at her. She gave him a half smile.

"What? You think I should go back to work, too?"

"I think your father is doing well. It's off season for Mick. He can be here to watch over your father."

"Yeah, Elizabeth doesn't want to lose another meal ticket."

Elizabeth tensed but didn't say anything.

Gavin's gaze shot to Mick. "You can stay out of this conversation."

Mick shrugged. "I'm in the room. Hard to stay out of it."

"Mick. Butt out," their dad said, then turned his attention back to Gavin. "But Elizabeth's right. I'm right. You need to be playing ball."

"I'll get back to it, Dad."

"When?"

"Soon."

The Rivers were up to bat. The kid—Chris Stallings—hit a line drive past the shortstop and got on base. Gavin tried not to wince.

"He can hit, too. He's been hitting the ball since he came up."

"Because pitchers haven't seen his stuff. Once they do, they'll strike him out. He's just lucky right now."

Mick snorted.

Fortunately, Tara and his mom got back. Elizabeth left to help them with groceries, and Gavin sank deeper in the chair as Stallings made a couple of diving catches and then hit a home run in the eighth inning to take the Rivers up two runs over San Francisco.

Shit.

Not that Gavin wanted the kid to suck. His team needed to win. But did Stallings have to be so damn good? Gavin wanted his team to win on some of the other players' shoulders.

"Come on. Time for your walk," his mother said to his dad after the game.

"It's a doubleheader."

"You'll be back before the second game." She looked at Gavin and Mick. "Girls are starting dinner. You two can fire up the grill."

"Yes, ma'am."

He and Mick took the chicken outside. Gavin grabbed a beer, Mick a soda.

"So do you agree with Dad? Should I head back?"

Mick flipped the chicken, then closed the grill lid. "I think you should do whatever the hell you want to do."

"If it were football season, what would you do?"

Mick lifted his gaze to Gavin's. "It's not football season."

"That's not an answer."

"It's your career, man. We've got it covered here, but I understand where you're coming from. I probably wouldn't want to leave right now, either. That was some scary shit that went down with Dad."

Gavin nodded. "I'm afraid if I leave, something will happen and I won't be here."

"Can't stay forever, though. In sports your name and your presence is everything."

"I'll know when the time is right."

"Yeah, you will."

AFTER DINNER, ELIZABETH HELPED WITH THE DISHES, then went looking for Gavin. She found him out back cleaning the grill.

"Chicken was good."

He smiled at her. "Yeah, it was."

"Your mother is awesome the way she's taken control over every-thing. How she handles it all . . ."

"She holds up well. She's got him home, and he's going to be fine."

She sat on one of the patio chairs. "Yes, he's going to be fine. Which means you need to get back to work."

He paused, stared at the grill. "Not yet."

"Gavin, you need to work."

"I'm not ready yet, Lizzie. A few more days, just to make sure he's okay."

"You're not really doing anything here, Gavin, other than driving yourself crazy. Your dad is on the mend. Mick is here to help out your mom. Jenna has the bar under control. Tara is local, too. Your dad has plenty of help."

His gaze shot to hers. "I said I'm not ready yet."

"What are you so afraid of?"

"The question is, Elizabeth, what are you so afraid of? That Gavin will be replaced, and you'll lose more money?"

She turned her gaze on Mick, who pushed the screen door open and stepped out back.

She knew this conversation should have waited until they were back at Gavin's house. But he'd been so tense lately, and watching that game today had nearly done him in.

He needed to get back to work. Not for her. God, not for her. For himself.

"Mick, please. Let me have a minute with Gavin."

"Why? So you can needle him about how important it is that he play for the Rivers? God, Elizabeth, don't you ever let up? Is the job always number one to you?"

She stood, wiped her hands down the sides of her Capris. "It's not like that. I was just—"

"I know what you were just. You were just going to convince Gavin that time is money. Play is money. Image is everything, and if he doesn't get out on the field, he's losing image points. Possible contract renegotiation position. I know how you think."

She shook her head. "No, you don't. If you'd just let me—"

"Can't you just for one second think about someone else besides yourself and your career and what's important to you? What about Gavin, my mother, my father? What about what's important to them? Did you once stop to think that maybe my mom needs Gavin here for emotional support?"

"I did. I thought—"

"No, you didn't think at all about that. All you thought about was getting Gavin back on the ball field, so millions of people could see him play. God forbid he's not out there front and center, on television, in the media. I know the game, Liz. I know your game. And this time I'm not going to let you use Gavin to play it."

Her gaze shot to Gavin, who hadn't said a word.

Didn't he know? Didn't he understand what she was trying to do?

He didn't. He believed every word Mick said. He thought it was about the money, the PR, the face time. Not about what was best for Gavin the person, what was best for him inside.

Tears pricked her eyes, and she'd be damned if she'd cry in front of them.

"I'm sorry."

She brushed past Mick and opened the screen door, past Tara and Gavin's mom.

"Elizabeth. What's wrong?"

"I'm sorry. I have to go."

Tears blinded her as she grabbed her purse and fled to the front door. She pulled it open and ran to her car, peeled out of the driveway and hit the street. She hoped like hell Gavin wouldn't come after her.

He wouldn't. She already knew he wouldn't.

Gavin had believed Mick. Mick's words had sunk in, had made sense to him. Otherwise, he'd have spoken up, would have said something, would have stopped Mick from saying those awful things.

But he hadn't.

Deep down Gavin believed Elizabeth was just as bad as Mick thought she was.

She should have seen it, should have known.

At least now she did.

It was over.

GAVIN WAS SUCH AN ASSHOLE. HE'D STOOD THERE AND listened to Mick make those accusations against Elizabeth and hadn't said a goddamned word.

So fucking typical, wasn't it? Mick, the big brother, who always knew what was best, right?

Only maybe this time he was right.

Gavin wasn't ready to go back to the game yet. Mom needed him. So did Dad. And Elizabeth was probably anxious about Gavin missing so many games. She had his professional interests in mind, not his personal ones.

Didn't she?

Mick had just stood there and stared at him after Elizabeth ran inside, then said, "You know I'm right about this. Open your eyes and see her for who she really is before she hurts you."

Then he'd gone inside, leaving Gavin alone out there with his thoughts.

All his thoughts.

Only he wasn't sure which thoughts were the right ones.

"Gavin, what happened?"

His mother stepped outside, a dish towel in her hand.

Gavin bent his head over the grill and scrubbed. "Nothing."

"Elizabeth ran out of here, and I'm pretty sure she was crying. That doesn't seem like nothing."

He shrugged. "I'll handle it."

"Did Michael say something to her?"

"Probably nothing that wasn't the truth."

She took a seat on the chair. "Expand on that."

"She wanted me to go back to the game."

"And?"

"Mick accused her of selfish interests. That she's only concerned I'll be replaced."

"And you said what to that?"

He lifted his gaze to his mother. "I said nothing."

"So basically you allowed your brother to insult the woman you love, and you didn't say a word."

He frowned. "I don't love her."

"Is that right?"

"Yeah."

"You're sure about that? Because from what I've seen of the two of you together, it seems to me you do love her."

"Don't tell me how I feel, Mom. We've had some fun together. That's all it is."

His mom tilted her head and gave him her trademark bullshit look. "You're so good at denying how you feel."

He didn't respond.

"But she's also your agent. It's her job to look out for your career."

"True."

"And her doing so means she should be lambasted by your brother just because he carries a grudge?"

"That's his issue to deal with."

"And you let him continue to do so, with a woman you've been seeing and should at least care enough about to defend. I raised you better than that, Gavin."

He inhaled, let it out, closed the grill, and jammed his fingers through his hair. "I don't know. This is all so complicated. It wasn't supposed to be complicated."

He sat in the chair next to hers. She smiled at him and took his hand. "Relationships are always complicated, Gavin."

"It's not what I set out to have with Lizzie. It was just supposed to be something fun."

"Have you been having fun with her?"

"Yes."

"So what happened?"

"No clue. I guess somewhere along the way something happened."

"Something like . . . love?"

He'd never wanted that to enter the picture. Not with Elizabeth. But maybe it had, and he just hadn't realized it. He sure as hell didn't want to talk about it with his mother. "I don't know, Mom. Honestly, I don't know. I feel something for her. I don't know what it is."

"Maybe it's time you stop running away from it and figure it out."

"I don't know if I want to. Elizabeth isn't easy."

She laughed. "Neither, my sweet boy, are you."

THE SECOND GAME WAS WELL UNDER WAY BY THE TIME Gavin joined his dad in the living room.

They sat in silence and watched for a while. Mick and Tara had gone home, and Jenna was at the bar.

The Rivers were behind one run in the seventh inning. The middle of the order was up to bat.

"Your replacement is two for three so far in this game. Stole a base in the third, and drove in a run in the fifth."

"That's good. Let's hope we can win."

More silence while one player hit a grounder to third for the first out, and the second batter popped out to right field.

Stallings was up next. Gavin leaned forward to study the kid. Decent batting stance; wasn't afraid of the pitcher's curveball or his fastball. Wasn't fooled easily as he took two balls and one strike. When a pitch came sailing over the plate, he launched it over the left field fence for a home run.

Shit. The kid was good.

"Too bad there wasn't anyone on base," his dad said.

"Yeah. Too bad."

Gavin leaned back.

"Saw Elizabeth hightailing it out of here earlier. You piss her off?"

"No. Mick did."

"About?"

"Don't worry about it, Dad. You just need to rest."

His dad leaned forward. "Stop treating me like an invalid. I never had high blood pressure so it's not like I'm going to explode over here."

Gavin glanced over to his mother, who was sitting in her chair sewing something by hand. She didn't look concerned or give him a warning look. In fact, she didn't look up at all.

"Well?"

"Elizabeth suggested I get back to the game. Mick accused her of trying to manipulate me for her own personal gain."

His dad snorted. "Your brother isn't thinking clearly where Elizabeth is concerned, and it's damn time he got over it already. And didn't I tell you the same thing? That kid is looking like a hotshot at first base. I'll bet he makes a damn site less than you do, too."

Gavin sank into the chair and didn't say anything. The Rivers were out as the next batter swung on a good pitch.

"So what did you say while Mick was reading the riot act to Elizabeth?"

"Nothing."

"You're dating her, and you didn't defend her?"

Gavin felt like he was eight years old again. Getting a lecture from his dad had never felt good then, and it didn't now. "No."

"Because you think she's manipulating you, that she only cares about your career and not you?"

"I don't know what to think."

"And here I thought I raised smart boys. Right now I'm thinking you're both dumber than dirt."

Right now that's about how Gavin felt.

TWENTY-ONE

IF ELIZABETH WOULD HAVE HAD HER WITS ABOUT HER, she could have gone toe-to-toe with Mick. She never let athletes knock her on her ass. If they got in her face, she got right back in theirs. So why had she let Mick do that to her? She should have stood up to him and told him exactly how he was wrong in his thinking. And then told him to stick his opinions about her up his ass once and for all, because she was tired of hearing them.

Dammit.

It was because of Gavin. Okay, and also because she didn't want to cause World War III at his parents' house. Not with his dad recovering. She'd never do anything to upset him.

She pulled into the parking lot at Riley's bar, not sure what the hell she was doing here. Hadn't she had enough Rileys for a while? Did she need to get her ass kicked by yet another one?

Maybe she was a glutton for punishment. After all, Jenna hadn't read her the riot act yet. Might as well let her have a turn.

It was mid-week, so a quiet night. She found Jenna at the bar tending to a few customers who seemed to be regulars. Jenna, dressed in a black tank top and jeans, was talking up her customers, so Elizabeth took a seat at the end of the bar. Jenna made her way over.

"Someone kick your puppy?"

"Your brothers suck."

She snorted. "Tell me something I don't know. What would you like?"

"A decent glass of wine. You choose."

"You got it."

Jenna poured a glass of red and set it down in front of Elizabeth. "Okay, I can give you a long list of why I think my brothers are assholes, but this isn't my party. You tell my why *you* think so."

She took a sip of the wine. "This is excellent."

"Of course it is. It's what I do. Now spill."

"Are you sure you don't want to take their side?"

Jenna leaned against the bar and cocked a grin. "Rarely."

"Gavin's been restless since your dad's surgery. Watching the game today, I could tell seeing that first baseman they brought up bothered him. The kid is talented, and I know Gavin feels threatened. Since your dad is recovering so well, I told him maybe he should go back to work. And Mick jumped all over me saying I had ulterior motives."

Jenna rolled her eyes. "Isn't he over that yet?"

"Apparently not. The worst part was that Gavin stood by and didn't say a word while Mick was reading me the riot act about how I was only interested in lining my own pockets at Gavin's expense."

Jenna looked livid. "What a dick. You're right. They both suck."

Elizabeth laughed, raised her glass, and tilted it toward Jenna before taking another sip. "And here I thought I might be making a mistake by coming here and venting to you, since you're their sister."

"Hey, I'll defend my brothers to the death when they're right. Problem is, they rarely are. They're men; therefore, they have the testosterone disadvantage. Screws them every time."

"I hope that's not a mark against everyone in my gender."

Elizabeth swiveled on her barstool and grinned at Ty Anderson. "Hey, Ty. What brings you here?"

"Stopping in for a drink and spotted you right off. Can I sit down or is this a male-bashing party?"

Elizabeth looked at Jenna, who shrugged. "It's your male-bashing party, Liz. They're just my brothers, and I'm always happy to play along."

Elizabeth laughed. "Ty, this is Jenna Riley, Gavin's sister. Jenna, this is Tyler Anderson. He plays hockey for the Ice."

"Ah. Nice to meet you, Jenna."

Jenna studied Ty, then sighed. "Another sports jock. My heart goes pitter-patter."

He grinned. "A fan, huh?"

"Yeah, you know it."

Elizabeth laughed and turned to Ty. "I think she gets bombarded with all the players here because of Mick and Gavin."

"Uh-huh. So I'm damned before I even start, huh?"

"Afraid so, cowboy. What'll it be?"

"I'll have a beer. Bottled. Not light."

"Careful there, Ty," Jenna said as she popped the top off and slid the bottle to him. "Don't want to put on too much weight, or you'll have trouble holding your stick."

He grabbed the bottle and held it to his lips. "Never had any complaints about my abilities with my stick so far."

Jenna arched a brow. "And you're here alone? With that charm? Shocking."

While Jenna went off to tend to one of her customers, Ty turned to Elizabeth. "Who pissed in her corn flakes?"

"She's always tough on the guys in here. It comes from having famous brothers and fending off all the jocks, plus coming from a family that lives for sports. I don't think guys like you are her type."

Ty took a long pull from the bottle, his gaze trained on Jenna as she worked the bar. "Fine with me since she isn't my type, either."

"Is that right?" Elizabeth studied Jenna's short dark hair, slender body, tattoos, and multiple ear piercings. She thought Jenna was sexy and adorable. "What about her isn't your type?"

"I like them with big tits."

Elizabeth rolled her eyes. From the way Ty hadn't once taken his eyes off Jenna, she figured Ty was full of shit and just hadn't enjoyed getting shot down.

"I think I'll go try my luck with darts. See you later, Elizabeth."

"Later, Ty."

Elizabeth emptied her wineglass, and Jenna was there to refill.

"Another egocentric jock. Just what Riley's needs."

"Huh? Oh, you mean Ty?"

"Yeah."

"He's actually a pretty nice guy once you give him a chance."

"One of yours?"

"Yes."

"Not my type."

Grateful to be discussing something other than herself and her miserable relationship with Gavin, Elizabeth asked, "Oh, really. And what is your type, Jenna?"

She laid her palms against the bar. "I like them cerebral. Poetic. Book smart. Lyrical. Musical. And interested in anything other than sports. Growing up with sports and being surrounded by them in this bar, I prefer to be with a man whose focus is on anything but."

"I can understand that. So you go for the office types or the teacher types. Or maybe a lawyer."

"I don't care what he does for a living as long as we don't have to talk about sports when we're together."

But Jenna's gaze strayed to Ty while she wiped down the surface of the bar. Elizabeth turned and watched Ty, now involved in a game of pool with a few other guys. His jeans stretched across his mighty fine ass as he leaned across the table to take a shot. His tight T-shirt showed off his bulging biceps, and Jenna would have to be dead not to notice.

As Elizabeth turned to face the bar, it was clear Jenna was noticing.

"Ty's not your type, huh?"

Jenna shrugged. "He has a great ass and that bad boy look that gets my panties wet. It's been a dry spell. I'm human. But I still don't date jocks. Too bad, because I could definitely take someone like him for a spin."

"I'm sure he'd take you up on your offer, too. He was giving you the eye when you weren't looking."

Jenna gave him another quick glance, then sighed. "Why does this place attract so many guys like him? Maybe we should do some kind of promotion to attract the men I want to date, instead of the ones I don't."

"That's a good idea. You should come up with something."

"Yeah," Jenna said, her lips curving. "In my spare time."

"I could help you. I'm kind of good with promotional stuff."

Jenna leaned over the bar. "That's true. It is your area. But you're probably busy."

"Not that busy. I'd love to help."

"You're just trying to avoid everything Gavin."

"You're right. I am." She lifted her glass and took a drink.

"So how are you going to solve that particular problem?"

"I have no idea what to do. I don't think he trusts me. And I don't honestly know how he feels about me. Being his agent and being in love with him is screwing everything up, both professionally and personally."

"How so?"

"As his agent, I should be kicking his ass back to the game. He's been gone way too long. As the woman who loves him, I understand how he feels. I'm empathetic to his concern about your dad and his need to be here."

"My dad is recovering just fine, getting stronger every day. This whole thing scared the shit out of all of us, so we're naturally hovering."

"That's to be expected, I think. It scared me, too. I love your parents."

Jenna smiled and reached for her hand. "I know you do. You've been family for a long time."

"But he is recovering well, and you all take such good care of him. And Gavin's restless. I can see it, can feel the tension in him. He watches the game and he knows he needs to get back to it, but something's holding him back. A sense of responsibility coupled with the fear that if he's gone, something bad will happen."

"So go put your agent hat on and kick his ass back to work. You're just going to have to realize that sometimes you can't be both girlfriend and agent. Sometimes you just have to be his agent and make him see that it's time to do his job."

She sighed. "Or I might find out that I can't be both at all, that I'm going to have to choose one. Or he'll choose one for me."

Jenna gave her a straight look. "Yeah, that might happen. If he loves you, it won't matter."

"And if he doesn't love me at all, it might matter a lot."

"Are you afraid to find out?"

"I think that's the million-dollar question."

TWENTY-TWO

GAVIN AND MICK WERE CLEANING OUT THE GUTTERS
when Gavin saw Elizabeth's car pull up in the driveway. A twinge of
guilt and something else pulled at his gut. His dad was sitting out on
the back patio, watching them. It was a perfect day. The sun was out,
a nice breeze blowing. Mom and Tara were out shopping.

"You know why she's here."

"Leave it alone, Mick."

His dad stood when Elizabeth came through the back door.

"Front door was open."

"Hi, Lizzie."

She gave his dad a hug and sat down with him, not even acknowl-
edging Gavin and Mick.

"She's playing you, man. Just like she manipulated me. And Tara
and Nathan."

Gavin glared at Mick. "This isn't about you. Not everything is
about you."

Mick shrugged and directed the hose into the gutter while Gavin grabbed a pile of dead leaves out of another section. Mick climbed down off the ladder to move it, and Gavin inched his way across the roof, trying not to focus on Elizabeth and his dad, who were engaged in conversation and laughing together.

"Hey, boys, Lizzie's going to take me for a little walk. Be back soon."

"I can do that, Dad," Gavin said.

"I think she can handle it. Just clear out the gutters. We'll be fine."

Gavin looked at Mick, who frowned, but they finished up the gutter, and by the time Gavin climbed down the ladder and went in search of his dad, he was in the living room with a glass of water, his feet propped up on the ottoman. Elizabeth was in one of the chairs next to him.

Damn, she looked good in her cream-colored suit with a pale blue silk blouse underneath. Her heels showed off her killer legs, and he wanted to eat her up from top to bottom. He suddenly wanted to be alone with her, to talk to her, to get past this distance between them, to figure out what had gone wrong. But he just . . . couldn't. There were things she just didn't understand.

She looked up at him and offered up a smile, but it wasn't the kind of smile he wanted to see from her. She was holding back, just like he was. "Your dad is doing so well. He walked all the way down to the corner and back."

His father grinned. "Going to be kicking your ass in a game of hoops in no time, especially with that horrible diet of chicken, turkey, and fish your mother is making me eat."

Gavin smiled. "It's good for you, Dad."

"Yeah, whatever. I miss French fries."

"You'll get over it," Gavin said. "And you'll lose that beer belly."

"I miss beer, too."

"You'll get over that, too," Mick said. "I did."

"Get those gutters done?"

"Yup," Gavin said. "All cleaned out."

"Good. Mick, how about you and I go rustle up a turkey sandwich? I'm hungry."

"Whatever you want, Dad."

His father got up and followed Mick into the kitchen. Gavin took a seat on the sofa across from where Liz sat.

"He looks good," she said.

"Yeah, he does."

"He's been home for a week and a half, Gavin. Your father is progressing remarkably well."

"Yes, he is."

"It's time for you to get back to the game. You've missed enough."

His smile died and he stood. "Don't tell me what to do."

She stood, too. "I'm your agent. It's my job to tell you what to do. You don't want to miss too much baseball. Your team is counting on you. You're paid to play, in case you've forgotten."

"I haven't forgotten anything. The Rivers said I could take as much time as I needed to. Why are you pushing this?"

"I'm pushing because you don't need to be here anymore. Mick and Tara are here to watch over your father and help out your mom. Jenna is taking care of the bar. Your father's health is good. Half of your games are local, and you can check up on your dad when you're here for home games. Your delay tactics are only hurting your career."

"I'm not ready yet."

"You're not the one who had a heart attack and surgery, Gavin. It's time for you to get back on the field."

"And I'll let you and the team know when I'm ready to get back on the field. Today isn't the day."

"Why are you being so stubborn about this?"

"Why are you being so insistent about it?"

"I'll tell you why. Because she's manipulating you for her own gain."

Gavin shifted his focus to Mick, who leaned against the doorway to the living room.

Elizabeth did, too. "You stay the hell out of it. This is none of your business."

Mick's lips curled into a sneer. "When it affects my brother, it becomes my business. And I won't let you do to him what you did to me."

"Butt out, Mick. This doesn't concern you. Gavin is my client, and I'm trying to get him to see that he needs to get back to work."

"Oh, right. Like your only concern is Gavin. Please. I know you too well, Liz. I know you're scared to death that you're going to lose another moneymaker, that if he doesn't get back to the game the Rivers might not pick up his next option, might not pay him so much money next time."

She whirled on Mick. "You know what? That's exactly right. And you know who that's going to hurt? It's going to hurt Gavin. And you know what else? If you'd pull your head out of your ass and stop thinking of yourself for one goddamn minute, you'd see that your brother is miserable and has been, that every time Stallings gets up to bat it kills him, that he wants to be on that field so bad it physically hurts him. But no, you're so happy that he's battling me that you can't see past your own anger and spite to what's best for Gavin. You only want to continue to get back at me, and by doing so you're sabotaging your brother's career when what you should be doing is kicking his ass right out of this house and encouraging him to get back in the game where he belongs. I'm ashamed of you, Mick. I thought you loved your brother."

She turned to Gavin. "Look, I don't know what your hang-up is about all this, but I love you and only want what's best for you."

He stared at her. "So do you tell all your clients you love them to get them to do what you want them to do?"

Her jaw dropped. "What?"

"You heard me. Is that your newest form of manipulation? A declaration of love? How many of them did you sleep with to get your own way?"

She went pale, and even as the words fell from his mouth, he couldn't believe he was saying them.

"Gavin, you should know better. I have never slept with a client before. But you know what, this was a mistake. Everything about us has been a mistake from the very beginning."

She cut her gaze to Mick. "Is that what you wanted? Well you know what? You got it. You win. I concede. Give Don Davis my regards when he signs Gavin."

She shifted her gaze back to Gavin. "Gavin, I can no longer represent your interests since it's obvious you want something other than what I can give you. At your earliest convenience please find other representation. I'll follow this up in writing immediately."

She turned and walked out the door before he could form a coherent response.

What the hell had just happened?

She'd told him she loved him, and he'd accused her of sleeping around with all her clients?

And then she'd fired him.

Of course she'd fired him, because he was a dick.

He fell into the chair and listened to the sound of her car pulling out of the driveway.

"What the hell was that all about?" his father asked as he came back into the room and took a seat.

Gavin couldn't form words to explain to his father what he'd just done.

"Did I hear correctly, or did Elizabeth just fire you?"

"You heard right, Dad," Mick said.

"And what part did you play in all of this?" his father asked Mick.

"A lot, I think."

"Michael, I try not to interfere in your life, and I understand that Elizabeth made some mistakes with you and with Tara and Nathan, but don't you think it's about time you got the hell over it already? I've never known you to hold a grudge."

Mick sat and put his hands in his hair. "I was mad. Really mad. I love Tara and Nathan like I've never loved anyone in my life. And what Elizabeth did, the way she manipulated them, hurt me. Hurt them."

"And she apologized and made it right, didn't she?" his father asked.

"Yeah, she did."

"But you couldn't let it go."

"I was afraid when Gavin started seeing her."

Gavin lifted his head, turned to Mick. "Why?"

"Because I was afraid she'd hurt you."

Gavin let out a laugh. "You didn't think I could take care of myself?"

Mick shrugged. "You'll always be my little brother, no matter how old we are. I was trying to protect you. I guess I overprotected. Shit. I fucked this up bad, man. I'm sorry. I have to fix this."

Gavin shook his head. "No, I think you've done enough. I'm the one who has to fix this. But I'm not sure I can. The things I said to her. She said she loved me, and I stabbed her in the heart."

"You realize she was only looking out for your love of the game."

Gavin looked at his dad.

"She knows you love the game. We talked about it on our walk. She sees what I see, how much you love baseball. It's never been about the money with you, ever since you first started playing. You would have played for nothing. Fortunately, you had Elizabeth in your corner to negotiate a good contract, because you would have signed for nothing. She told me she'd never known anyone else who would have played for the pure love of the game. And watching you the past couple of weeks has killed her, just as it's killing me, because the light has gone out of your eyes. She wanted you back in the game because your joy is gone. I told her to do whatever it took to convince you to get back to work."

Gavin stood and dragged his fingers through his hair, the burn in the pit of his stomach so intense he didn't think he'd survive it.

God, he'd hurt her. He was so afraid of leaving his dad, so afraid of losing him. What if he wasn't here and something happened?

And yet his dad and Elizabeth had pegged the loss he'd been feeling.

He missed the game.

He had to go back.

He turned to his dad. "I have to go back."

His dad smiled up at him. "I know you do. I want you to. It's what you do. It's what you love. I'd be disappointed in you if you stayed here because of me."

He went to his father and kneeled down in front of him. "I was afraid something would happen to you again if I left."

His dad leaned forward and touched his shoulder. "I'm gonna be fine, kid. I'm not made of iron, but I'm not made of Jell-O, either. I had my wake-up call. I'll take care of myself, and I promise not to fall. But you can't watch me every second of every day. You have to let go."

Gavin shuddered in a breath and stood. So did his dad. They fell into a hug, Gavin careful not to squeeze his dad because of the incision.

"I'm not gonna break, kid."

Gavin fought back the sting of tears, then pulled back and nodded. "Okay, time for me to go back to work."

"Gavin."

He turned to Mick.

His brother looked miserable. "I'm sorry. I fucked this up, made it worse."

"You did. But that's on you, and between you and Elizabeth. And I have to take the blame for not stopping it when I should have. I let it go on too long."

Mick quirked a grin. "You can't stop me when I'm being a bull-headed ass."

Gavin smiled. "True."

"I'll fix it. At least my part of it. So you love her?"

Gavin had thought he'd hesitate when it came time to say it out loud, but the words fell from his lips. "I do love her. So you're going to have to live with that."

Mick grasped Gavin's shoulders. "I can live with it if she can put up with me. Now go get your girl. And get your ass back to work."

Gavin left his dad's and went back to his house. He'd called the Rivers and told them he was ready to play. They'd be back in town from their road trip by the weekend, so Coach told him to be ready to suit up then. In the meantime, he was going to Elizabeth to fix things between them.

He called her. She didn't answer. He called again, left a voice mail, and waited. She didn't call him back. He called her again. And again. She wouldn't pick up.

Dammit.

He drove to her house, knocked, but got no answer. Maybe she'd gone to her office, so he tried there, but the receptionist said she wasn't in, which meant she either really wasn't in or she was refusing to see him.

He checked the parking lot and didn't see her car.

Well, hell, she wasn't going to make it easy for him, was she? Then again, after what he'd said to her, he didn't deserve easy. And he damn well wasn't going to apologize via cell phone or text message. This had to be done in person.

He drove back to her condo that night and didn't see her car parked in the parking lot, and there were no lights on inside. He waited like a damn stalker in her parking lot for three hours, calling her cell several times, but she still didn't answer.

And she never came home. He waited until one in the morning before giving up and going home.

It was going to be hard to apologize to her if he couldn't find her. Her office was no help, refusing to tell him where she was, and the next day she wasn't at work, either.

He had one more day before he had to report back to the team, and he couldn't find Elizabeth.

But he knew someone who could help.

GRATEFUL FOR THE TRIP OUT OF TOWN, ELIZABETH stared out the window of her New York hotel room. Contracts and negotiations for a potential new client had kept her busy for the past two days, and she was so damn glad for that, too, because the last thing she needed was surplus time to think.

Time to think meant time to dwell on Gavin, and she'd already wasted too much time on that man.

She crawled onto the bed and picked up her laptop, putting the finishing touches on the contract language for her new client, an up-and-coming NBA player for New York. Not quite as high profile as Gavin, but a couple of more players added to her roster would make up for what she lost by dumping Gavin. She'd put some feelers out and gotten the line on a few guys unhappy with their current representation, and she was well on the way to evening out the loss with some stellar gains. First the basketball player, next up was a running back for Baltimore she intended to meet with the first part of next week. And that guy was a moneymaker. If she could sign him, she'd not only have a coup, but a laugh at Don Davis, his current agent.

It was all in keeping the balance. And she *would* maintain the balance.

Her cell buzzed, and she grabbed it off the table, hoping it wasn't Gavin again.

It wasn't Gavin. It was his mother.

Shit. Her stomach dropped, and she clicked the phone, hoping like hell Gavin's father hadn't had a relapse.

"Hello?"

"Elizabeth? It's Kathleen Riley."

"Hello, Kathleen. Is Jimmy okay?"

"He's fine, dear, don't worry."

She blew out a sigh of relief. "Oh, thank God. I'm so glad to hear that."

"I'm calling about Gavin."

"Oh."

"You really fired him?"

This was going to be difficult. "It was getting to be too hard, Kathleen."

"You don't have to pull punches with me. I understand. Was he awful to you?"

There was only so much she was going to tell his mother. "There was a conflict of interest I couldn't deny any longer. I was in love with him. I couldn't represent his best interests with that kind of conflict. I had to make the break."

"He said you won't answer his calls."

And he had his mother call to run interference? Really? "I'm working right now so I've been busy."

"He said you haven't been at home or at your office."

Looking for her, was he? Good. "No, I'm in New York on business. Whatever he and I have to say to each other will have to wait."

"I told him I wasn't going to pressure you or pretend that this call was anything other than a fact-finding mission on his behalf."

She smiled at that. "Thank you, Kathleen."

"I hope you two are able to work things out."

That wasn't going to happen. "I'm glad you called. Please say hello to Jimmy for me."

"I will, honey. You take care."

Elizabeth laid the phone down on the nightstand and stared at her laptop, but the contract language had lost its appeal. She closed her laptop and sank under the covers, grabbed the remote and turned on the television, randomly flipping channels, hoping she could find something mindless to tune into until she fell asleep.

Her phone rang. She grabbed it from the nightstand, her heart squeezing when she saw it was Gavin. She laid it back down and focused on an animal show on the television.

When her phone buzzed again, she let the tears fall, no longer able to hold them inside.

TWENTY-THREE

GOING TO RILEY'S WAS PROBABLY A MISTAKE, BUT ELIZABETH wanted to talk to Jenna. It wasn't like she had a lot of friends. She missed Shawnelle and Haley, but she wouldn't be hanging out with them anytime soon now that she and Gavin were no longer a couple, and she wasn't Gavin's agent. Since she didn't represent any other Rivers players, at least not at the moment, there would be no reason for her to attend any of their games.

Wasn't it just so funny that someone who never had any female friends suddenly craved them?

She pulled up a seat at the bar and waited for Jenna, who spotted her, waved, and dealt with a few of her customers before moseying down Elizabeth's end.

"What's up, girl?"

"Just got back into town after a few days of traveling. How about you?"

Jenna held out her arms. "Another day in Riley paradise here. What can I get you to drink?"

"Hit me with something strong and mighty."

"You talking a man or a drink?"

Elizabeth laughed. "I'll start with the drink and work my way up from there."

Jenna filled a glass with ice and whiskey, straight up. "Hard and mighty. It's Gavin's favorite."

"Ouch."

"Yeah, Mom told me you two had a falling out and you fired him. Care to elaborate?"

Elizabeth took a long swallow, her eyes watering as the whiskey burned its way down her throat and into her belly. "Whoa."

Jenna laughed. "Lightweight. Don't get into a drinking contest with me, ever."

"Duly noted."

"Okay, girlfriend. Spill. What did my dumb-ass brother do to fuck things up?"

"I'm not sure it was entirely his fault."

"Oh, I'm sure it was. Go on."

"I pushed him to get back to the game. It's my job as his agent."

"Yes, it is."

"Anyway, your other brother stuck his nose in our business and accused me once again of manipulating Gavin. I told Gavin I loved him."

"Wow. Big step," Jenna said.

"Yes. But I wanted him to understand that I cared about him and wanted only what was best for him. I could see he was miserable."

Jenna nodded. "We all could see that."

"So he asked me if I told all my clients that in order to get what I wanted, then he asked me how many of my clients I slept with."

Jenna's eyes widened, and she pushed off the bar. "Get the fuck outta here. He did not say that."

Elizabeth hoisted her glass and emptied it, then laid it back on the bar. "Afraid so."

Jenna refilled the glass. "This one's on me. What an utter fucking prick. I can't believe he said that to you. What was he thinking?"

"I have no idea." She took the shot in one swallow this time. Jenna refilled it again.

"I'm so sorry, Liz. I know Gavin can be a little dense and unfeeling at times, but that was just uncalled for. I know he cares about you. Where was his head at the time?"

She shrugged and took the shot again, feeling warm and buzzed. "Don't know. Don't care anymore. At that point I was stunned, pissed, and disappointed as hell. I told him it was obvious we weren't seeing eye to eye on business or personal agendas anymore, so I fired him and walked out on him."

"Good for you, sister." Jenna refilled Elizabeth's glass, then poured another. "I'll have a shot with you this time."

Elizabeth giggled. "Can you do that since you're on duty?"

Jenna lifted the glass. "Honey, I can do anything I damn well please. I'm the owner. Or at least part owner. Cheers. And men suck."

They clinked glasses and Elizabeth chugged the shot. Her face was getting numb, but she felt a hell of a lot better now. She knew coming here was a great idea. In no time at all she'd forget all about Gavin Riley.

GAVIN SAT IN HIS LIVING ROOM PLAYING XBOX, TRYING to get his mind off Elizabeth. Sometime soon she'd get home, and he'd stop stalking her condo.

Okay, maybe tonight he'd go back there and see if her car was there yet. He'd try around midnight. She couldn't stay gone forever. Eventually she'd have to go home, and she'd have to face him.

And he'd have to face her.

His cell buzzed. He picked it up, saw Jenna was calling.

"Hey, baby sister, what's up?"

"Hey, dickhead. I need you to come to the bar for a pickup."

He frowned. "Pickup. What kind of pickup?"

"Your girlfriend—or should I say ex-girlfriend—Elizabeth, is ten sheets to the wind here, and it's 100 percent your fault, asshole."

His heart thudded against his chest. "Lizzie is there? Why?"

"Getting stinking drunk because you're a prick. You coming or should I call for relief so I can take her home?"

"On my way. Don't let her leave."

Jenna laughed. "Not intending to."

He launched out the door, grateful he'd had an early game today. It was only eleven, but still, he might not have been around to take Jenna's call, and he didn't want to miss the chance to talk to Elizabeth.

Fifteen minutes later he pushed through the door of Riley's and headed straight to the bar, ignoring the shouts and waves from the patrons calling his name.

"Where is she?"

Jenna motioned with her head. "Holding court at the pool table."

He started to turn but Jenna grasped his wrist.

"What?"

"You were a jerk."

He nodded. "I know. I'm an asshole. I hurt her, bad. You can lecture me later, and I deserve every word. I'm going to fix this."

Jenna nodded. "See that you do."

Geez. Women and bonding. He was so screwed. As if his mother hadn't already read him the riot act about what he'd done to Elizabeth. His own family was turning against him. Not that he didn't deserve it. He did, in spades.

He headed over to the crowded pool table and stopped in his tracks at the sight of Elizabeth bent over the table with about eight sets of horny, eager eyes focused on her ass. She wore black Capri pants and a sleeveless stretchy top and little canvas shoes. Her hair was in a ponytail. She looked hot and sexy, and oh, God, no wonder they were looking at her ass—those pants cupped the globes perfectly. She did have such a great ass, especially when she bent over like that.

She couldn't shoot pool for shit when she was drunk though. He winced when her cue scraped the cloth. She scratched—twice in a row. But he didn't think the guys watching her gave a crap about her pool-shooting abilities. They were watching the woman, who laughed with them, flirted with them, and leaned against them, probably because she was having trouble standing.

What was her intent in getting drunk and hanging out with all these men?

It occurred to him he had no right to wonder, since he'd tossed her declaration of love in her face and basically called her a slut. He cringed again at the thought, as he had every day since he'd flung what she'd said out the window as if it had meant nothing. She'd told him she loved him—in front of his brother, who she knew had the capacity to hurt her, and in front of his father.

And he'd crushed her under his heel. He was a callous, no good son of a bitch, and he didn't deserve her.

He was no better than dirt. He couldn't blame her for never wanting to speak to him again. And he sure as hell couldn't blame her for dropping him as a client.

Now it was time for him to man up and take whatever she flung his way.

He moved into the circle by the pool table.

"Excuse me, guys, time for me to take my woman home."

They all backed away, whether it was because they knew him or whether they didn't want to get in the middle of a guy and his girl, he didn't know. Didn't care.

Elizabeth lined up a shot, though he knew she had it lined up wrong. He got up behind her and pressed his body against hers. She giggled.

"I hope you don't think you pressing your crotch against my ass to help me with this shot in any way means you're coming home with me."

She had no idea it was him. He hadn't said a word. He slid his arm alongside hers, held her hand steady, lined up the shot, and hit the ball. It slid into the corner pocket—without scratching.

"Wheee!" she said, lifting and turning around with a wide grin.

Her smile died as soon as she saw him. "What the hell are you doing here?"

"Jenna called me. I'm your ride home."

She shot a glare at the bar. Jenna waved.

"Traitor."

He laid the pool cue on the table. "Come on, honey, I'll take you home."

She backed away from him. "I'm not going anywhere with you. I'm staying here with my guys. Right, guys?"

Gavin scanned the gazes of the men surrounding the table. None looked ready to jump to her defense. Smart dudes. The last thing they wanted was to get in the middle of what they probably thought was a domestic dispute.

"Party's over, Elizabeth. Let's go." He reached for her hand, but she jerked it back.

"Leave me alone. You don't love me. And I fired you."

"Do we have to do this here?"

She nodded her head up and down like a goddamn bobblehead. "Yes. Yes we do. Right here. Right now."

Not a good idea. She couldn't even stand up by herself. She was weaving back and forth, and looked like she was going to drop to the floor any minute. In fact . . .

He caught her before she fell. "Okay, here we go." He scooped her up in his arms. Jenna was right there with Elizabeth's purse and a kiss to his cheek.

"Here you go. Good luck."

She held the door for him.

"Thanks, sis."

Elizabeth lifted her head and glared at him. "I don't want you to take me home. You're fired."

"So you told me. I'm taking you home anyway. You can fire me again when we get there."

"Okay." Her head dropped to his shoulder, and she was blissfully quiet on the ride home. Only instead of taking her home, he took her to his house, where she'd have less of a chance of making an escape when he tried to talk to her.

She passed out on the ride home, didn't wake up when he carried her into his house and up the stairs to his bedroom. He took off her shoes and covered her, and she didn't move.

She was out. Totally and utterly out. Whatever he wanted to say to her was going to have to wait until tomorrow.

Shit.

He turned out the light and closed the door.

He went downstairs, picked up where he'd been on his Xbox game, and figured he was going to be up for a while tonight, figuring out what he was going to say in the morning.

ELIZABETH WOKE WITH A START AT THE SOUND OF A door closing, shot up in bed, and blinked her eyes open.

Ugh. Cotton mouth.

Whiskey.

This was all Jenna's fault.

Not really, but always nicer to blame someone else for your own stupidity.

She needed coffee, stat. She forced her eyes open, and that's when she realized she was not in her own bedroom.

Even worse, this was Gavin's bedroom.

Double shit.

She vaguely remembered him showing up at Riley's last night. Thank God Jenna had the presence of mind not to let her drive home. Not that she would have been foolish enough to do so, but drunks never had common sense.

She didn't remember exchanging much in the way of verbiage with Gavin last night, so maybe they hadn't gotten into it. She'd likely been too drunk to have any sort of intelligent conversation anyway.

Good. She had nothing to say to him anyway.

She glanced over at the clock on the nightstand.

Holy crap, ten a.m.

She really should give up alcohol. Or at least alcohol binges when you're mad about a man.

Good thing she didn't fall in love often. Or ever.

At least she never intended to fall in love again. The wear and tear on the body, heart, and soul was too great. She'd already invested enough years of her life in Gavin, and for what? To be called a whore?

She should have listened to her mother. Love hadn't worked for her mother, and it sure as hell hadn't worked for her. She was going to take up Tori's lifestyle in the future. Career first, men were to be thought of only as recreation, and there was no such thing as love.

She swung her legs over the side of the bed and stood, checking her status.

A little shaky, slightly nauseated, and desperate for a cup of coffee. Other than that, she was okay. Now she had to get out of here.

She found her shoes and slipped them on, then opened the door.

She smelled coffee. Oh, God. She didn't care if she was forced to have a civil five-minute conversation with Gavin. She was going to have a cup of coffee. She tiptoed downstairs, hoping he was asleep or, even better, gone.

As she rounded the corner into the kitchen, she spotted Gavin leaning against the counter. He lifted his gaze from the newspaper to look at her. He wore a pair of faded jeans and a T-shirt, and oh, God, he looked so good. His hair was messy, and she wanted to go up to him, put her arms around him, and mess his hair up a little more with her fingers. She wanted to kiss him and ask him why he couldn't love her as much as she loved him.

This was why she was a cold-hearted bitch. Love just fucking hurt too much to risk the attempt. She'd tried. She'd failed. It sucked.

She walked into the room.

"You're awake," he said, laying the newspaper on the counter.

"Apparently."

"Feel okay?"

"I'll live."

"Coffee?"

"Desperate for some."

He grabbed a cup and poured, held it out for her.

"Thanks."

He didn't try to engage her in conversation while she drank down the sobering, life-affirming brew. For that she was grateful. She needed to consume an entire pot of it, but not here. Not with him.

She laid the cup down and fished in her purse for her phone. "I'll just call a taxi to take me to my car."

"I'll drive you."

"No."

He laid his hand over hers. "Elizabeth . . ."

She pulled her hand away. "Gavin, save it. I don't want to hear whatever you have to say."

"I'm not going to go away until you let me say it."

She dialed the taxi company, gave them Gavin's address, then hung up.

She blew out a breath and walked around him to the coffeepot, refilled her cup, then leaned against the counter. "Fine, then. Say it, so I can go home. They said fifteen minutes for the taxi."

He turned to face her, tried for a smile. She didn't smile back, so he raked his hands through his hair. "You're not going to make this easy for me, are you?"

She had no answer for him.

He inhaled, let it out. "Okay. Look, I know I hurt you that day. When you told me you loved me, I wasn't thinking straight. All I heard was you telling me what to do. Telling me I had to go back to work. I had already heard my dad telling me, my mom telling me. And then on the other side I heard from Mick saying how you were manipulating me, how all you were interested in was the money and career aspect, that you didn't care about me."

She let out a small snort at that one but didn't dignify it with a response.

"I know, I know. I should have known better than to listen to my brother. Believe me, he's got a lot to answer for in all this. But the blame lies on me. All of the blame is on me. And I'm sorry. You laid your heart on the line, and I stomped on it as if it didn't mean anything. I guess it kinda scared me when you said you loved me."

She waited for more from him. Nothing.

"That's it? It kinda scared you?"

"Yeah. I knew you and I were headed for . . . something. At some point. I just don't know that I was ready for . . . it."

She arched a brow. "It?"

"Yeah. You know. Love."

She rolled her eyes. "You act as if love is some kind of communicable disease, Gavin."

He shook his head. "That's not what I meant. I'm messing this up. I just wasn't prepared for you to tell me you loved me in the midst of browbeating me about going back to work. I mean you're my agent and you were my girlfriend—or something. I didn't really know what we were to each other. And then all of a sudden you're telling me you love me in front of my brother and my dad, and I'm not sure about anything anymore. And I knew I felt something big for you, but I was messed up over my dad, too, and I—"

She didn't know what she'd expected from him, but this wasn't it. He was stumbling over his words, and maybe she'd expected a straight out apology and declaration of love.

Stupid. Once again, reality hadn't met her expectations.

When had it ever?

The sound of a horn honking was a giant slice of relief. This whole thing was mortifying. Elizabeth wasn't sure she could put up with one more second of Gavin's painful explanations.

"Look, Gavin. Let me make this easy for you. I'm not your agent anymore, and I'm not your 'whatever' or your 'something,' either. You're off the hook. I'm sorry I embarrassed you in front of your brother and your father with my inept declaration of love. Trust me, it won't happen again."

He frowned. "That's not what I'm trying to—"

She laid down the cup and grabbed her purse.

"We're over. You want to know what we were to each other? Fuck buddies. A fling. Call it whatever you want. I mistook it for love. That's on me, so don't feel responsible. I'll get over it. You should, too."

"Elizabeth, wait."

She wasn't going to wait. She'd waited long enough. For five damn years she'd been in love with a man who was never going to be able to love her back. Not the way she needed him to.

Because he was incapable of loving her. Possibly incapable of loving anyone.

She walked out the door and slid into the taxi, keeping her gaze focused straight ahead. She wouldn't look back.

Not anymore.

GAVIN SAT IN THE KITCHEN AND STARED AT ELIZABETH'S cup of coffee, now cold. He should toss it in the dishwasher, but he couldn't seem to move.

How had he colossally fucked that up? Again. Twice now he'd hurt her.

Christ. He'd always been so good with women, could charm them, smooth talk them, convince them of anything he wanted.

And with the one woman he needed to be smooth with, he was like a tongue-tied teenager incapable of uttering a simple syllable, let alone get his point across. He hadn't been able to tell her how he felt. He'd swung and missed.

What the hell was wrong with him? How hard was it to say he was sorry? How fucking difficult was it to tell a woman he loved her? It should have been so simple. He had the words in his head, and he couldn't get them out. The most important conversation of his life and he'd struck out.

No, he hadn't just struck out.

It was bottom of the ninth, bases loaded, and he was up to bat.

Facing down Elizabeth had been bigger than the World Series.

And he'd just lost the game. The biggest game of his life.

He'd lost the woman he loved.

Game over.

TWENTY-FOUR

"YOU GOING TO SIT AROUND MOPING ABOUT THIS FOR-ever, or are you going to do something about it?"

Gavin knew he should have stayed home today instead of going to his parents' to see his dad. He'd had a week out of town where he'd blissfully drowned his sorrows in baseball and at the bar. He'd sucked at his game, which hadn't helped his mood any, and the bar hadn't offered any answers, either. Neither had the women who'd tried to approach him. He wasn't interested in any of them, because they weren't beautiful redheads with emerald green eyes and chal-lenging attitudes.

Now he was home, and home reminded him of Lizzie, too. So he'd gone to his parents, figuring he could do some fix-it work for his dad. He visited with his father, who hadn't said anything about Elizabeth. His mother, on the other hand . . .

"Nothing to do about it, Mom. It's over. I tried to talk to her and only succeeded in screwing things up again."

She stood in the kitchen chopping vegetables but paused to offer him a not-so-sympathetic look. "I've never known you to be a quitter, Gavin."

"And you only get so many strikes before you're out."

She waved the paring knife at him. "Don't try that baseball analogy on me, mister. Elizabeth isn't a bat that you can swing, try three times, and go sit down when you don't get a hit. She's a woman you claim to love. You get out there and keep trying until you get her back."

"You make it sound so easy."

"It's not easy. It's hard. Love is hard, just like baseball. You think it should come easy to you just like all the other women in your life since you became famous."

He laughed. "I'm hardly famous, Mom."

"You're not a nobody, either. And you need to admit that you're well known, especially around here. It's not like you've had to go trolling for women since you went to the major leagues."

His mom had said "trolling for women." Jeez. "Okay, I admit women have been pretty available."

"Exactly my point. And then you hook up with Elizabeth, and suddenly it's not so easy. You have to work at the relationship."

"No, she's definitely not easy. In fact she's been a giant rockin' pain in my ass since we first got together."

She continued to slice carrots. "Yeah, and you're a real walk in the park."

"Hey."

She laid the knife down and looked at him. "Well, let's just take it from her side. She's your agent, and she's been in love with you for years, but at the same time she has to see you on the arm of these bimbos year after year and not say anything. Then suddenly you show interest in her, and she probably thinks she's just going to be another notch on your bedpost. How's she supposed to react to that? A little standoffish, I imagine."

Gavin frowned. "Wait. What? She's been in love with me for years? Where did that come from?"

His mother rolled her eyes. "Men are so dense sometimes. I guess I wasn't supposed to say anything about that, but yes, Gavin, Elizabeth has been in love with you for many years. She just never said anything to you about it because of your professional relationship."

"I didn't know."

"Of course you didn't, because she didn't intend to ever do anything about it."

Until that night in Florida when he made the first move. And everything changed between them. And before then. He remembered the night Mick fired her. That kiss that had knocked him out of his shoes. And the look in her eyes that had made him wonder what the hell was going on. No wonder she was so reluctant, and so willing to keep things light and easy between them.

She hadn't wanted him to know. And she'd been scared.

"I never knew, Mom. Why didn't she tell me?"

"Because she was guarding her heart against you, because you could hurt her."

Aw, hell. "And that's exactly what I did."

"Yes, you did. The question is, are you going to give up on her now, or are you going to fight for her?"

ELIZABETH BURIED HERSELF IN HER WORK. HAVING two new clients helped with that. There were contractual issues to go over, and she'd met with them to discuss their current team contracts and their career goals, which meant more travel. While she was on the road, she'd also stopped in at a few of the games of her other clients to meet with them and give them a little attention.

Getting out of town again had been the best thing for her. She'd needed to clear her head.

Now that she was back she intended to concentrate on her client portfolio and give all her clients her attention. She'd given one client too much of her time for too long.

That was over and done with. Time to focus on her career, on what she loved, on the one thing that fulfilled her and loved her back.

Besides, with her assistant on vacation for two weeks, she was utterly swamped.

Perfect. It would give her a chance to clean up and reorganize her office, something she desperately needed to do.

She was on the floor, her head buried in a box of files when her door opened.

"That had better be either my lunch or more boxes."

"Neither, sorry."

She whipped around to see Mick standing in her doorway.

She stood, wiped her hands down her skirt, not at all mentally armed for this battle. "Look, I've stayed away. What the hell more could you possibly want from me?"

"Is it okay if I come in?"

Wary, she motioned with her hand. He walked in and shut the door.

"Your receptionist sent me back. She seemed to be in a hurry to head out to lunch."

Damn Felicia and her crazy diets. Hunger made her stupid.

"You're here. Might as well sit down. Do you want some water?"

"That would be good, thanks."

He was being polite. That was new. She fixed him and herself a glass, handed his to him, and took a seat behind her desk. Her spacious office suddenly seemed too small as she waited for him to say whatever it was he came to say. Finally, she tired of the suspense.

"Why are you here, Mick?"

"To apologize for being so hard on you. I've never been one to carry a grudge, and for some reason with you I have been." He stood, dragged his fingers through his hair. "I've never been in love before. It's made me a little crazy and overprotective of Tara and Nathan. And what you did really set me off."

"I—"

He held up his hand. "Let me finish, please."

"Okay."

"What you did hurt them. And I know you realized it and you fixed it. You apologized over and over again, and made peace with both of them. You're even friends with Tara now. But I couldn't let it go. For some reason I just couldn't let it go. I kept on punishing you. And when you and Gavin got together, I didn't want that to happen. I wanted you out of my life, out of Tara and Nathan's lives, too. Seeing how happy Gavin was with you made me think we might never get away from you. It also made me think I made a mistake firing you."

She had no idea what to say to that, so she said nothing while he paced and talked.

He stopped, turned to face her. "I hate Don Davis. I signed with him because you hated him, too. I knew he was your nemesis, that his number one goal in life was to take business away from you. I did it to get back at you, to hurt you the way you hurt the people I love. And maybe it did hurt you, but it hurt me, too. He doesn't know shit about promoting me and my career the way you did."

Wow. Just . . . wow.

"I mean, obviously, I can't have you throwing women at me anymore. Not with Tara in my life. But you really understood me and my career goals and what was important to me. And you listened. Davis doesn't listen. He doesn't know me and my family and my life like you do."

He sat in the chair and faced her. "I'm sorry, Elizabeth."

She got up and moved around the desk and sat in the chair next to his. "I'm sorry, too, Mick. Truly sorry for what I did to Tara and

Nathan. I do learn from my mistakes and try never to make them again. I've missed having you as a client and as my friend. Losing you as a client hurt me professionally. Losing your friendship hurt me on a much deeper level.

"If you'd like, I can recommend some very good agents who aren't as slimy as Don Davis, people who'll listen to you and who'll be very good for your career."

He arched a brow. "You'd do that?"

"Of course. I've always wanted what was best for you. And Tara's my friend. Your career is beneficial to her, too."

"How about I re-sign with you as soon as I can get out from under the Davis Agency?"

She leaned back in the chair. "You'd want to work with me again?"

"Yes."

"I don't know, Mick. There's a lot of history, not all of it good."

"And sometimes you have to leave the past in the past. We had a great working relationship. You get me. And your negotiation skills are the best out there."

She smiled. "They are, aren't they?"

He laughed. "That's what I like about you—your humility."

"Can't have humility in my job. Not when it counts the most."

"I signed with him for a year, told him I wanted to test the waters. When the contract's up for renewal, you and I will talk. If you're interested . . ."

"You know I will be."

He stood. "I'm sorry I've been so hard on you. And I'm sorry I came between you and Gavin."

Her smile died. "You wouldn't have come between your brother and me if he hadn't allowed it. It just wasn't meant to be. Too much conflict there."

"Is that Gavin talking, or you deciding it for him?"

She shrugged. "Doesn't really matter, does it? You heard him that day at your dad's house."

"Yeah, I did. And I was part of it, instigating it all. I can't apologize enough for it. You have every right to kick my ass forever for it."

She lifted her gaze to his. "I think there's been enough ass kicking to go around for a lifetime, don't you think?"

"Probably, but I still deserve it. Tara sure did her part when she found out. She was mad as hell at me."

Her lips lifted. "Well, that's good enough, then. You don't need me to add to it."

"Still, I feel bad. I should have butted out. What's between you and Gavin is none of my business and never should have been."

She turned away to stare out the window. "There isn't anything between us. Not anymore."

"He loves you, Liz."

"No, he doesn't."

He laid his hands on her shoulders and turned her to face him. "Yeah, he does. He's never been in love before, and loving you scared him as much as my dad's heart attack did. He didn't know how to handle it. Give him another chance."

"Thanks, but I gave him all the chances he's going to get. It's better this way."

"Now who's scared?"

Her eyes widened. "Me? I'm not scared. I'm sad. And maybe a little fed up. I gave everything and it didn't work out. He didn't love me."

"Try harder."

"What?"

"Try harder. You didn't try hard enough."

She laughed. "Please. I gave everything to Gavin. I gave him my heart, and he threw it back in my face. I don't know what more I could possibly give."

"Give him a chance. First, he's a guy. And he's never been in love before."

"Oh, and I have?"

"Yeah, but you're a woman. It's like being a female agent in this field of sports where you're surrounded by all these men. You have to work twice as hard at it to be taken seriously. But you're also twice as good as most of them."

"Well, thanks for that."

"Love's the same way. Women are so much better at it. Better at communicating what's in their hearts, better at showing the one they love how they feel. So maybe this was your first time, too, but you obviously handled it better than Gavin did. And he's fumbling it bad, and he's fucked it up, and now he doesn't know how to fix it, but he's trying. Or he wants to try. And he's afraid to fuck it up again."

She wrapped her arms around her middle. "I can't. I just . . . can't."

He nodded. "That's your call, but I hope you'll at least think about it. He's worth it, Liz. And I really do think you two are good for each other. Give him another shot."

"Thanks, Mick. For coming here, for talking to me, and for giving me another chance."

He pulled her into a hug. "You're family, Elizabeth. I'm sorry I forgot that for a while."

He left, and she fell into her desk chair, kind of stunned that Mick had been here. She thought about everything he'd said about her and about Gavin.

She was trying so hard to get over him. A plea from his brother on his behalf wasn't going to change her mind.

And she wasn't going to go to him. She'd done that too many times already.

No matter what Mick said, no matter how much her heart hurt, no matter how much she missed Gavin, she couldn't take that step.

Not this time.

She threw herself back into her office project, until her phone rang. She picked it up, surprised to hear Dedrick Coleman on the line.

"Dedrick, how are you?"

"Fine, Elizabeth, and you?"

"Great, thanks. What can I do for you?"

"You can possibly become my agent, if you're interested."

Wow. Was it going to be a good day or what? "Definitely interested. Is your contract up with your current agent?"

"Yeah. The guy is a dumb-ass. Overlooked some clauses in my last contract and tied me up with a few things that made me pretty unhappy."

"That's not good."

"I've given him his thirty days so he knows I'm looking. Can we talk?"

"Certainly. What does your schedule look like?"

"Well, you can see our game schedule if you look it up. Problem is, my grandparents are flying in on Saturday for this big anniversary party we're planning for them, and I'd like to get this settled one way or another as soon as possible. I don't want it weighing on my mind with my grandparents being here and Shawnelle breathing down my neck about it. She's already stressed enough about the party."

"I understand. My calendar is clear the next few days. You just let me know when you'd like to meet."

"We have a day game tomorrow. Can you come to the game? Shawnelle would love to see you, and we can go somewhere right after, have a chat, and hopefully get things ironed out."

"Uh, Dedrick, I assume you know I'm not seeing Gavin anymore."

"Yeah, believe me, we all know about that. He's been moping around the clubhouse ever since you dumped him."

"I didn't dump him."

"Whatever you say, honey. Look, I like you. Your shit with Gavin is between the two of you. I just want a good agent, and I think you're a good agent. But if you think there's a conflict because me and Gavin are friends . . ."

"I didn't say that. I can meet with you after the game."

"Shawnelle would be disappointed if she didn't get to see you. You aren't going to cut off your friendship with her just because of you and Gavin, are you?"

Now that he said it, it sounded petty of her. And selfish. "Of course not."

"Good. I'll leave a ticket for you at the box office, and I'll see you after the game tomorrow afternoon."

"That sounds fine, Dedrick."

"And thanks for agreeing to do this on such short notice."

"It's no problem at all. I'll see you then."

She hung up, laid her phone down, and sat in her chair. Well, hell. She was hoping to avoid the Rivers—and seeing Gavin—at least until she could get her riotous emotions under control.

No such luck. She was going to have to suck it up. No way was she passing up on the chance to pick up another new client just because she might see Gavin.

Besides, he'd be out on the field. She'd be in the stands. It was unlikely he'd even be aware she was there.

IT WAS UNSEASONABLY HOT IN THE STANDS. SHE'D much prefer to be in the owner's suite, where it was shady and air-conditioned.

Then again, there was nothing like seats behind the dugout as far as the best view. And hanging out with Shawnelle and Haley again was wonderful. She'd missed her friends, and their excitement at seeing her again made her feel warm and gooey inside.

"We were afraid you had dumped us just because you fired Gavin and broke up with him," Haley said.

Ah, nothing like the brutal honesty of youth. "I would never do that."

"You haven't been around," Hayley said.

"I've been really busy."

"Busy avoiding us and Gavin. You weren't planning on hanging out with us anymore," Shawnelle said.

"That's not true."

Even though that's exactly what she'd planned to do. Now that she was here though, she was ashamed of herself for even thinking it. So what if she and Gavin weren't together anymore? That didn't mean she couldn't have spa days with Shawnelle and Haley or have lunch with them or even go out for drinks and dinner once in a while.

She'd gone her whole life without girlfriends. And then she'd found a few in Shawnelle, Haley, and even Jenna. She didn't intend to close herself off just because all of these women were in some way connected to Gavin.

She'd have to deal with it. And so would he.

It was nice to be at a Rivers game again. This was her home team since she'd moved to Saint Louis ten years ago, and she wasn't going to pretend otherwise. Of course as an agent, she wasn't supposed to have an allegiance to any professional team since she represented so many players from so many different teams.

But no one had to know the Rivers were her favorites, did they?

She ate a hot dog, had a soda, and enjoyed catching up with Haley and Shawnelle.

"Where are the kids, Shawnelle? I thought they'd be at the game today."

"They came to the last day game, but they're at the pool with my mom and dad today, while Dedrick's parents get the house ready for his grandparents arrival. It's one big coordinated effort for their sixty-fifth wedding anniversary."

"Awww, that's sweet. And how nice of you to throw a party."

"Dedrick loves his Gamaw and Paw-Paw. They were instrumental in helping him go to college, so he feels like he owes them. And they're just so damn proud of him."

"It's nice to have that kind of family support, isn't it?"

"Yes, it is."

"And how about you, Haley? How have you been?"

"Great. Enrolled in school for the summer semester, and excited as hell about taking classes."

"Good for you. Settled on a degree program yet?"

Haley grinned. "I want to teach. Elementary education."

Elizabeth reached for Haley's hand and squeezed it. "I can so see you as a teacher. That's wonderful."

Shawnelle nodded. "I told her she'd make a great teacher. She's incredible with my two kids. She has more patience than I do."

Haley laughed. "It's always easy when they're not your kids. You don't have to keep 'em. But I do love children. Always have."

Shawnelle nudged her. "Ready to have one of your own?"

"Nope. Not 'til I finish school. I'm still too young. Not ready to settle down and have a family yet. I have goals."

"And maybe you also want to stick it to your family and home town?" Elizabeth suggested.

Haley arched a brow. "Maybe just a little."

"Ahh, there's nothing like a little vengeance to stir the juices of motivation," Shawnelle said.

Elizabeth laughed. She knew all about that. Her family might never know what she'd amounted to, but she knew, and that's all that mattered.

As the game got under way and the Rivers took the field, Elizabeth's gaze was riveted to Gavin. She swore she wasn't going to pay attention to him, but how could she not when she loved him?

As he stretched out to catch practice balls at first base, she sighed. She knew every inch of that man's body, and it was absolute perfection. His uniform clung tight to his muscular thighs and stellar ass, and his biceps bulged out underneath his shirt as he pulled the ball from his glove and threw it to second base.

Shawnelle smoothed her hand over Elizabeth's back. "You miss him."

She nodded. "I do."

"Then fight for him."

She shook her head. "I tried. It's over."

"Who walked out, you or him?"

"I did."

"Has he been trying to contact you?"

"Yes."

"And you won't let him."

"No."

"Then bullshit. If you still have this much feeling—and I know you do because there are tears you're trying not to shed—then it's not over yet. Whatever it is that he fucked up, and God knows men fuck things up all the time, give it another try. If he hasn't given up, then why have you? It's obvious you love him, honey."

Tears blurred her vision, and she blinked, swiping at the ones that broke free. "It's complicated."

Shawnelle laughed. "Honey, love is always complicated. If it was easy, there'd be no fun when you win at the end."

"What Shawnelle says is true, Elizabeth," Hayley added. "There are so many pressures on a relationship sometimes. Often it's outside stuff that has nothin' to do with the two of you that gets thrown into the mix and can muck things up. Wade through it all, and focus on what's important. If you love him and he loves you, isn't that what's really important? The rest of it's just fluff."

Elizabeth inhaled a shaky breath, feeling as if she were balancing on a high wire with no net underneath her.

Maybe she was being too stubborn, or too afraid. Maybe she should talk to Gavin and figure out if there was anything between the two of them. Maybe he was afraid, too. He'd come to her, had tried to talk to her, and had apologized. She hadn't given him much of a chance. She'd decided his apology wasn't good enough, had cut him off and walked out. That had been her fear and her anger preventing communication. So maybe she owed him—owed them both—another shot at this.

"Thanks, both of you. I'll give it some thought."

Shawnelle smiled and squeezed her hand. "That's good enough. Now dry your tears, and let's root these boys on to a win."

Elizabeth did exactly as Shawnelle suggested. She shoved Gavin to the back of her mind and focused on the Rivers. By the seventh-inning stretch the Rivers were up by three runs, and Elizabeth was relaxed and into the game.

"Ladies and gentlemen, we have a very special announcement. One of our Rivers players has asked that instead of singing 'Take Me Out to the Ballgame' during the seventh-inning stretch tonight, he be allowed to take the mic and ask a question."

The crowd went silent. Elizabeth frowned and turned to Shawnelle and Haley. "What's going on?"

Shawnelle shrugged. "No clue."

Haley shook her head.

"Would Elizabeth Darnell please stand up?"

Oh, shit.

Shawnelle elbowed her. "Stand up."

She shook her head. "No."

"Go on, stand up."

She shook her head again. Vehemently.

Shawnelle and Haley both shoved her, then the people around her started clapping and yelling and pointing her out. She had no choice. She stood, and suddenly her face was beamed up on the giant JumboTron screen.

Oh, hell.

Then Gavin climbed up on top of the dugout, much to the raucous delight of the fans. He waved his hands down and the cheers subsided.

He found her in the stands and turned his attention on her.

"Elizabeth, you know the last time we talked things didn't go so well."

Good God, he had the mic in his hands, and everyone could hear what he said.

"And that was my fault. This time I hope I can be a little more eloquent."

He wasn't playing to the crowds. He was looking right at her. He came down off the top of the dugout and Shawnelle pushed her. She went to him and met him in the aisle.

He took her hand, and when she saw him swallow, she knew he was as nervous as she was. That gave her comfort.

"Elizabeth, I love you. I've loved you for a while now, but I was afraid to say it. Maybe I was afraid you wouldn't love me back. But I'm not afraid anymore, and I need you to understand that. So I figured the only way to get you to believe me was to tell you in front of forty-five thousand people."

And then he got down on one knee.

Oh. My. God.

Her legs were shaking.

"Marry me, Elizabeth."

The chorus of awws and cheers was deafening.

But she only saw Gavin, only focused on Gavin. She saw the truth in his eyes. She saw the love.

This time, she believed.

She burst into tears and threw herself into his arms.

And then he kissed her. And oh, what a kiss. Her heart swelled with so much love she couldn't believe it was real. Her fantasy, what she'd always wanted. The man she'd always wanted.

The cheers and clapping of the fans told her it was real.

He broke the kiss and swiped the tears from her cheeks. "Sorry, we'll have to wait 'til later to continue this."

She laughed. "Go win the game."

"So does this mean you said yes?"

She took the mic from his hand. "I said yes."

More cheers, and Gavin climbed back down to the dugout.

The rest of the game was a blur. The Rivers won. Even more shocking was seeing Kathleen and Jimmy Riley, Jenna, and Mick and Tara after the game. They had just been a few rows over. Gavin had told them his plans, and after he'd gone back to the dugout, they'd surprised her. She flew into Kathleen's arms for a hug.

Even Mick hugged her and welcomed his new sister into the family.

"What if I'd said no?" she asked Kathleen.

Kathleen gave her that all knowing look. "You weren't going to say no. You love my son, and I had every confidence he wasn't going to screw this up."

She looked to Mick. "So, you think we can put up with each other?"

"Hey, if I can put up with Jenna, I can put up with you."

Jenna elbowed him in the ribs. "Jerk."

Tara was thrilled for her. "We've come a long way, haven't we?"

Elizabeth hugged her. "You're the most forgiving of all, and I'm so grateful. I need family and sisters." She hooked her arms with both Tara and Jenna. "I'm going to have sisters now. I've always wanted them."

Jenna gave her a wry grin. "Be careful what you wish for."

Elizabeth laughed.

After she said good-bye to the Riley family, she and Shawnelle and Haley headed down to the team locker room to wait for their guys.

Shawnelle told her Dedrick really did want to change agents, but it could wait. They'd been in on Gavin's proposal, and it was Dedrick who came up with the idea to use his interest in changing agents to get Elizabeth there tonight.

"You are such a sneaky bitch," she said.

Shawnelle just waggled her brows. "All in the name of love. And speaking of love . . ."

The door opened and Gavin walked out. The rest of the world ceased to exist as she walked into his arms and was greeted with a kiss that rocked her world.

"Uh-huh. I think we'll leave these two alone, Haley. I'm going to go find my man."

"Me, too," Haley said.

"Talk to you tomorrow, girl," Shawnelle said.

Elizabeth waved them off, her lips and her mind and her heart focused only on Gavin.

TWENTY-FIVE

SOMEHOW, GAVIN HAD GOTTEN IT RIGHT. HE'D MAN-
aged not to strike out when he'd gone up to bat in the most important game of his life.

Now he stood outside the locker room with his lips locked with
the woman he loved.

He'd won the girl.

Elizabeth slid her fingers into his hair and curled her body
against his. God, it felt like it had been months since he'd touched
her, since he'd breathed in the sweet honeyed scent of her, since he'd
been inside her.

They stood in a hallway outside the locker room in a baseball
stadium, and he was getting a hard-on.

Not good. Not good at all.

He broke the kiss and stared into her eyes, still not believing that
he'd been forgiven for all he'd fucked up, that she'd said yes. He still
felt like he had so much to make up for.

Time. He needed lots of time.

"We have to get out of here. I need to get you alone."

Her lips lifted. "That's a very good idea."

"Follow me home?"

She nodded. "Try not to break any speed limits, but hurry."

HE STAYED AT OR JUST ABOVE THE SPEED LIMIT THE entire way to his house, glancing in his rearview mirror every few seconds to make sure Elizabeth was right behind him. He kept expecting her to ditch him, that maybe he'd dreamed everything that had happened today.

They pulled into the driveway together and got out of their cars, and he linked his fingers with hers as they strolled up to the front door. He held it open for her, his heart pounding the entire time.

"Your hand is sweaty," Elizabeth said after they stepped inside and he closed the door.

"I'm nervous."

She arched a brow. "Why?"

"I keep waiting for you to bolt. I keep thinking this isn't real."

She turned to him, wrapped her arms around his neck. "I'm not leaving you, Gavin. Not now, not ever."

He laid his hands on her hips. "I messed up bad. There were so many things I wanted to say to you today, to make you understand how sorry I am for what I said. But there isn't a decent excuse for hurting you the way I did."

She pressed a finger to his lips. "And sometimes you just have to let it go. We could rehash everything we've both said to each other during our relationship, the stupid things we've said and done, but what would be the point? Every step we've taken led us here, right?"

"Yes."

"Do you love me, Gavin?"

"I do."

"I love you, too. I've loved you for so many years, and I was afraid to tell you. I was afraid if I let you know how I felt about you, I'd lose you."

"Why?"

She dropped her hands and stepped back. "I don't know. The fact that I was your agent, that I'm a few years older than you, that you went through women as fast as you went through underwear."

"Hey."

She laughed. "It's true, isn't it?"

"I played the field a little."

She cocked a brow. "A little? Gavin, you were all over women all the time. And that's fine. It was good for your image and good PR. I played it up as much as possible."

He stepped up to her, smoothed his hand over her hair. "And you loved me. Didn't it hurt you?"

She shrugged. "A little. But I did my job. I did what was best for you."

He inhaled, blew it out, took her hand, and led her to the sofa. She sat, and he kneeled in front of her. "I'm sorry I never knew, never picked up on it. What kind of man does that make me?"

"It makes me a very good agent who made sure you never knew."

He didn't smile. He lifted her hand. "I'll spend the rest of my life making it up to you."

"Not necessary. I have you now. It's all that matters."

"I really don't deserve you."

"Yes, Gavin, you do. As much as I deserve you. We belong together."

He lifted up and brushed his lips against hers, feeling like the luckiest man alive. His heart swelled with so much love his chest felt like bursting.

This was what love felt like. This feeling of joy, of knowing you'd never be alone again, never feel like something was missing from your life; the feeling that you now had someone to protect, to keep safe from harm.

He got it now; he understood where his brother was coming from.

He'd die to protect Elizabeth.

He pulled a box out of his pocket. "This part I didn't want to do at the stadium. I wanted it just to be the two of us."

ELIZABETH STARED AT THE BLACK VELVET BOX.

She hadn't expected this. She raised her hand to her heart, then looked at Gavin.

"Oh."

He opened the box and inside was a princess-cut diamond in a platinum setting. And wow. The diamond was huge, the band covered in tiny sparkling diamonds, too.

It was perfect. Gorgeous and everything she could have dreamed of.

"Oh, Gavin. It's the most beautiful thing I've ever seen."

He held her hand. "Elizabeth Darnell, I love you. I don't care how old you are or how old I am. I want you to be my wife. I want to have babies with you if you want them, too. I want you to continue to love your career as much as I love mine. I want us to love and respect each other forever. Will you marry me?"

This time she didn't try to fight the tears. She let them flow down her cheeks and nodded enthusiastically. "Yes, Gavin. I love you, too. And I'd be honored to marry you."

He slid the ring on her finger and pulled her off the sofa and into his arms. On her knees, she met his lips with equal passion. Her carefully coiffed updo was gone in an instant as he pulled the pins from her hair and shook it out, his hands diving into the strands as he fell onto his back on the floor and pulled her on top of him.

God, it felt good to feel his body against hers again. She'd missed his touch, the way his hands glided over her back and to her hips, the way he dug his fingers into her as if he couldn't seem to get enough of her.

She'd missed his passion, his almost desperate need for her, because she always needed him. Would it always be like this between them? She hoped so.

She lifted, stared down at him, smoothed his hair away from his brow, and listened to his heavy breathing, felt his heartbeat jamming away against her chest.

He tilted his head and smiled up at her. "What?"

"I was just wondering if it would always be like this between us. This hunger we seem to have for each other."

He cupped her face and brought it down to meet his. "Hell, yes."

He kissed her with such deep longing that she had no doubt he was right. Her heart melted, and so did her panties as he lifted against her, his erection driving against her sex. She planted her hands on his chest and surged against him, the need so powerful to have him inside her she quaked with it.

He broke the kiss, and she was breathless, especially when she saw the passion in his eyes. She sat up and began to unbutton her blouse, her fingers shaking. Gavin watched her undo each button, and try as she might to be slow and sexy, all she could do was fumble it.

Maybe him lifting and teasing her with his hard cock had something to do with it.

"You're distracting me."

He cocked a brow. "Hurry up."

"Trying."

She let her blouse slip from her shoulders. His hands were on her breasts in an instant, his thumbs sliding over the swells, then her nipples. The silk of her bra was no defense, and her nipples hardened as he swept his fingers over her bra.

He sat up and undid the clasp, and she shrugged the bra off. He pulled her forward and caught one aching bud between his lips, suckling her and driving her mad with his tongue, teeth and lips while using his hand to roll the other nipple between his fingers. She tangled her fingers in his hair and tried to hold on through the myriad of sensations shooting pleasure sparks straight to her core.

This wasn't happening fast enough. She pulled away and scooted down his thighs, reaching for the button of his jeans. He leaned back on his palms and let her unzip him, her knuckles brushing his erection, causing him to jerk against her in response.

Yes, he was as primed as she was. And she wanted him in so many ways, all at once. She pulled his jeans and shoes off and got them out of the way, then dragged his boxers down, too.

His cock sprang up, hot and hard and delicious. She circled it with her hands, loving the soft, steely feel of it, the way the skin moved around the erect muscle, the engorged head just begging for a taste. She bent over the shaft and put her lips over the wide purple crest and swept her tongue over it, loving the way Gavin thrust against her mouth and groaned, then grabbed a handful of her hair as if he couldn't control his reaction.

She wanted him out of control, wanted to see how far she could push him.

"I haven't come since the last time we were together, Lizzie. If you're going to suck me, I'm going to come in your mouth."

She lifted her gaze to him, then took his cock all the way in her mouth. He thrust, giving her more. She took it, wrapping her hand around the base of his cock, stroking him as she wound her tongue around his shaft, dragging her tongue down the underside and licking him all the way down to his balls. She took them into her mouth and flicked her tongue over them. Gavin let out a guttural groan.

She swept her tongue up his shaft again, then took it between her lips.

"Suck it. Suck it hard." She pressed his cock between her tongue and the roof of her mouth, and gave him the suction he asked for, cradling his balls in her hands and massaging them.

He tightened his hold on her hair. "Yes. God, yes. That's going to make me come, Lizzie."

She bobbed up and down on his shaft, her hands on his thighs, feeling his muscles tighten, feeling the sheen of perspiration coating his skin as he thrust upward into her throat.

"Yeah, like that. Suck me. I'm coming."

She loved listening to him, loved knowing she could give him this pleasure. And when he let out a wild groan, his whole body jerking as he jettisoned into her mouth, she swallowed, gripping his thighs and taking all he had to give her.

He smoothed his hand in her hair, and she licked his shaft, then moved up to kiss his belly. She rolled his shirt in her hand as she kissed up his abdomen, loving the rock-hard feel of him. He lifted and allowed her to pull his shirt off, then surprised her by rolling her over onto her back and laying a deep, penetrating kiss on her that left her breathless. He plundered her mouth, licked against her tongue, rubbed his lips against hers until she was mindless and her bones felt like butter.

"Now it's my turn," he said, kissing his way across her neck, her collarbone, and when he got to her breasts, he licked her nipples, taking his time to enjoy both until each peak stood hard, wet, and aching. Her body vibrated from his touch and his kisses as he moved down her body, dragging her Capris down until all she wore were her panties.

"These are pretty," he said, kissing her hip bone where one of the ties of her cream silk panties lay.

"Thanks."

"It's like a present for me." He untied one of the bows, kissing her next to her sex, then went to the other tie and undid the bow, pulling the material free and baring her sex to him.

She shuddered. "Gavin, I haven't come either since the last time we were together."

He lifted his gaze to her. "I'm going to fix that right now."

He pressed his mouth to her pussy and laid his tongue on her.

"Oh," was all she could manage, because he moved his tongue across her clit and any coherent thought was gone. Now she was merely a center of pleasure, focused on everything Gavin's hot, wet tongue did to her as he glided across her sex.

Tension built in a hurry, and as he slipped a finger inside her, she quivered and knew she wasn't going to last long. It was amazing the way he knew her body so well and could take her right to the edge in minutes. He pumped his finger in and out of her and moved his tongue in a slow circle over her clit. The sensation was like a lazy Sunday afternoon; her reaction anything but.

"Harder. Faster. Take me there, Gavin."

He listened, inserted another finger inside her, pumped up the tempo, put his lips around her clit, and sucked.

"Yes. That's it." She arched against him and came, the torrent of sensation almost unbearable because it was just so damn good. She thrashed against him, and he placed a hand on her belly to hold her in place as he continued to lick her while she climaxed on his face and his fingers, rolling from one orgasm right into another in an endless stream of pulses that left her weak and shaking.

And when he hovered over her, smiling down at her, she reached for him, and he covered her with his body and his lips, rolling them over again while he was kissing her, placing her on top once again.

His cock was hard, and she slipped it inside her still-pulsing pussy, then sat up, linking her fingers with his as she surged against him, burying him fully inside her.

His gaze narrowed, and he lifted against her. "Ride me."

She placed her hands on his chest and leaned forward, then lifted, setting the pace as she fucked herself on his cock, drawing out each movement for maximum sensation, loving the feel of his cock thickening inside her.

Gavin reached up and grasped her breasts, sliding his thumbs over her nipples. She arched into his hands, filling them with her breasts. He rose up and took alternating nipples in his mouth, sucking them deeply, making her shudder at the shock of pleasure that shot straight to her pussy.

Connected to him like this was a slice of pure heaven. She wanted it to go on forever, but as she rode him, rocked against him, and felt the stirrings of orgasm once again, she couldn't help but drive toward that finish, only to back off, to pull away, and pause just to look at him. She tried to memorize his face, the way he looked when he was buried inside her. His muscles tightened and strained as he clenched his jaw, his heavily lidded gaze seemed so intently focused on her, yet he held her gently in his grasp. His fingers flexed and unflexed against her hips as she surged forward and then back. His hair had fallen over his forehead, and she brushed it away, then leaned down to press a kiss to his lips.

She'd only meant to brush his lips, but, oh, how she loved his mouth, and the way he kissed her so deeply, the same way he was buried so deeply inside her, physically as well as emotionally. He was part of her and always would be. Making love like this sealed the deal.

She lifted, her face only inches from his as she slid down on his cock once again, so close to orgasm she had to fight to keep from coming.

"I love you, Gavin."

His jaw clenched; he swept her hair from her face, brushed his thumb over her cheek. He rolled her over, then plunged deep inside her. She cried out with her climax, and as she was coming, he looked at her and said, "I love you, Elizabeth."

As he came, he groaned and called out her name, his fingers tightly wound with hers.

Her eyes filled with tears, and she realized she would never forget this moment.

After, they stayed tangled together, their legs entwined. She didn't want to move, and Gavin didn't seem to be in any hurry, either.

"Will you move into Castle Grayskull with me?"

She laughed at the use of her insult for his house. "Yes. Will you let me redecorate it?"

"Any way you want to."

She lifted and laid her chin on his chest. "You trust me?"

"Of course I trust you." He frowned. "You aren't going to do any rooms in pink, are you?"

"Ugh. Are you kidding me? Maybe the baby's room, if we have a girl."

His eyes widened. "Are you pregnant?"

She laughed. "Not yet, but I imagine with a concerted effort you could get me that way. I'm not getting any younger, you know. We should get started on that as soon as possible."

He rolled over and got on top of her. "I'm ready if you are."

She looked up at this man she loved and realized that though she had never thought she would have a perfect life, somehow, some way, she'd gotten everything she ever wanted. She'd worked so hard to have the career she'd always wanted. And for a while that had been enough for her. She never thought she was going to fall in love.

But she'd been wrong.

She'd hit a home run. Together, they'd pitched the perfect game of love.

She giggled at the baseball metaphors.

"What are you laughing at?" he asked.

"We won."

He looked at her. "Won what?"

"The game of love."

He rolled his eyes. "That was lame."

"Wasn't it? Come on, get up," she said, climbing off the sofa and smacking him on the butt.

He cocked a brow. "What? Why?"

"We have to go to the grocery store."

"Again, why?"

"Because it's time I baked you a pie."

He laughed and rolled off the sofa. "That's worth getting up for. Let's go."

JENNA RILEY HATED SPORTS.

Which was ironic, considering she owned and operated her family's sports bar. Doubly ironic, considering one brother was an NFL quarterback and the other brother was a Major League Baseball player. And triply ironic, considering her entire family loved sports of all kinds.

Personally, she was fed up with sports, having grown up with them shoved down her throat her entire life. And now she lived with it twenty-four hours a day, hearing about it every damn night at work. The bar was constantly filled with nothing but sports, from football to baseball to hockey to basketball to racing and everything in between.

She was in the wrong line of work. She should quit her job and be a roadie for a rock band. She snickered at the thought. Like she could ever be free from the chains of familial responsibility. Ever since her father semi-retired from the bar, Riley's had become her responsibility, which meant, like it or not, sports had become her life. Big-screen televisions broadcast every sporting event, blaring out the excited voices of obnoxious announcers calling plays right behind her, in front of her, and to the side of her. Excited fans filled the bar after every game, so not only did she have to listen to the games on television, she also had to hear the patrons' recaps after the game.

And if that wasn't bad enough, there were the sports networks rehashing player stats and player drafts and all the game replays with analyst commentary.

For someone who hated sports, she had a head full of statistics on every player who had ever played any sport.

Which meant every patron at Riley's loved her.

"Hey, Jenna."

She glanced up from wiping down the bar. Steve Mahoney, one of her regulars, signaled for another beer. She grabbed a bottle, popped off the top and slid it over to him, then added it to his tab.

"You see the game tonight?"

She smiled and nodded. "Of course." As if she had a choice.

"Two goals for Anderson. The Ice scored a winner by picking him up last year, didn't they?"

"Yeah, he's great."

Dick Mayhew got into the action, sliding onto an available barstool someone had vacated. He lifted one finger and Jenna grabbed a beer for him.

"He and Boudreaux make a hell of a team at center," Dick said. "I think they're unbeatable."

Steve nodded. "I think we have a serious shot at the cup this year. What do you think, Jenna?"

Jenna thought she'd like to extricate herself from this conversation and go refill some of her customers' drinks down at the other end of the bar. Instead, she did what she always did when talk of sports came up. She grinned and leaned her elbows against the bar and did her best PR. "I think you're right. Anderson is quick on his skates and he's magic with his shots. It's like he knows right where to put them. I've never seen anyone who can shoot a puck like he can. And we already know Boudreaux is a proven winner at center. That's why the Ice have held on to him as long as they have. Together they make a hell of a duo. Their combined stats on goals are off the charts."

"Not to mention power plays. When one is down, the other picks up the slack," Steve said, and he and Dick launched into their own conversation, which freed Jenna up to grab a few drinks for her other customers and see to the bar orders from the waitresses who served the clients sittings at tables throughout Riley's.

Rileys always got packed after a game, which meant Jenna lost all track of time. She'd been here since before noon and it was now midnight. Her feet hurt, she smelled like food and alcohol and she was ready to go home, fall into bed, and sleep for twenty-four hours.

Too bad she had to be here tomorrow and start all over again.

It was midweek. Maybe people would start clearing out soon. After all, it was a work night.

But the sounds of raucous cheers made her cringe. She took a quick glance at the door and her worst fears were realized when she saw a half dozen of the St. Louis Ice players stroll through the front door.

Crap. Now no one would leave until closing time, which meant almost three more hours for her and her team. And the players were probably hungry. She headed into the kitchen.

"Players just walked in," she said to Malcolm, her head cook.

Malcolm, who had the patience of a saint and always took things in stride, just nodded. "I'll get out the steaks."

She laughed, shook her head and went back to the bar, refilled a few drinks, and decided to let her waitresses handle the players.

She'd go over there and say hello when she had a free minute. Right now she was slammed filling drink orders. Something about players coming in made everyone thirsty.

It was good for business, though. She loved having the players frequent Riley's. She had Mick and Gavin—and Elizabeth—to thank for that.

"You look busy."

She lifted her head and stared into the steel gray eyes of Tyler Anderson. He wore his raven hair a little long and shaggy, just the way she liked . . .

No. She did not like this guy. He was a jock, a hockey player, and she most definitely did not like sports players. Especially not Ty.

"Yeah, Ty. I'm a little busy here. What can I do for you?"

"Thought you could use some help. Why don't you have two bartenders?"

"Because I can handle it by myself. Is Lydia taking care of your table?"

"She is. We're fine. Steaks are ordered."

She planted her palms against the side of the bar, sucking in a quick breath. "Then what do you need?"

He came around the open end of the bar. "Nothing. I came here to help you."

Her eyes widened. "Get out of here. You can't be back here."

"Sure I can. You need help."

"No, I don't." She shoved at him, but she might as well be trying to move a car. "Go away."

The crowd thickened around the bar as soon as Ty made himself at home back there. He filled drink orders while Jenna stared dumbfounded. He popped the tops of bottles of beer like a pro, poured hard liquor, fixed mixed drinks, and operated like he knew what the hell he was doing behind a bar, then took the customer's money or credit cards and handled her cash register, too.

What. The. Hell?

He slid a glance her way. "You have customers at the other end of the bar."

She finally gave up and took care of her patrons while Ty drummed up more business.

"Hey, Ty, your steak is ready," Malcolm said a half hour later.

"Just leave it behind the bar. I'll eat it here."

"You got it."

Jenna rolled her eyes and watched as Ty ate his steak standing up while he visited with the guys at the bar, then went back to serving drinks.

By two thirty she called for last round and everyone began to leave. Jenna started cleaning up while the last of her patrons made their way out the door. She called taxis for those who needed them, helped the waitresses bus tables, and cleared her bar registers.

She let the waitresses go, locked the front door and headed into the kitchen to find Malcolm and Ty chatting. The kitchen had been cleaned up, the other cooks and the busboys had left, and only Malcolm remained, with Ty—the two of them talking about football.

"What are you still doing here?" she asked.

"Sorry. Got involved talking postseason with Malcolm."

"Who is now leaving," Malcolm said with a yawn. "Want me to walk you out, Jenna?"

"No, thanks. I've got a few things left to do."

Malcolm narrowed his dark brown eyes on her. "Go home. Don't stay here all night doing paperwork."

She laughed. "I don't intend to."

She locked the door behind him, then turned to tell Tyler to go, but he wasn't in the kitchen. She found him in the bar pouring a whiskey.

"Hey. Last call was an hour ago."

He didn't look concerned as he smiled at her, tipped the glass to his lips, and downed the drink in one swallow, then put money on the top of the bar. She grabbed the money and slipped it into her pocket.

"Pocketing the profits, I see."

"No, smart-ass. I already closed out the register. I'll add it in tomorrow."

He shook his head and leaned against the bar. "This is how you talk to your customers?"

"You stopped being a customer when you came behind my bar and served up drinks."

"You needed help."

"No, I didn't."

He folded his arms. "Are you always this bitchy, or just to me?"

"Just to you. Now get your ass out of here so I can finish closing up."

He didn't seem insulted, just smiled instead, showing off perfectly straight white teeth. Weren't hockey players supposed to be missing a bunch of teeth because of all their fights on the ice? Why did he have to be so gorgeous? The damn man made her panties wet and had a habit of showing up here fairly regularly, which did make her bitchy because he hit all her hot buttons and she hadn't had sex in a really long time.

She needed to get laid soon. Real soon. By someone who didn't play sports.

She hit the master light switch, bathing the bar in darkness.

"Scared of the dark?"

She jumped, not realizing he was right behind her until she felt his hot breath on the back of her neck. His body was warm and she'd turned the heat down so now she was freezing. She bent down to grab her purse and sweater, brushing her butt against his crotch. He felt solid. Hard. Yummy.

Damn. She straightened, her eyes adjusting to the lack of light.

"No."

"No, what?"

"I'm not afraid of the dark."

He turned her around to face him. The light from the full moon cast him in grayish shadow. She could see his face, though, as he cocked a grin. "Too bad."

"Why?"

"Then you might have to lean on me to protect you?"

She took a step back. "Why the hard-core press here, Ty?"

"Come on, Jenna. You're not a kid. You know why. I've been coming to the bar a lot, hanging around. I like you."

"I don't like you."

He laughed. "Liar. I see the way you look at me."

"You are so full of yourself, Anderson. Go pick up another girl. I'm not the least bit interested in you." She brushed past him and headed to the door, waiting for him to meet her there so she could set the alarm.

He did, his coat in hand. She had her fingers on the keypad ready to turn the alarm on.

"Wait a second," he said.

"Did you forget something?"

"Yeah." He hauled her into his arms before she could take her next breath, and his mouth came down on hers.

For a fraction of a second she thought about objecting and pushing him away, but hell, it had been a really long time since she'd been kissed. It was January, cold as the polar ice cap outside, and Ty's lips were warm. His body was hot and as he folded her against him, she felt that heat seep into her.

She dropped her purse and coat and went with it, letting his lips claim hers.

It was just as she'd imagined it would be, and okay, she'd thought about this a lot. His mouth was firm and demanding, a hint of whiskey on his lips. He didn't kiss like a sissy, thank God; wasn't hesitant at all. He just took the kiss, sliding his tongue inside her mouth to wrap around hers.

She tingled all over, her toes curled, her panties got wet, and her sex pulsed with a roaring need to be fucked. If he put his hands down her pants, in two or three strokes she could come. The kiss was that good.

He reached up and cupped her breast and she moaned against his lips, pressing her breast into his hand. She wanted more, wanted it all, and wanted it right now. Her mind was filled with images of him lowering her to the floor in the back of the bar, or bending her over the pool table.

But that would be going against everything she wanted. And didn't want.

She wasn't going to let him have it. Not this guy. Not ever this guy. She pressed her hands to his chest and broke the kiss.

"Stop. We can't do this."

He stepped back, his eyes dark with passion.

"Why not?"

She fought for breath, for her bearings and some semblance of sanity.

"Because I don't want to." She licked her lips, bent down, and grabbed her coat and purse. She turned away from him and with shaky hands she set the alarm, walked outside, and locked the front door, Ty right behind her.

She started to walk away but he grabbed her wrist, burning her with a look that melted her to the cold cement sidewalk.

And then he smiled at her. "Good night, Jenna."

She pivoted and walked to her car, conscious of him standing there watching her. He waited, hands in his coat pockets, while she got in and drove away.

Bastard. Her body was on fire from his kiss and she was going to have to take care of herself when she got home tonight.

She was never going to let him kiss her again.

TY WAITED UNTIL JENNA PULLED OUT OF THE PARKING lot and onto the street before he climbed into his car to head back to his place.

He had known Jenna for almost a year now, had met her through his agent, Elizabeth, and Jenna's brother, Gavin.

Jenna wasn't at all his type. Oh, she was beautiful, all right, but she was skinny with small breasts. He liked his women full and lush with big tits.

He liked his women with long hair he could run his fingers through. Jenna had short, spiky black hair that had weird purple tips of color at the end, which was kind of wild and funky.

Jenna had multiple piercings in her left ear and that tiny little diamond in her nose. It always made him wonder what other parts of her body were pierced. And those tattoos he'd only gotten glimpses of intrigued him. He wanted time to explore them, to study them, to strip her down and see where else she was tattooed.

But her eyes were what really drew him to her. They were an amazing sapphire blue that were so expressive and so vulnerable, even though she liked to play the tough chick.

Okay, so maybe she was a little different. And maybe he was drawn to how utterly different she was.

So he played with her, irritated her and baited her because he knew he could get a rise out of her.

And not interested? Yeah, right. That kiss had told him just how interested she really was. He'd bet if he'd gotten his hands into her panties she'd have been wet.

Just the thought of getting into her panties made his cock throb. He could still taste her on his lips—peppermint and some kind of cherry-flavored lip gloss. He licked his lips, wanted more.

Yeah, he wanted a lot more of Jenna.

And just like in hockey, when the goal was in sight, he never gave up.